THE LOST VOICE
By Allison Agius

Other books by the author:

Non-fiction
Hidden Secrets Buried Treasure: a spiritual guide

Fiction
Treading Water
The Cross Over

Coming soon:
Nothing But The Truth

For more information see www.allisonagius.com or follow on twitter @writer_agius or Facebook page at Allison Agius Writer

'It is the province of knowledge to speak and it is the privilege of wisdom to listen.'

Oliver Wendall Holmes
The Poet at the Breakfast Table (1872)

Chapter One

Entering the corner shop was a braver move than Kate Gregory realised that day, for in a few minutes she would hear something that would blister her soul and upend her guarded life. But for now, as she pushed open the door, she was oblivious to what lay ahead.

The bell rang through the empty store and Kate was pleased she had the shop to herself. It was an 'electro magnetic day', so if she wasn't careful, other people's thoughts would pour into her head until it felt like it would explode. She wouldn't normally venture out at all on days like these, except she had run out of milk.

The smell of plastic bread, newspaper print and sugar hung in the air. A radio buzzed quietly in the back room, and Kate silently sang along to 'Jimmy Mac' as she headed to the refrigerator.

Dot Kimble hobbled in and one thought dropped into Kate fully formed as clear as if the woman spoke to her.

'Oh my piles, oh my God that cream's done nothing for me. Bloody doctors. Prescription bloody cost enough.'

Kate turned away from the woman and smiled, picking up a litre of semi-skimmed she took it to the counter.

'You want an Echo with that love?' Dot asked.

Kate nodded.

'£2.75.'

Kate handed her three pound coins and watched the woman shuffled to the till.

'You all right?' Kate asked, even though she knew she wasn't.

The lie tripped off Dot's tongue. 'I'm fine, it's these blasted new shoes,' she rolled her eyes. 'Silly really, I know I shouldn't but there you go.'

Kate smiled and nodded. 'I do it all the time.'

The bell rang a warning, someone had entered the shop. Kate took it as her signal to go; experience had taught her that too many people in so small a place would be difficult on a day like today. People's thoughts ricocheted off the walls and the jumble of voices became a scene from Babel's Tower in her head.

'Your change love.'

Kate smiled and turned to leave. Behind her stood Lucy Newton, a neighbour's girl from across the street. The girl was about nine, but small for her age, with the spindly limbs of a sapling tree. Her blonde hair hung in strands around her elfin face, and Kate wondered if she were undernourished. Despite the grubby clothes and ingrained dirt, the girl had an inexplicable angelic presence about her. You just had to stop and look at her.

Lucy peered over the counter, her deep blue eyes wide.

'Yes, Lucy?' asked Dot Kimble.

'My mam says can she have ten regal blue?'

'Sorry Sweetie, you know I can't sell 'em to you.'

Kate saw the girl shrink.

'Please Mrs. K, me mam's ill.'

Kate knew it was a lie.

'Don't make no difference, it's the law. I'd be closed down if I did.'

Lucy's eyes swept to the floor.

'Here y'are,' Dot Kimble said, and handed her a yellow sherbet lolly. 'This is for you, and tell yer mam I'm sorry.'

'Thanks Mrs. K.'

Kate moved to the door, her eyes still on Lucy and bumped into someone as they entered. She stopped, turned her head to apologise and recognised her next door neighbour, Ray Montford.

As the large man moved to close the door, a stale damp smell rose up from him. His clothes had been left too long in the washing machine. She stepped back to let him past. He turned slowly, and looked at her with grey watery eyes, then he looked over at Lucy as she walked towards them, heading for the door.

'Nice, very nice, very...peachy.'

The lascivious thought sent cold shivers of fear through Kate, splinters of ice through her veins, causing the hairs on the back of her neck to rise. As she squeezed past him a waft of his body odour hit her. She reached the street and leaned back against the shop window, catching her breath. The brief glimpse into his mind had left her shaken, like a slip on ice. It wasn't so much the thought, it was the *way* he thought it. The implication and intension behind the words.

Kate watched Lucy Newton emerge from the shop and skip down the street, sucking on her lolly, her silver bangle catching the sun. She was so diminutive among the buildings and cars. Kate's thoughts returned to the giant that was Ray Montford. He was going to hurt that little girl, she was sure of it, and there was nothing she could do.

There was a reason people couldn't hear thoughts...there were some things nobody should ever know about another.

Chapter Two

The following day heat pressed down on Kate, forcing itself into her nose, thinning the air. She woke with an aching head, damp with sweat. The clock read 9:35 but she didn't know if it was morning or evening, until she saw the light through a gap in the curtains. A gnawing in her stomach reminded her she had come to bed without eating. So desperate was she to complete the transcribing yesterday, she had worked late into the night and into exhaustion.

Kate rolled over, kicked off the duvet and lay, waiting to gather enough strength to rise. Flotsam from the previous night's dream rose up on a wave of memory, and washed itself onto the shore of her consciousness.

She didn't dream like other people. Kate dreamed of normal things like taking out the rubbish, shopping, talking with friends on the phone. Her life was inside out, a duvet cover on the wrong way. Her life a dream and her dreams her life. That was what had so intrigued her about the transcript the night before. A university student's thesis entitled 'Reality: Fact or Fiction?'

Kate wouldn't claim to have understood all his philosophies, or those of the people he quoted, but she could certainly sympathise with the writer's confusion between the two. She could give him more material to work with, and wondered what he would make of her ability. Ray's whisper came back to her, she shuddered and pushed it away.

She tuned in. Some days, like yesterday, she had a crackle around her, like a magnetic field and she knew she would pick up everything. Today was not one of those days. Today, other than a mild headache, she could pretend her life was normal.

The incident in the shop reasserted itself, but she forced it to the back of her mind. Today she *would* be normal.

She disregarded the throb in her temples, the whisper of yesterday, and began to whistle as she stood to peel off the clothes she had fallen asleep in the night before, determined to enjoy the day. These rare days of normality were pearls among the plastic beads of her life, and she would not let anything spoil them.

Kate threw her jeans and T-shirt into the wicker laundry basket in the corner. She caught sight of her long limbs in the cheval mirror and admired her lean athletic figure. She didn't like her face shape so much; her jaw was too square, unfeminine even, but thanks to Angelina Jolie her thick lips were now in vogue. She puckered at her reflection, then smiled. Not bad, she thought. Still, she envied her friend Sam, envied her soft rounded face, gloriously framed with apricot hair.

Kate's jet hair stood in short tufts off her head, more from the way she'd slept than design. She tried to console herself that some people paid a fortune to get her 'just out of bed hairstyle', but it didn't work. She pulled her fingers through it, trying to get it to lay flat, then gave up. Who would see it anyway?

She padded across to the wardrobe, her hot bare feet sticking lightly to the floorboards. This year the weather had been glorious, more of a Mediterranean summer than a British one. It was hot already, not a day for jeans. She selected a red mini skirt and sleeveless white T-shirt, sprayed deodorant under her arms and washed her face in the bathroom.

In the kitchen she switched on the radio, put some coffee on and opened the back door. A soft breeze blew in, bringing the smell of newly cut grass. Kate stepped onto her balcony, her foot soles shrinking against the cold metal like a slug on salt, and looked down into the garden below.

She saw Felix immediately, sitting at his white cast iron table below, and considered retreating. She knew he'd once stolen a pair of her knickers from the washing line. She had never approached him about it, never would. She hadn't even mentioned it to Sam, afraid she would blurt it out, but she had stopped hanging out her smalls and, whilst Felix seemed okay on the surface, she was now wary of him.

He was reading his paper and hadn't seen her yet, she could stay inside...but it was too pleasant to be indoors, and besides, she wouldn't be able to hear him today.

She took a deep breath and called down. 'Morning Felix.'

He looked up and smiled. 'Hey! Great day.'

'Wonderful,' and today she didn't just mean the weather.

'Thought I might pop down the Red Lion for a pint tonight,' he stood up and folded his paper. 'Fancy coming?'

Kate hesitated, reluctant to encourage Felix.

'Sam can come,' he added.

'Okay. What time?'

Felix shrugged. 'You know better than that.'

Kate laughed; Felix had a pathological aversion to planning, which was ironic, given that he worked in the local planning department. She ran her fingers through her spiky hair. 'Text me when you decide and I'll invite Sam.' Felix couldn't possibly think it was a date then.

'No problem. Got to go, people to piss off, things to fuck up,' he picked up his mug, his paper wedged under his arm.

Kate laughed again and went inside, glad she had said hello. He was just a little odd, she thought. The smell of coffee pervaded her small grey and chrome kitchen. She filled a mug, added milk and then went back onto her balcony to enjoy her coffee.

She noticed Ray Montford, plodding down to his shed at the bottom of the garden, and was reminded of yesterday. She watched him, his gait uneven, suggesting he was using someone else's legs. They had been neighbours for years, but rarely spoke. He lived alone, was a quiet, insular man, and Kate had liked that.

In his late fifties with grey greasy hair combed over a bald patch, he had that unkempt look old bachelors sometimes developed. She remembered from her brief encounter with him yesterday, that he emitted a stale fug when you got close, and she shuddered at the memory.

On his return he stopped and looked up at her, and Kate, instead of waving, froze, retracted back into her doorframe, goose pimples rising over her body. After a few moments, Ray continued to his house. When he was gone Kate released the breath she didn't know she had held, and the band of pain tightened round her head.

Sam sat in her small windowless office at the back of the boutique, hunched over her desk, absorbed by the sales report. A cloud of cigarette smoke hung in the centre of the room, and the air smelt stale and fetid.

Anne Fletcher, the owner of Mocha's was due in shortly to discuss the sales figures, and Sam was preparing for the meeting. The shop floor was looking good. Sam had come in early to change the display, and Tracey and Stella were sorting out the stock to make sure everything was in order.

She returned to the sales report open on her desk. The new range of dresses by 'Donna Michelle', that Sam had gambled on last month had sold well, and with a significantly higher mark-up than the other lines they carried. She increased this month's order in the stock order book to include a few separates from the same designer. If they did as well as the dresses, Anne would probably give her a bonus. The task completed, Sam closed the black order book and left it in Tracey's in-tray for her to action, the sales report she left on her desk, she would need it for her meeting with Anne.

Sam leaned back in her chair, lit another cigarette and wondered if there was another reason for her boss's visit. Whilst she would call in briefly once in a while, she rarely made a specific appointment to meet like this, except for the end of year accounts. It smacked of a formality unprecedented in the previous three years of Sam's employ. Well, she'd find out soon enough.

She pulled on her cigarette, drawing the thick satisfying smoke deep into her lungs, and contemplated her next move, for it was time to move. As much as she loved Mocha's and enjoyed the freedom and trust Anne Fletcher gave her, she was bored. All her ideas were now in place, and the boutique was doing better than ever. There wasn't much left to do. The trouble was, she didn't know what she wanted to do next.

She tucked her hair behind her ears, and flicked the tower of ash that had grown on her cigarette towards the ashtray. It missed and exploded across the desk. Sam didn't notice.

Her husband Paul would not be pleased when she told him she wanted to move jobs, again. The fact that she had been in one job for three years now, would not impress him at all. Three years was nothing to a man who had stayed with the same building firm for fifteen. Still, he would come round, he always did. Eventually.

The phone rang and Sam crushed her cigarette out in the overflowing ashtray before answering it.

'Sam, it's Kate.'

'Hi. How's you?'

'Fine except I've got the headache from hell.'

'Another one! Overdone it again, huh?'

'I think it's coming from my shoulder blades...or my neck. Actually, I'm not sure where it's coming from. I seem to ache everywhere.'

Sam laughed at her friend's melodrama. 'You should see Paul's chiropractor. He has this amazing way about him. I swear Paul's a new man since he's been seeing this guy.'

'That must be interesting.'

'Not THAT new,' Sam shook out another cigarette and lit it.

Kate heard the click of the lighter and Sam's sharp intake of breath.

'Young,' Sam continued, holding the smoke in her lungs. 'But excellent according to Paul. Knows his stuff.'

'How young?'

Sam shrugged, 'late twenties?'

'That's not young!'

Sam blew out a long stream of smoke. 'It is when you're over thirty kiddo. Apparently he's a bit of a dish.'

Kate's voice rose an octave. 'Did Paul say that?'

'No, don't be daft. Sheila from the pub.'

'I was worried for a minute there.'

Sam laughed. 'Apparently, he's a pleasure to get your kit off for.'

'Sam!'

Sam laughed again. 'What you up to tonight?'

'Felix asked if I wanted to go to the Red Lion.'

'You up to it?' Sam didn't know why, but Kate had days when she looked as fragile as a light bulb.

'I'm good today. Apart from this headache...thing.'

'Give this guy a call.'

'If it doesn't clear up I might do, bring his number with you tonight will you?'

Sam glanced at the clock. 'Look Kate, I gotta go. I'll see you tonight. I need to talk to you about something.'

Sam stubbed out the cigarette and counted the butt ends. Ten. It was eleven in the morning and she'd smoked ten already. Ten in two hours, was that even possible? At this rate she could try for a Guiness World Record. Checking the last cigarette was out completely, she tipped the evidence of her sin into the waste paper bin and returned the empty ashtray to her desk.

She threw three extra strong mints in her mouth, and began to spray the room with an air freshener that promised to eliminate all odours including tobacco. That done, she put the can back in the bottom drawer, squirted herself with perfume, and wiped the ash off her desk with the back of her hand. As she finished Tracey poked her head round the door.

'Mrs Fletcher's here,' she said.

Sam nodded and Tracey disappeared.

Sam straightened her jade Roccobarocco dress, pushed her hair back from her face, and launched herself onto the shop floor to greet her boss.

By lunchtime, the dull ache Kate had woken with, had intensified into hot needles, sending electric shots of pain from between her shoulder blades, up her neck and into her head. Paracetamol had no effect. This, she concluded, was no ordinary headache.

She sealed up the box containing the manuscript with brown tape, and had just completed the address label when the doorbell rang. It would be Toby the courier.

'You okay?' he asked, taking the parcel from her.

'Headache.'

He handed her his clipboard to sign and gave her a receipt.

'How's your mum?' Kate asked, taking it from him.

Toby's face tensed under his unruly hair. 'How did you know about that?'

Kate cursed herself. She was usually so careful, but today the pain had lowered her guard.

'You told me last week,' she said, praying he would accept her explanation.

He looked sideways at her, his dark eyes wary.

'Well?' she asked, trying to cover her mistake by brazening it out. 'How is she?'

Toby nodded. 'She's on the mend. Doctor says it's benign.'

'Good, good.'

He went to walk back to his van then stopped. 'I don't remember telling you,' he said.

Kate smiled and shrugged. 'Then how would I know?'

Toby nodded, pulled the corners of his mouth down as he considered her reply. 'True,' he said, and walked away satisfied.

Kate closed the door with a sigh of relief.

Sam was pleased to see that Stella had arranged fresh flowers on the shop counter; a pink and purple mixture of orchids and lilies. The heavy scent of the lilies hung in the air, clogging in the back of Sam's throat. The flowers were beautiful, but she found the scent cloying.

Anne Fletcher stood talking to Stella, giving Sam an opportunity to take in the woman who was her boss. Immaculately turned out in a well-made ivory

13

cotton trouser suit and pearlised shoes. This wasn't a woman who emptied the rubbish bin at home. Her brown hair was short and layered with highlights of grey, an expensive cut that would defy wind and rain and hold itself in place. Anne's face was worn, and there was a severity around the eyes and mouth that suggested a woman you didn't want to argue with. She was smiling now, a benevolent bend to her head.

Sam took a deep breath and strode over to her. Anne's eyes flickered over to Sam and back again to Stella. She placed a hand lightly on Stella's arm, thanked her for her hard work and turned to Sam, effectively dismissing Stella.

'Sam, how are you?'

'I'm well thank you Mrs. Fletcher, and you?'

'Good,' she spun round, gesturing the shop floor. 'The place looks good Sam.'

'I'm glad you think so.'

'And the sales too.'

Sam smiled and nodded.

'Shall we go into your office to talk?'

'Yes, Tracey could we have some coffee please?' Sam said, and turned to follow her boss into the back, her chest thumping. Sam had thought Anne wanted an update on how the new ranges were going, but if she knew the sales were good, why the meeting?

'Still smoking Sam?' Anne said, when they entered Sam's office.

''Fraid so.'

'Not ideal.'

Sam sat in her chair, unsure what to say. Was she here to give Sam an appraisal?

'No,' she said eventually.

'And how's Paul?'

'He's good thank you, and your family?'

'Fine. Julie's getting married next month and Julian finally finishes University next summer, with this PhD I thought he was going to be the perpetual student. Frank's retiring in a few months, so it's all change.'

'Sounds exciting.'

'Yes, yes it is.'

Tracey entered with a tray and set it down on the desk between the two women.

'Thank you Tracey,' Anne said, and Tracey left.

Sam poured the coffee and they helped themselves to milk and sugar.

'I've been through the sales figures this morning for the last month,' Sam said, breaking the silence. 'They're up again.'

'Yes, I'm very pleased. You've done well, Sam. Very well.'

Another silence poured between them, setting like concrete. Sam waited, unsure what else she could do to chip it away.

Finally Anne spoke. 'Frank and I have been talking. We think it's time we reviewed our future. Perhaps make some changes to our lifestyle.'

Now Sam knew why Anne had visited. She intended to sell, and if so, Sam would be out of a job. Whilst part of her was ready for a change, another part resented it being thrust upon her. She didn't like the idea of no longer being required.

'Obviously the boutiques, this one and the ones in Durham and York, have been my life. I built them up with my own hands. They are, as it were, my babies.'

Sam had never seen this side of Anne and she didn't care to now. She just wanted her to get to the point.

'I have many fond memories of beginning the business, building it, and I'm very proud of it.'

Sam smiled and nodded, wishing the woman would just get on with it.

'There's no doubt the work and ingenuity you have injected into this particular boutique, has paid dividends over the last twelve months. You have increased the turnover by forty percent but, more importantly, because of the increased mark-up of the lines we're now selling, profits have risen even further.'

She liked the sound of this. This suggested she was going to get a pay off, and she warmed to the woman's monologue.

'It would be foolish of me to sell when things are going so well. However, as I said, times change.'

Sam was itching to light a cigarette. Anne seemed to be talking very slowly, spinning out each word, rolling them round her mouth like marbles.

'But I would be sorry to pass my business onto someone else, particularly as I believe there's potential to both duplicate the success here at the other boutiques, and perhaps to open more, Harrogate for example,' she paused to sip her coffee.

Sam watched the slow exaggerated movements of her boss.

'There is, of course,' she said, replacing the cup in its saucer, 'an alternative. One I would like you to give considerable thought to before you answer.'

Sam's brain scrambled round trying to take in the words. She wasn't selling, or was she going to suggest Sam buy from her? That was ridiculous. Sam didn't have that sort of money.

'I need to be free of the business so I can spend more time with Frank. We want to travel more, enjoy our twilight years before the lights go out, so to speak. So, I need someone I can trust to run the business, someone who understands it, has a proven track record, and has the age and energy to take the business forward.

'I need someone to oversee the current boutiques, putting staff in where needed, and to oversee the general running of the organisation, as well as the selection and ordering of stock. That person will also need to source new locations, seek new opportunities to expand the business, obviously within the financial limitations of the company. In exchange there will be a company car, a good basic salary, plus with profits bonus and shares in the company.

'What I'm proposing Sam, is that you become the new managing director of Mocha boutiques.'

Kate had gone back to bed in the afternoon and woke refreshed. Now she sat in the beer garden at the back of the Red Lion, and watched the smoke rise lazily from the end of Sam's cigarette as her friend downloaded her woes. They were woes Kate had heard before, so she could safely tune out. Sam didn't want a conversation, more a sponge. Felix was inside getting more drinks, and Kate relished the loose feeling inside her body.

She still had a dull ache between her shoulder blades, but the headache was gone, and at least today she could hear people talk clearly, if she wanted to listen. Often she had to strain to pick out conversation from a background of hissing whispers, rather like panning for gold.

She watched Sam pull on her cigarette and enjoyed the break in the word stream. They were an odd mix she concluded. Different in so many ways, and Kate thought that, had it not been for the voices, they wouldn't have been friends at all.

They met five years ago when Sam was temping in Bruce's office. Kate didn't go into the office much now, but in the beginning, when she was establishing a working relationship with Bruce, endeavouring to prove herself as a transcriber, she went in more often. Mainly to hound him for more work.

Kate avoided contact with people unless it was necessary, and rarely instigated any meaningful conversation for fear they would notice something odd about her. So when Sam approached her she did not respond. It was usually enough to put people off, but not Sam, Sam was persistent. Every time Kate went into the office Sam would try to strike up a conversation. She was candid and comic and, Kate realised after a few meetings, self-absorbed.

She found herself looking forward to seeing Sam, and eventually Kate relented and handed over her telephone number. The following week when Kate went into the office Sam was gone.

At first Kate missed her. The relationship had been one-sided, she knew that, but it had suited them both. So she thought. Sam wanted someone to talk to, and Kate was happy to listen, at least, most of the time. With Sam gone there was a gap but, like an ebbing sea repairing a hole in the sand, time slowly filled it.

Then out of the blue, on one of Kate's good days, Sam called. They talked for a long time, and finally arranged to meet. As Kate got to know Sam better, she realised they were as lonely as each other. Sam didn't have as many friends as Kate had imagined. But then, she could be hard work.

Night was slowly gathering and the heat of the day had dissipated. Felix was approaching with the drinks. Kate glanced at her watch.

'Going somewhere?' Sam asked, with a sharp twang.

Kate ignored it. 'I was just noticing how the nights were drawing in. It's only just after nine.'

'Something big happened today,' Sam said suddenly.

'Oh?' asked Kate, interested now.

'Anne Fletcher, my boss? She's planning on retiring and she offered me the post of MD of her company.'

'Wow! That's fantastic...so why has it taken you this long to tell me, and why the long face? Did you turn it down?'

'No, I said I'd think about it.'

'What do you need to think about?' asked Kate, even though she knew, Sam had never confided in her so she had to pretend she didn't.

'There's a lot to think about.'

Kate heard a whisper under Sam's words, it moved through her, in the river of quiet thoughts that was always with her, even on good days like today.

'Why do people do that?' asked Felix, dumping the glasses onto the bench in front of them.

'What?' asked Sam.

'Jump in.'

Sam and Kate exchanged glances. They turned to Felix and in unison said, 'What?'

Felix stepped over the bench and sat down. 'At the bar, it was clear I was waiting, but they just pretend they don't see you. It's damned rude.'

Sam drew on her cigarette and threw the end into the car park.

'I wish you wouldn't do that,' Kate said.

'It's only a fag end. It's biode-watsist.'

'It's still littering.'

Sam sighed and drank her pint of lager. Kate watched, amazed that she could look feminine even when she drank out of a pint glass.

'So what are you going to do?' Kate asked Sam, turning back to the original conversation.

Sam shrugged and looped her hair over one ear. 'That's the trouble. I don't know. I should probably talk it over with Paul.'

'What?' asked Felix. Kate brought him up to speed then turned to Sam. 'He'll be okay about it,' she said. 'He's a pussy cat really. He just wants you to be happy.'

'Am I missing something here? Shouldn't he be jumping for joy?' Felix asked.

'He doesn't like me...changing jobs so often,' Sam sighed. 'I suppose he just wants me to be like him. Settled.'

'Have you asked him why it bothered him so much?' Felix asked.

And there is the rub, thought Kate, but bit back her words, remembering her gaff earlier with Toby the courier. Sometimes she forgot what she was and wasn't supposed to know. Her head had started to throb again, making it difficult to concentrate.

Sam shook her head, her eyes glistening.

'Sorry I didn't mean...' Felix stopped and focused on his drink, looking pink. He glanced at Kate and smiled. She observed him, hearing on the breeze words she was grateful she could not make out today, and shifted her focus back to Sam.

18

Kate knew the bone of contention between the couple, but was powerless to say anything. How would she explain her knowledge if she and Sam had never discussed it? If they had been alone, she might have guided Sam in the right direction, but not with an observer. Often people weren't very observant at all, and then, when you least expected it, noticed far more than you thought. She had made that mistake before. No, she could do nothing at the moment except watch her friend's misery. Frustration chewed at her insides, causing her headache to sharpen further.

Chapter Three

Kate headed for the discount store in town. It was a large shop ranging over three floors, and sold everything from embroidery thread to garden tools. Each department consisted of one or two stands with little thought to display. Instead, goods were piled up in cheap heaps. The results of a visit here were mixed. Sometimes it was a long fruitless search, and at other times a real gem of a bargain was unearthed.

Kate moved slowly through the store, making her way to the crockery department downstairs. She nodded as she passed the sales girl pricing up a large batch of blue and white mugs. Each to be ticketed individually, no bar codes here. The slow click of the gun suggested a deep seated boredom in the girl.

Kate picked her way through the discounted china. Last night, while washing up, she had chipped her yellow butter dish, and she was now looking for a replacement. She knew from experience it was pointless asking the staff for help, either through apathy or lack of organisation, they would simply shrug and grunt. She would just have to search for herself.

After several minutes Kate was close to giving up and crossing the road to the department store to pay high street prices, when she saw the dark blue dish. She leaned over and picked it up. It was heavy and solid with a good fitted lid. Kate would have preferred a different colour but, after scanning the shelves one final time, decided that at £1.99 it was a bargain.

When Kate woke the following morning and made toast she reached for the butter dish, only to notice she was still using her chipped one.

'Where did I put the new one?' she asked the fridge.

Slowly she put the pieces together. The nod to the girl. No voices, not one. Not even a whisper. She remembered the slow clicking of the pricing gun. She would never hear that because she would never go into town without being plugged into her i-pod, without her music she was too vulnerable to the voices that weaved and danced through the air, wrapping themselves around her, tugging at her attention, dropping into her head unexpectedly.

It was then she knew. It had been a dream. Another of her inside out duvet cover moments. It was only a butter dish, but she could have cried with disappointment.

After breakfast, disappointment shelved, Kate scheduled the work sent by Bruce into her diary and closed the book. It was Saturday, officially her day off, but she could relax better now she had organised her work for the following week.

She moved away from the desk and flopped onto the sofa. Her head still ached and the pain in her neck and shoulders, whilst intermittent, clawed at her. Maybe she should dig out the number Sam gave her for the Chiropractor and book an appointment? But it was manageable, and she didn't want to get that close to someone if she could avoid it.

As she lay back, tracing a crack in the ceiling with her eyes, she thought again about Ray Montford and Lucy Newton. It was two days ago, and she was still haunted by the incident. Was she being paranoid? Had she imagined it all? What was she imagining anyway? How could she be sure she hadn't made it up? After all, if she could dream about buying a bloody butter dish and not realise it was a dream until she couldn't find it...how could she trust herself about this?

It wasn't as if she had any control over her ability. Some days it was just a great cacophony, with the occasional unclear comment coming through, like a fog light in bad weather. At other times, nothing but a clear formed thought dropping into her head unbidden. Ray Montford's comment had been just like that. No, it was very clear, and she wasn't confused by its meaning. There was danger there, at least...she thought so. The way the man looked at the child, his voice so...lascivious. It sent shivers down her spine just to think about it.

She glanced at the clock on the mantelpiece. It was time for lunch. She hauled herself off the sofa and, as she made her way down the hall to the kitchen, she heard a knock on her door. Her heart sank.

She knew it was Felix. Anyone else would have had to ring the doorbell on the street door, that both flats shared. Only Felix would be able to knock directly on her door. She wasn't really up to dealing with him today, but

21

maybe she could talk to him about her concerns over Ray, get a another perspective?

'Hi, come in,' she said, swinging the door wide.

'You okay?' Felix asked, following her upstairs.

'Sure why?'

'You look peeky.'

Kate laughed. 'Peeky? What kind of a word is 'peeky' for a grown man to use?'

They both laughed as they entered the kitchen.

'Was just about to make some lunch, want some?'

'Depends. What is it?' Kate was not renowned for her cooking.

'Could you pretend to be polite?'

Felix thought for a moment. 'No, sorry, not possible. Not when it comes to food.'

Kate pretended to punch him and he dodged behind the kitchen table. 'I'm making scrambled eggs,' she declared, pulling the whisk from the drawer as if it were a sword.

'God no. Your scrambled eggs are like rubber.'

'Felix!'

'Sorry, no offence, but they are quite dreadful.'

'You're not gay by any chance are you?' She knew he wasn't, but there was something about him, something she had been unable to uncover. Not that she had really tried. She didn't like to pry, it was too easy for her.

'I take exception to that. I'm all man.'

'I should think that's very appealing to a gay man.'

He screwed up his face. 'Very funny.'

Kate laughed hard. She was glad Sam had insisted on inviting him to the pub the weekend he moved in. She had to be careful around Felix, he was more observant than Sam, less self-absorbed, but he was good company. She only wished things could be different, that he didn't find her attractive...or that she felt the same way about him.

'You make them then,' she said, handing him the whisk.

'I've got a better idea, let's go out for lunch, my treat.'

Kate stopped dead. 'It's Saturday.'

'So?'

Kate took the whisk back from him and turned away. 'It'll be busy,' she mumbled.

'So?'

Kate took a deep breath and turned to face him. 'I don't like busy places, remember?'

Kate heard the thought stir and rise up.

This woman is neurotic, beautiful, but neurotic. Nightmare scenario.

Her insides shrank.

'Actually Felix, I've got a headache, I think I'll go back to bed.'

'What? What did I say?' his disappointment was noticeable.

'Nothing, I'm just not up to this.'

'Look, we don't have to go out. I'll cook.'

'No, really please, I don't feel so good.'

'Can I get you anything?'

'No, I just need to lie down.'

When he'd gone Kate curled up on the bed. There was a reason she didn't get close, and sometimes she forgot why, until something came along to remind her. She hadn't even asked Felix about Ray, she thought with misery.

Sam phoned that night. She talked incessantly about her relationship with Paul, had it all been a big mistake? She felt stifled, unsupported. Why was it always his way? Where was the partnership? If her relationship was so great, how come she couldn't talk to him about the opportunity of a lifetime?

Usually Kate didn't mind Sam's incessant need for it to be all about her, but for once Kate had something she wanted to talk about, and felt impatient with her friend.

Any normal person this close to Kate would have long since noticed something unusual about her, but not Sam. Until now Kate had considered that an advantage, and in truth she knew it was the only reason Sam *was* allowed to get so close. Still, tonight it irked her.

'Are you still there?' Sam asked, irritated.

'Yes,' Kate replied, her voice a monotone.

'Are you alright? You sound...funny.'

Kate sighed. 'Actually I am worried about something.' There was silence on the line. 'Sam?'

'What is it?' There was a mixture of intrigue and irritation in Sam's voice.

'It's my neighbour. I think he's getting too friendly with a girl in the street.'

'Eh?'

'I think he wants to do something to her.'

'What are you on about?'

That was the question. What *was* she on about? 'A little girl and...'Kate sighed. 'Oh, never mind.'

There was another long pause. 'Oh, you think he might be a pervert?'

'Sam!'

'Is that what you mean though?'

'I suppose.'

'Why, what's he done?'

'Nothing especially, it's just a feeling I've got.'

'And?'

'I don't know what to do about it.'

'Why not have a word with the kid's mother?'

'What?' asked Kate.

'Talk to the kid's mother. Have a word about your concerns to her. Then it's her problem.'

'That's a great idea!'

'You're welcome. So, what do you think?'

'About what?'

'Should I tell Paul before I've made a decision, or just take it and present him with a fait accompli?'

Kate shook her head in exasperation. Only Sam, she thought.

Chapter Four

'Felix? It's Phoebe. How's your weekend been? Refreshed and ready for work tomorrow?'

'Yeah, not bad, quiet, you know. How's the kids? Still a handful?'

'They're eight year old boys what d'you think?' she said with amusement. Felix chuckled, leaned back into his armchair and put his feet on the coffee table.

'You need laugh,' she said. 'I got called into the school last week because they'd plaited two girl's hair.'

'That sounds nice.'

'Together. In class. They'd plaited two girl's hair together – as in, attached them!'

Felix laughed. Phoebe started to giggle. 'It's not really funny Felix. Apparently, when they went to stand up and walk away they snapped back and banged their heads together.' Phoebe's giggles multiplied.

'Priceless,' Felix roared.

'No,' she said, regaining control of herself. 'It's not funny. Really it isn't.'

'So why are you laughing?'

'Because I'm a dreadful mother?'

The tone sobered.

'I suspect that's why you called?' said Felix.

'Yes, it's that time again.'

'Comes round fast...must we?'

'Felix!'

'I know, I know, it's just...I so don't want to do this.'

'And you think I do?'

'No. I suppose not. How's she been?'

'The same, though you'd know if you went and saw her occasionally, she is your mother too.'

Felix sighed, the walls of his living room suddenly closing in. 'I can't do this,' he said, in a small voice.

'Felix you've got to.'

'Can't you deal with it? You're the oldest.'

'Oh no you don't, I'm not doing this alone.'

'I know, but you can deal with her. It's always so...she messes with my head Phebes, you know?'

'I know. When was the last time you saw Dr Carmichael?'

The line hung taunt as a wire between them, humming with shared memories and pain.

'Felix?'

'What?'

'Answer me.'

'I don't need to see him.'

Phoebe sighed into the phone. 'Well, at least tell me you're taking your medication?'

Felix felt the pressure on his chest, they were always getting at him, his family. Always on his case. He was the odd one out, the broken one and boy, didn't they like to let him know...except for Phoebe. No, she was on his side. He had to remember that.

He heard her take a deep breath. 'Felix?'

'What?' he felt she was on the verge of saying something important, but her answer proved him wrong.

'Are you okay?'

'Yes, I'm fine. When are you going?'

'Sure?'

"*Yes*. When are you going?' He repeated.

'Friday, I'll leave the boys with Gertie and set off in the afternoon. David's in Dubai at the moment.'

Gertie was Phoebe and David's Dutch au pair, although Felix could never figure out why they needed an au pair when Phoebe didn't work.

'Friday!'

'Yes, spend Saturday with her and come back Sunday lunchtime.'

'But that's nearly forty-eight hours!'

Phoebe sighed. 'I know that. You think I don't know that?'

'But why so long? Why nearly forty-eight hours?'

'She needs us at this time of year.'

'But it's *every* year.'

'I know, but it'll take me nearly three hours to drive up.'

'It only takes me an hour. I can come over on the Saturday morning. I don't have to stay over,' he pleaded.

'Felix! She needs us, and I need your support. You'd be sorry if you didn't do this.'

'No, I wouldn't, you're just a better person than me.'

'I don't think so. I'm a mum, maybe I'm trying to store up some karma points for myself, for the future, just in case.'

'Don't compare yourself to her.'

'I'm not, it's just, I'd like to think my boys would come if I needed them. If something happened to David...well, especially the circumstances of Dad's death...you know?'

'Of course they would.'

'I do my best, but I'll have made mistakes. All parents do. Mum's no different. She loves us, *both* of us.'

'What about you stay here? I've got space, we can drive over from here?'

'Felix, it's only once a year. You barely see her as it is.'

Felix sighed. 'Okay. She just...terrifies me.'

Phoebe laughed. 'I know what you mean. Great battle-axe of a woman that she is.' Their mother was five foot one and weighed seven stone. Both Phoebe and Felix towered over her.

Felix laughed. 'Alright, I'll meet you in the Crown in the village okay? I don't want to arrive there alone.'

'I tell you what, to soften the blow let's meet for a long late lunch, my treat? Can you get the time off work?'

'Shouldn't be a problem, I've got loads of TOIL stacked up. Needs taking, so, yeah, okay, why not?'

They set up a time for the following Friday and Felix replaced the receiver.

He licked his dry lips and swallowed, his stomach churning. He hated being around his mother, almost as much as she hated being around him. The woman reduced him to a gibbering wreck with that look of hers. She had devil eyes, he was convinced that one day she would snuff him out, or gobble him up, or destroy him in some way.

Still, he reminded himself, he was a grown man now. A grown man with a flat of his own, a career and a few friends. So why did the thought of visiting his mother make him did feel so small and impotent? And why, did he get a nagging feeling that Phoebe was not telling him something?

27

Chapter Five

Kate raised her head slowly from her work, suddenly aware of the tension that had taken hold over the last few hours.

Her neck and shoulders ached, signs that she had overdone it, again. When would she learn? She stood up from her desk in the corner of the living room and walked over to the window, twisting her body as she moved in an effort to release the knots of discomfort. She stopped at the window and looked down at the street below as she slowly rotated her shoulders.

It was a warm day. The street was deserted, except for a woman with a pushchair on the other side of the road. She walked quickly and was soon out of sight. A taxi chugged by.

The pain began to ease and she was just considering phoning the chiropractor Sam had recommended, when she saw Lucy leaving her house on the other side of the road.

Kate stopped and watched the girl. Shouldn't she be in school, or were they on holiday at the moment? Lucy was struggling to get her pink pram over the door frame when her mother, Rachael, appeared and effortlessly lifted it onto the garden path.

It had been five days since she heard Ray in the corner shop, and for the last two days, since Sam's suggestion, Kate had practiced what she might say to Rachael, but she still hadn't been to see the child's mother.

What would she say? How could she explain that for no apparent reason, she thought Ray Mountford had ill intent towards her daughter? She wasn't truly convinced herself half the time. Until she recalled the tone of his thought that day in the corner shop, but how could she explain that? If she told the truth Rachael would dismiss her as a deranged, and anything else she tried just sounded...lame.

Kate watched as the woman said something to her daughter, probably a warning to not go far, or mind the road. The girl nodded, then pushed the pram down the path, through the wooden gate and out onto the pavement.

Rachael Newton watched her daughter and Kate watched Rachael Newton. She was a beautiful woman with a long straight nose, a wide mouth and arched eyebrows over deep eyes. Classic Hollywood features tainted by too many cigarettes and too much alcohol. The deep lines across her forehead and around her mouth suggested a woman who had suffered.

She brought Lucy up on her own, and Kate thought that must be hard, to have sole responsibility for another human being. Just then the woman looked up and Kate waved. The other woman nodded and sent her a small smile before retreating into the house, leaving Lucy to play.

Kate observed Lucy travel up and down the street chatting away, occasionally she stopped to check on her doll before tucking her back in and continuing back and forth like a Buckingham palace guard. Children were tireless Kate decided, as she turned from the window to make some coffee.

Five minutes later, mug in hand she returned to the window, curious to see if the child was still playing the same game. A hard lump formed in her throat at the sight below.

Ray Mountford had joined the child. His bulk bent over the pram, preening the doll and talking to Lucy. Lucy responded with animation, clearly enjoying the attention and interest of an adult. The little girl looked even more minute next to the giant of a man.

Kate wasn't sure what to do. Panic beat in her chest and she found it hard to breathe. She stood and watched, transfixed in the window frame, gripping her mug of coffee, the heat burning into the palm of her hand unnoticed.

She couldn't just stand by and watch the man squirm into Lucy's confidence like this. She should have found the courage to speak to the mother about her fears, but it was too late now. And she couldn't just stand here and do nothing at all.

The panic heightened and Kate felt the belt of tension tighten round her head. Her breath shortened further, causing pain in her chest. What should she do? What could she do?

The moment Ray took the child's hand in his Kate ceased to ask questions. She slammed the coffee down onto the desk as she rushed out of the room, slopping hot coffee over her hand.

She sped down the stairs, her feet barely keeping up with her. She stumbled down the last few, causing her to career down the hall and bang hard into her door with the momentum. Righting herself quickly she burst out of her flat door, but with trembling hands fumbled over the lock on the outside door. Cursing she stopped and took a breath, knowing that every second counted. He could be leading the child away at that very moment.

29

She tried again, her hand, wet with coffee, slipped again. She wiped her hand down the side of her jeans. Finally, the lock turned and she was out of the door and into the street.

'Leave her alone!' she screamed. She tore across the road towards them. A drum beat in her ears, her breath coming out in short rasps.

They looked up at her. Ray scowled, Lucy's eyes widened.

'Leave her!' Kate shouted, although it wasn't necessary now she was only a few steps from them.

Ray dropped the child's hand and shrugged. 'We're just chatting,' he said, with a voice like gravel.

'Get away from her.'

'Look, I don't know what your problem is-'

'Just keep away.'

Rachael Newton emerged from her house and ran down the path. 'What's going on?' she asked, her brow creased with concern.

'I'm not sure Rachael,' Ray said. He sounded calm, if bewildered. 'Just having a chat with your Lucy here, when Kate came bursting out of her house shouting the odds.'

Kate looked down at Lucy. 'You okay?'

Lucy nodded, her eyes wide, a worried expression on her face.

Rachael crouched by her daughter, took hold of her upper arms gently and turned her so they faced one another. They were close, their noses nearly touching.

'What's going on Lucy?' the woman's voice was soft.

Lucy looked at Kate, then Ray. Little pools formed in the child's eyes and, as she shrugged, the movement caused them to spill down her face. 'I don't know mam. Ray was just asking me what my doll's name was.'

Rachael gave her daughter a hug and cast a scornful glance at Kate.

Kate's heart shrank as she realised how this looked. It was she, not Ray, who looked like someone who would harm the child.

'I...it's just that...' It was just what? This was exactly why she hadn't gone to see Rachael in the first place. How could she explain, especially with a street audience? What did she have to go on anyway? A lascivious thought in a corner shop a few days ago. For all she knew about men, they did that all the time. But no, even she knew enough to know they didn't over nine year old girls. Or if they did, they shouldn't.

A crowd had begun to gather around them. A couple of other neighbours had come out to see what was going on, and a few passers-by had stopped to join them.

'I'm sorry, I thought...'

Voices were beginning to swirl and clash in Kate's head as the group of people grew. She was unable to think clearly. What would she say anyway? What possible explanation could she give? Even if she were prepared to expose her ability to read thoughts, she would not be able to disprove the natural scepticism she would encounter, she had tried that before. She had never had much control over what she tapped into it, and now, since hiding from it for so long, she had even less.

Besides, even if she could, she had nothing but a hunch that Ray was dangerous. She hadn't actually heard or seen anything to back it up. She looked at him now. His grey eyes glared at her, but could she blame him?

'It's all a misunderstanding,' he said. 'Kate was looking out for a neighbour's child. We all need to do a bit more of that these days.'

She heard the words, but there was something underneath, thoughts she couldn't decipher among the pan crashing cacophony of all the others around. She wished the crowd would disperse so she could hear it more clearly.

She strained to listen, unsure what she was doing. She had never wanted to hear anything in the past, had always prayed it would just go away. Now that she was trying it was as unnatural as trying to breathe under water, and, she decided, she might drown in the noise.

It was malevolent, she was sure of that, but towards her or something darker, something aimed at the child? She couldn't be sure.

'The sentiment's lovely Kate, but would you mind not scaring us all half to death next time?' It was Rachael.

Kate tore her eyes off Ray and looked at her. 'I'm sorry,' she said. Her voice sounded rough and broken up, the result of strangling high emotion.

What was she doing? Mortified she returned to her flat. As she turned to close the front door she saw the group looking back at her.

She shut the door quickly, retreated to her flat and closed that door too. She leaned back on it and took a few deep breaths, the voices receding to a dull whisper and hiss.

'I think I'm going mad,' she said out loud. 'This cursed thing is finally sending me mad.'

Chapter Six

Kate piled the cushions to one end of her pale blue sofa and reclined against them, hoping to ease the gnawing pain that ate across her upper back and into her neck. To add to her trouble, the weather had become changeable, and the blue skies of yesterday had been replaced with steely grey clouds and strong winds.

Kate sat in her lounge cowering from a wind that rattled the window frames in rage and, like a spiteful child, threw pebble rain against the glass.

She always hated the wind, but today the combination of the wind, the voices, the humiliation of the previous day, and this pain were too much for her, and she hunkered down in misery.

She could kick herself for not phoning the chiropractor before, and now she couldn't. What would be the point? She wouldn't be able to go out in this. Kate knew from experience that even headphones blasting music into her ears, wouldn't be able to drown out this wind.

When the wind blew like this, voices dropped into her head from all sorts of places. They crashed together, fighting with one another inside her. They could come from anywhere, and her imagination ran as wild as the wind.

Enigmatic yearnings of the dead, wise whisperings, linguistic yearnings to be heard. Visceral verbiage. Hints of another world, another dimension. Overlapped lives, unseen occurrences, confessions and guilt, like the the primary colours in purple, necessary to make it, but invisible once it's done. Voices, like shadows in pale light, soft, without definition. Blurred, muted and rubbed out. A hissing bubbling cauldron of words. The blue, black and grey of emotion. The red, violet and pink of desire.

It all came to her on the wind, picked up like dandelion seeds and, looking for fertile ground, dropped into her head. It terrified her to go out in it, because at any point she could become unstable, unable to think, unable to function.

The phone rang again for the third time today. It would be Sam, desperate to share the latest episode of her life, but Kate wasn't up to it today, so she had characteristically ignored it. She did the same yesterday after the incident in the street.

She shrank into the sofa, refusing to let the world in, waiting for the pain, the voices and the weather to leave her be. Wondering if she had imagined it all, that Ray was just a harmless old bachelor, and she an omen of gloom.

Sam sat on her telephone seat in the hall looking through the frosted door, listening to the phone ring in her ear.

'I hate that door,' she muttered.

It was a conversation she had with herself every time she was on the phone, but she hadn't done anything about it, because she promptly forgot the moment she replaced the receiver.

The ringing clicked onto Kate's answer machine and Sam hung up without leaving a message. It was pointless. She'd left three already and Kate hadn't responded to any of them. She returned to the living room and Paul.

It had been four days since Anne's offer, and Sam still hadn't broached it with him. She had tried, but just didn't know where to start. She really needed to talk to Kate, and felt disgruntled that her friend wasn't there for her when she needed her.

'She's done it again,' she said, slumping into one of the armchairs.

'What's that?' asked Paul, without taking his eyes off the television. He was watching a documentary on Meerkats. Cute little things Sam thought, watching one stand up and look around, arms folded in front like an anxious old lady who'd misplaced her handbag.

'Kate. She's done it again. Cut herself off from civilisation. I haven't been able to get her for two days now.'

'Shouldn't worry. It's not the first time.'

'I know. It's weird though don't you think?'

Paul shrugged. 'We all do weird things sometimes.'

'What do I do that's weird?'

Sam knew Paul hadn't been paying attention to the conversation when the comment had slipped out, and she watched him squirm.

'What?' he asked, clearly playing for time while his brain scrambled round for a suitable answer.

'What do I do that's weird?' Sam persisted.

'You want a list?' he said, smiling.

'No, I just want you to name one thing.'

He stopped smiling and thought.

'Well?'

'I'm thinking,' he told her.

'I can't be that weird,' she said. 'If you have to think about it.'

He smiled again. 'No, I guess not. I know, you like eating in the bath.'

'Is that weird?'

'Weird, but cute. More...quirky.'

'That's good.'

'Wonderful,' he said, relief evident.

Sam nodded in satisfaction and Paul returned to his programme.

'So you think it's okay?'

'I told you, more quirky than weird.'

'No, Kate I mean?'

'She'll be fine. You said yourself, she does this from time to time. Maybe she's in the middle of an important job; maybe she just needs some peace and quiet.'

'I think she's not keen on the weather.'

'Mmm.'

'She's afraid of wind.'

'Who's afraid of the wind? Lightening yes, but not wind.'

'I think she is.'

'Has she said that?'

'No, but she's always a bit odd when it's windy. Doesn't like going out in it.'

'Fear of a bit of wind – now that's weird.'

'Yes, yes it is,' Sam said, and settled down to watch the remainder of the documentary with him.

Chapter Seven

Kate woke the following morning to sun streaming through her bedroom window. After breakfast she picked up her phone and caught up on her calls.

First, she rang Bruce, who ran the agency, to explain she had been ill. She confirmed the priorities from the outstanding packages on her desk. He was used to Kate taking time off, but as she always met the deadlines he never complained.

Next, she called the number of the chiropractor Sam had recommended, and secured an appointment for Saturday. Finally, she phoned Sam and braced herself for the inevitable interrogation. She wasn't disappointed.

'Kate? What the hell are you playing at?' she said, and before Kate could answer Sam continued. 'I've been worrying my arse off. Where the hell have you been? For all I know you could be lying dead, or worse.'

Kate wondered what Sam thought was worse than dead.

'Well?'

'I'm sorry. I wasn't feeling well.'

'So you couldn't pick up the phone and tell me? I could have brought you things, looked after you.'

Kate couldn't imagine anything worse than being nursed by Sam. She would surely finish off even the most robust patient. 'I didn't need looking after.'

'Don't argue. That's what friends are for. God, you piss me off.'

Kate smiled. 'I'm sorry. I didn't mean to worry you.'

'Well, you did.'

Kate heard Sam suck on a cigarette.

'So, you okay now?' Sam asked.

'I'm feeling better. I've got an appointment with the chiropractor you recommended.'

'Make sure you wear your best knickers.'

Kate giggled. 'Sam!'

'I'm serious.'

'I'll bear that in mind when I'm selecting my knickers for the day.'

'You do that. So, what was wrong this time?'

'I told you.' Kate wasn't going to tell Sam about the fiasco in the street earlier in the week.

'This head, neck, shoulders thing?'

'Yes.'

'I thought it was the weather. I told Paul that you're scared of wind.'

Kate forced out a laugh. 'What did he say?'

'He said that was weird.'

Kate forced another laugh. 'He's probably right. Look I've got to go, I've got a ton of work to catch up on.'

'Do you want to go to the cinema tonight?'

Kate hated the cinema, but it was preferable to a pub, and in order to maintain the friendship and not arouse Sam's suspicion, a sacrifice was needed from time to time.

'Sure. Ring me later.'

Kate sat back in her office chair. 'Weird,' Sam had said. Weird. The word cascaded through her body. A red hot rash that burned. That word had haunted her as a child, especially when she learnt that others didn't hear people's thoughts on the wind. Only her. Weird. Odd. Strange. Creepy. Freak. Abnormal. Perv. She'd heard them all, and more, at some point.

What was that one from Felix the other day…oh yes, neurotic. And now all the neighbours were saying the same things. She had been so quiet and unobtrusive since buying this place, and over the past few years she had slowly carved out a life for herself bordering on normal. Now she felt she was back in the school playground, with all the loss of control and subsequent fear that entailed.

She was six when she first discovered the truth. A few weeks into starting back at school after the summer break. Kate was in the playground with her best friend, Shelly. It was windy and the whispers danced round her like autumn leaves, tugging at her hair and skirt, wanting to play. The wind made her laugh then.

As a child Kate could easily distinguish between the multitude of voices in her head, picking out a voice in that chorus and listening. But she was less able to distinguish between someone saying something out loud, and them thinking it.

Shelly and Kate were prodding the grass with sticks hoping to see some creepy crawlies. They were doing mini beasts in class.

'My dad left home last night,' Shelley said.

'Why?' Kate asked.

'Why what?'

36

'Why did he leave?'

'Who?'

'Your dad.'

'How did you know about that?'

'You just told me.'

'I never did. I never said anything.'

'Then you must have thought it.'

'But you can't hear people's thoughts.'

'Why not?'

'You just can't.'

'I do.'

Shelly stood up and looked at Kate.

'That's weird,' she said.

'Is it?'

Shelly nodded. 'You better stop or else people will think you're a freak.'

'OK,' she said, sensing it was the best response to make, secretly she didn't know how to.

The bell went to signal the end of playtime. Shelly poked Kate hard in the arm with the stick.

'Ow!' said Kate, rubbing her injury.

Shelly threw the stick down and ran off.

The rest of the day she noticed Shelly staring at her, whispering with Andrea Emmett, a mean girl who pushed the smaller children when the teacher wasn't looking. She couldn't push Kate because Kate was the same size as her, but she could make fun of her, and Kate knew Shelly was giving her the ammunition.

That wasn't the worst of it. Kate didn't really mind that Shelly had run off and stopped being her friend; she knew she was just scared. She didn't even mind about Andrea Emmett, because she knew her mum hit her a lot at home.

What bothered Kate the most was the idea that having the voices was somehow wrong. The thing that helped make sense of her world, the thing that helped her understand others, was considered weird, odd, a transgression of some sort.

Learning that other people didn't have this ability confused her. How did they manage? How did they understand one another? She decided to listen to her voices, but keep them a secret.

In order to keep her secret, she stopped talking so she didn't give herself away. As she got older that exposed her to other types of bullying, and she found it tiring, staying on guard all the time; standing remote in the playground. She didn't make close friends, because if they got close they sensed something unusual about her, sensed she was…weird.

At the age of fourteen Kate decided to stop listening, and during the past thirteen years they had slowly receded. Now, most of the time, she could ignore the hubbub in her head, except in the cacophony created by a crowd, or the uproar forged from a strong wind, both of which, through careful planning, could be avoided.

The only clear thoughts she got these days, were either highly charged and emotional, or inexplicable and fully formed, dropping into her mind from nowhere. Like Ray's.

She had built a good life: finding this flat, making friends with Sam and now Felix, even sourcing work that allowed her to manage her contact with the outside world. Kate thought she had found the right balance, and could make believe she was like everyone else, ordinary.

But Sam's off the cuff remark reminded her that she wasn't really. The word 'weird' broke up into tiny shards and dug into her flesh, rubbing her raw, fibre glass massaged into her skin. If that was what her friend thought of her, what were the neighbours saying?

Kate drew herself into a point of focus, switched on her computer, plugged in her iPod and smothered the pain in the noise of her work.

That afternoon Kate returned laden from the supermarket. She didn't have a car, having never learnt to drive. Her parents had bought her driving lessons for her seventeenth birthday, but the experience of a lesson in a confined space with a sex obsessed driving instructor put her off. She told her parents it wasn't for her, and although her father had tried to encourage her to change her mind, claiming it was a life skill she needed, Kate refused to try again.

The supermarket was only a twenty minute walk, it was one of the things that had attracted her to the flat, and usually Kate dashed in like an SAS raid for a few things and ordered the remainder on-line. Today, her usual raid had been a little more leisurely, and as a consequence she had bought more than she realised.

Her neck and shoulders were shrieking by the time she set the bags down at her front door, Marvin Gaye crooning in her ears. She was rummaging in her handbag for her keys, when she spotted Lucy walking down the other side of the street towards home.

Kate shouted and waved. 'Lucy, Lucy.' Then, realising her mistake, Kate pulled out one of the earphones and quickly crossed the road.

'Sorry I was shouting,' she said, as she neared the child. 'I had my earphones in,' she stopped in front of Lucy and smiled. 'How are you?'

'Okay,' the child responded, her head lowered, wide eyes fixed on Kate.

Kate had read that adults got a better rapport if they were at the same level as the child, so instead of towering over her, Kate leaned over so her face was level with Lucy's. 'You're not afraid of me are you?'

Lucy's gaze fell to the ground and Kate didn't need the voices to know the answer. Damn!

She stood up and sighed audibly. 'Look Lucy, it's just I'm worried for you. That man, Ray, he's a…well, I'm not sure he's as nice as you think. You know what I mean?'

Lucy nodded, still gazing at the pavement. Kate knew she didn't, the child didn't have a clue. That was part of the problem. In frustration she caught hold of the girl's arms to make her look at her.

'Just stay away from him, okay? He might…well, he might hurt you. Just, stay away.' She let go. 'You understand?'

Lucy nodded.

Kate ran her hands over her face in exasperation, and returned to her shopping across the road.

It was no use she thought, as she picked up the heavy bags, as much as she didn't want to, she would have to find a way to speak to the girl's mother, and convince her there was a problem. Before it was too late.

That night, Sam and Kate were heading back to the car after the cinema. It was dark and dry now, but it had rained whilst they were inside, the air carried the scent of hot wet stone.

Kate found it difficult to follow films at the cinema at the best of times, but after her recent run in with Ray, and then her disastrous encounter with Lucy earlier that day, she was finding it even harder to concentrate. Fortunately, the film was predictable so it didn't need any effort to keep up, and Kate had the added bonus of a near empty cinema tonight.

'Want to go for a drink?'

'No sorry, I'm tired. This head.' Kate shrugged an apology.

Sam nodded and unlocked her cherry red mini with the remote key. It clicked and reverberated around the dark car park.

'You okay?' Sam asked.

'Yes, just the –'

'I know,' Sam interrupted. 'The head.'

Kate smiled at her friend's lack of compassion. Sam reversed from her parking space and pointed the car in the direction of Kate's home.

'I think Felix has a thing for you,' she said, after they had been driving for a few minutes.

'What?'

Sam looked sideways and grinned.

'He does, you know?'

'Don't be ridiculous, we're just friends.'

'Would you be interested, if he did?'

Kate said nothing. Instead she watched the streetlights get caught in the drops on the car window as they drove by.

'Well?'

'Well, what?'

'Stop stalling, Gregory.'

'I don't know,' she lied. 'I've never thought about Felix in that way.'

'Have you thought of anyone in that way?'

Kate watched two youths punch one another in fun as they walked down the street. Why did young men do that she wondered?'

'Kate?'

'What?'

'In all the time I've known you, you've never had a boyfriend.'

'So you think I should go out with my neighbour?'

'You could do worse.'

'I'm fine.'

'Suit yourself.'

Sam's hurt was palpable. The car space around them shrank.

'I'm sorry, Sam, but I'm just not interested.'

'In Felix, or anyone?'

Kate shook her head, but smiled. Sam was like a tenacious terrier.

'In anyone at the moment. I like my own company. Have you told Paul yet?' Kate asked, knowing Sam would not be able to resist talking about herself.

'No,' she flicked the indicator and Kate felt soothed by the rhythmic click. They turned and it stopped. 'I thought I'd wait until I'd made a decision. Present it as a fait accompli.'

Kate sensed the soft breath of a whisper beneath the noise, and strained to listen, recognising Sam's voice. *I'm afraid of what it will do to us. I don't want to have that conversation again.* Kate understood the message, but was unsure how to broach a subject they had never discussed. She thought for a moment.

'So, what are you afraid of?' she asked.

'I didn't know I was.'

'Aren't you?'

'God yes, I think I am. How do you do that?'

Kate shrugged. 'I'm a genius.'

They pulled up outside of Kate's flat.

'Am I that obvious?'

'Only to me, and only because I know you so well.'

'I don't think I'm very good at commitment.' Sam sounded miserable.

'You married Paul.'

'I know, but like I've said before, I'm not sure about that now.'

'Don't you think it would be better to talk to Paul about it?'

'Maybe.'

'What is stopping you?' Kate knew, and Sam did too, she just wasn't facing up to it.

Sam shrugged. 'I don't know. I guess while I'm not clear about what I want, I don't want to listen to someone else's advice on what I should do.'

'In case they want something you don't?' she ventured.

Sam shrugged. 'Maybe, or maybe it's because I don't think Paul can let me be the person I want to be.'

It was as honest as Sam was likely to get tonight, and besides, Kate was too tired to pursue it any further.

The women hugged and promised to call each other later in the week. As Kate watched her friend drive away she knew Sam would not take her advice and talk to Paul, not yet anyway. Sometimes the voices helped, sometimes they didn't.

Chapter Eight

The following morning Kate sat at her computer playing her favourite simulation game, The Sims. She clicked on the bookcase and ordered Jayne Shield to study mechanical skills so she would achieve promotion at work. At the same time she ordered Kevin Shield to serve a lunch of grilled sandwiches. All the while Joss Stone poured into the room signing of how she had a right to be wrong. Lucky you, thought Kate.

She was having another good day, with no threat of the voices, so she had decided to take some time out to play her favourite Sims family, the Shields. The computer game involved creating characters, building a home, finding them jobs, loves and marriages, and eventually having a family. Kate was intelligent enough to realise that, given her withdrawal from everyday life, marriage was unlikely to happen for her, and she was also aware that the game gave her a virtual fulfilment of that need, if only in a small way.

It hadn't always been this way. Kate had dated in the past, and experienced the customary courting rituals: dinner, cinema, kissing, and sex. But it was unsatisfactory, for both parties.

She, for obvious reasons, held herself back, afraid of relaxing into the dark void of the voices, that could so easily overwhelm her. And in turn her suitor sensed something was wrong, they felt the distance she created, and unfortunately, demanded more than she could give.

There had been angst ridden conversations with boyfriends, but only Michael Ward, her last foray, had truly pinpointed the problem. It was the relationship that finally convinced Kate she should retreat into a Sims game, and leave real relationships for normal people.

They were sat in Bonhomie, a pretentious French restaurant in town. Michael had asked her to go away with him for the weekend to Edinburgh. He planned for them to catch the train on Friday evening, and stay in a hotel in the centre of the city. She had declined.

Kate couldn't bear the idea of being trapped in a railway carriage for several hours. And then the hotel and the city – wherever they went it would be crowded. Anything could happen.

Michael's jaw tightened and Kate felt her body retreat from him, tighten around her bones in preparation, she knew what was coming. It was the third time he'd asked her to go away with him in their six month relationship, and she knew what was going to happen next. The inevitability was exhausting.

'You know your problem?' he said to her. And she did but didn't say anything.

He didn't need to say anything, she knew, she could already hear. That was the other part of the problem. Kate had come to learn that she didn't really want to know what others thought of her, not without the filter of the social niceties we grow up with, the cream to sweeten the gooseberry. It was too crude, too raw, too sour if you just got it served straight up.

Equally significant, people didn't want you to know them that well either; they didn't want you to delve into them that much. It prevented the games for a start, and our whole social life is based on games, which is tiresome, if you can't play.

What's wrong with me? Why does she keep doing this?

She heard it and sighed inwardly, wishing she had words that could take away his pain. But without revealing her secret, there was nothing she could do but listen.

He pulled his hands through his hair. 'You just can't let go can you?' He looked sad and Kate was sorry. He wasn't a bad man, she liked him.

'You're right,' she said, simply.

'Is it me?'

How often had she heard that question? She shook her head and focused hard on a red wine stain on the table cloth. Pink, deep into the grain of the white linen.

'Then what?'

She wanted to tell him, to lay it all out there for examination among the wine stains and the breadcrumbs, but she couldn't. She tried. She opened her mouth to speak, but the words formed unfamiliar lumps that choked her.

Misunderstanding her silence for disregard, Mike ended the relationship that night, and Kate decided to stick to playing with make believe characters instead. It was subtly satisfying, and if something happened she didn't like, she could simply erase it.

She was just contemplating whether to get Jayne and Kevin to try for a baby, when her street doorbell rang. She put the game on pause and made her way downstairs. The couple already had two children, one boy and one girl, both with an A+ report card of course, and Kate wondered whether she wanted the couple to tip the status quo. Bringing her attention back to reality she opened the external door.

Rachael Newby stood on her doorstep. Although the two women had lived opposite each other on the same street for over seven years, they had barely exchanged the smallest of polite conversations until recently. And they had never knocked on one another's door. Kate's heart skipped, thinking the worst. Lucy!

'Kate,' Rachael said, and nodded sharply, her voice like brittle toffee, hard and edged.

'Rachael,' the word came out breathless. Kate relaxed a little, clearly the child was okay. She hesitated then stepped back and opened the door, unsure. 'You want to come in?'

'No. I'll say what I have to say right here.' She pulled in her mouth as if holding back the words till they were in the right order.

Kate waited. Anxious.

'I don't know what you're playing at, but you've near scared our Lucy half to death. *Again.* ' She laid heavy emphasis on the last word.

Kate said nothing, shocked by Rachael's aggressive tone.

'I know Ray comes across a little...odd, but he's alright. He can be a bit off putting to some I know, with his size and everything, but he's a gentle giant, *if* you took the time to get to know him. You think I'd let someone round her I thought would hurt her?'

'No I...'

'It's not right you trying to poison the minds of people round here just 'cause you don't like the man.'

'I didn't, I mean I don't...it's not like that.'

'Why you think scaring a little girl is acceptable is beyond me.'

'I didn't mean to.'

'Our Lucy tells me you grabbed her arms.' Rachael waited, her face tight, eyes hard. Kate knew this was all wrong, could hear the thoughts. *Bloody mad, mad as hell. Scaring children and making up poisonous stories about people. Little hermit mad crab, she needs to get a life and stop interfering. Cheeky cow. No wonder she hasn't got a fella herself. Who would? And she needs to get her bloody hair sorted out. Look at it!*

'It isn't like that,' Kate said, loudly over the voices in her head, subconsciously trying to flatten her hair.

45

Rachael, misunderstanding Kate's raised voice, raised hers in return. 'Did you?'

Kate slumped in despair. She had, but she was unable to explain properly, the story of her life. But this time she had at least got to try.

'Look,' she said, in a deliberately quiet voice, barely able to hear herself, but trusting the right words were coming out. 'I didn't mean to scare Lucy, it's just, I don't think Ray's safe around children, well, Lucy anyway.'

'What makes you say that?' Kate heard the element of doubt and fear in Rachael's voice and seized it.

'He looks at her in a...particular way, Rachael. There's something about him that's...not right.'

'What's he done? What's he said?' Alarm filled the woman's voice.

'I...' how to explain? 'It's not so much what he's said or done, it's just... the way he looks at her sometimes.'

'And?'

'And...well, that's it really.'

'That's it?'

It wasn't, and Kate wanted to explain. She had the familiar choked feeling. How could she explain? What could she say?

'Do you think I'd let my Lucy be round someone I thought would hurt her?' The anger was back. The moment for further explanation lost.

'No. No, I don't.'

'I've known Ray for over ten years; he's known Lucy since she was a newbie. He's helped me more than anyone I've ever known. When Lucy's father did a runner, Ray, bless him, told me not to worry. He's bought fags and bread round for me when I've not had two pennies to rub together, and he's not loaded himself.'

'No, no I see that. I just don't think that's all there is to him.' As soon as she said it she knew it was wrong.

'Kate, I don't think Ray is the problem in this street, I think you are.' And she jabbed a hard pointed finger in Kate's direction. 'And I'm not the only one. You can't go slandering people, saying the things you're implying about Ray. It's not right. It was better when you kept yourself to yourself. At least we didn't have all this...' she flayed her arms around looking for a word. 'Drama,' she said eventually.

She turned back to Kate. 'It's a wonder Ray hasn't called the police on you yet. But I'll tell you something for nothing, you come anywhere near me or my Lucy again, and I won't hesitate. The law will be down on you lady, like a ton of bricks. Is that clear?'

Kate nodded and watched as Rachael turned and stomped back to her house. She could see some of the neighbours looking on. She closed the door and crept back to the safety of her flat. The computer game sat waiting, everything frozen.

She sat at the desk and stared at the stationary figures, knowing there was no pause button, no command she could click, that could save Lucy. All she could do, was hope that she was wrong.

Felix pulled into the car park of the Crown pub where he'd arranged to meet Phoebe. He couldn't see her car, but she could have changed it again. Her husband David was a director in a stationery firm, and enjoyed all the trappings of a workaholic lifestyle. Felix didn't know there was so much money in stationery, until his sister had married David.

Although she had never said anything, Felix thought that Phoebe was not happy with this lifestyle. As children he wanted flash gadgets and fast cars, whilst Phoebe talked of goats, chickens and living off the land. As a young woman she was poised to go and live on a Kibbutz in Israel, until her mother intervened; a month later Phoebe met David. Felix believed that had their mother not interfered, his sister's life would have been very different, and probably more fulfilling for her.

On reflection maybe Phoebe was right; his mother did mess with her head as much as she did with his. After all, Phoebe was now in a relationship Felix thought his mother was happier about than his sister.

He pushed open the door and was comforted by the beery smell of the pub. It was quiet, and he spied Phoebe in the far corner opposite the door. She wore a pink tailored dress suit and killer black heels. He waved and strode over, looking more confident than he felt. Two drinks sat on the table; a red wine for Phoebe and a Marston's bitter for him. He sat down and took a long drink.

'Something to fortify us,' Phoebe said laughing.

Felix licked his lips and smiled. 'It's not enough. New car?'

'What?'

'I didn't see the BMW.'

'Oh yes, you know what David's like, likes to spoil me.'

'What with this time?'

'A Merc. SLK model. It's gorgeous!'

Felix recalled the sleek blue Mercedes in the car park but said nothing.

'Should we develop a game plan?' Phoebe asked, an artificial note of cheer in her voice.

'You think we can outwit her?' Felix gave a shy smile.

Phoebe laughed. 'No, probably not.'

They chatted idly for a few minutes, catching up on each other's news when Felix asked, 'How do you stop from being pulled in?'

Phoebe shrugged. 'I don't always.'

Felix listened to a clock ticking somewhere. The rumble of male laughter rolled in from the bar next door.

'I know,' he said, his voice soft. 'But more times than not you manage to keep out of the drama. She just seems to wash over you. How?'

'This story might help. Buddha is walking into the city market one day, when an old bitter man starts cursing him, telling him how pretentious he is, how worthless he is, but Buddha just keeps walking and smiling. The next day Buddha returns to the market and once again the old man is there, this time his cursing intensifies and he's screaming and yelling at Buddha as he walks by, cursing his mother, cursing his father and everyone else in his life. This goes on and on until eventually, the old man's curiosity overcomes him and he asks Buddha, "How can you continue to smile when I insult you, your family and everything you believe in?" Phoebe took a sip of wine and licked her lips before placing the glass back on the table and continuing her story.

'Buddha, still smiling asks, "If I were to bring you a gift and you refused it, who would this gift belong to?".

"It would still belong to you of course" answers the old man.

"And so the same goes with your anger, when I choose not to accept your gift of anger, does it not then remain your own?"

'In a nutshell, you choose what you accept and what you don't accept,' she smiled. 'I choose not to accept the crappy bits of mum, at least, that's the theory. There's a lot of good stuff too you know?'

'You make it sound easy.'

'But it is Felix,' she insisted.

'No, it's *not*,' Felix insisted back.

Phoebe nodded. 'I suppose there is more of a challenge for you, but you know what Dr. Carmichael said.'

'Yeah, yeah, keep taking the pills.'

'They do help, don't they?

'I suppose.'

'And are you?'

'God, *yes*, I told you. Do we always have to talk about it?'

'I'm sorry, you're right. It's just...it was an awful time. For all of us. I don't want to see you going back there.'

He nodded.

'So,' she said brightly. 'Are we ready?'

'I'm ready to try.'

She raised her glass. 'That's all any of us can do.'

Sam stubbed out her cigarette into an overflowing ashtray and sighed. It had been over a week since Anne Fletcher had made her the offer, and she still hadn't plucked up the courage to discuss it with Paul. She wasn't usually such a coward, but she knew why she was avoiding the question, knew what was holding her back, and she couldn't discuss anything with Paul while she couldn't see a solution to their stalemate.

She heard footsteps and Julie, their part-time assistant, appeared in the doorway.

'You okay?' she asked, fanning her ridiculously long white nails across her black skirt.

'Yes why?'

She shrugged. 'Dunno, you just look...funny.'

'Funny ha ha or funny odd?'

'Dunno, just...funny.'

'Julie your insightful commentary and grasp on the English language never fails to astonish me.'

'Eh?'

Sam shook her head at the irony of the girl's grunt. 'Did you want something?'

'Yeah, Tracey asked me to ask you if you wanted a sandwich,' she paused. 'From the sandwich shop. She reckons you haven't eaten anything today.'

'No I'm fine thanks.'

Julie clicked back down the hall to the shop and Sam smiled. The girl was as thick as two short planks, but fantastic at putting the right pieces together on the right people. Many of her clients specifically asked for Julie now, and Sam was going to have to think about increasing her hours.

It amused Sam, all those well to do ladies with plums in their mouths taking advice from Julie, as if she were the goddess of fashion. Under normal circumstances few of them would acknowledge someone like Julie, except to order another G&T.

Sam lit up again and sat back in her chair, her thoughts returning to something Kate had said when she had dropped her off after the cinema. Kate was right of course, she always was. She should talk to Paul, and soon.

It was just that, the idea of having a deep and emotional conversation was, for Sam, like eating worms, unappetising and she wasn't convinced she'd get a great deal from it. Besides, she had heard it all before. What was the point of dragging it all up again? She had her viewpoint and Paul had his. Having an angst ridden conversation wasn't going to change that, not unless she had a compromise. Trouble was, there was no compromise.

The house their mother now inhabited was a small, unremarkable two-up-two-down terrace, set in one of the many streets stemming, like spokes of a wheel, from a park in the centre. Nets were essential as the front door sat on the pavement, and offered no privacy otherwise.

He hung back as Phoebe slammed the knocker against the door, it made his heart thump. The sound reverberated around the street, rattling windows and startling its occupants, he half expected the whole street to emerge.

They heard shuffling inside and Felix's gut clenched. He glanced at the back of Phoebe's head, watching the gold in her hair glint while they waited for the door to open.

'Hello mum,' Phoebe said. Her tone was breezy, and Felix wondered if it was a tactic to cope with this visit.

'Did you have to knock so hard love? Nearly jumped out of my skin.'

No welcome, no how do you do, no thanks for coming, thought Felix. No, first words out of her mouth are criticisms. Why was he surprised? He didn't have to wonder why his father did what he did, afterall, he nearly did the same thing himself.

'Sorry, it just sort of slipped,' Phoebe laughed. 'Don't know my own strength.'

'You always were clumsy.'

Felix could feel the mercury rising and he bit his lip, determined not to argue with her before he'd even got in the house.

'You'd better come in. Is that Felix lurking?'

Felix popped his head round Phoebe. 'Hi mum, not lurking, just stood here, waiting to be invited in.' He had meant it as a joke, but even he could hear the sharp edge to the words. Phoebe glowered at him and he shrugged an apology at her.

Mary Shelly pulled open the door to allow her children entry, and they stepped directly into her living room. It smelt stale and the air had a chill to it. A gas fire hissed in the fireplace, the metal clicking as it heated up.

'You've just put the heating on mum.' Phoebe said. 'Mum, how many times have I told you? It's important to keep the house warm.'

The older woman brushed off the comment and eased herself into the armchair.

Felix stood by the door, his nose assaulted by the familiar smell from his childhood of furniture polish and boiled cabbage. It brought it all back, and was why he avoided his mother's place. It suddenly occurred to him that he should tell Phoebe why he didn't come, she would understand, perhaps she would stop making him come here.

'Shut the door if you're coming in,' Mary said.

As if I have a choice, thought Felix, as he closed the door, and a flutter of panic tapped against his breastbone.

His mother looked older and smaller than the last time he saw her. How long was that? He quickly calculated and realised with surprise it had been almost nine months. No wonder Phoebe had insisted he come.

Her hair was whiter, she more shrivelled, and there was an air of defeat she hadn't had before. It depressed him. An image of the mother he had once known flashed before him. Strong, laughing and fun, chasing them with the 'tickle' finger, splashing them in the bath. What happened to her? How did she get to be this person in front of him today?

Now she had nothing and no one. She was alone in this cold box. The thought made his stomach knot up. Life sucked the best of you and left you a husk; bitter and alone. Or was it just her?

'Are you listening Felix?'

'What? No sorry, what were you saying?'

'I said,' she repeated, with thinly disguised irritation. 'You'll have to take the sofa. Phoebe'll have the spare room.'

'Mum, I can drive home tonight and come back in the morning.'

Phoebe stepped in quickly. 'No, you can't. Remember we decided?' she arched an eyebrow.

He tried again. 'But I don't want to be any trouble.'

'It's no trouble Felix,' Phoebe said, through gritted teeth.

'Right. No problem.' He turned to his mother, 'thanks.'

His mother looked him up and down. 'You've grown tall,' she said, a softness creeping into her voice. 'I wonder if you'll fit.'

Felix smiled. 'I'll be fine mum,' he said.

'I forget how tall you are,' she said. 'Don't see you often enough to remember.'

And she's back, thought Felix, deciding not to respond to the criticism.

'I'll be fine,' he insisted, and Phoebe smiled her thanks to him.

Mary drew herself up and took a breath. 'Yes, I suppose you will. It's always easier when you're young.'

'What is mum?' asked Phoebe.

'Life dear, life.'

Felix insisted on going to the bottom of the street to bring back fish and chips, his treat. It was a relief to be out, but as he trudged down the street, his hands buried deep in his pockets, his head down, the weight of his mother still pressed on him. This was dangerous territory, he remembered, and he was sorry he'd lied to Phoebe about his medication. If he'd told her the truth, maybe she wouldn't have made him come.

Kate took two paracetamols with a large glass of water, hoping to take the edge off the pain in her neck and shoulders, glad she had the appointment with the chiropractor tomorrow.

She flopped onto the sofa and turned on the TV, hoping there was something she could watch that would shift the hard rock that had set in her stomach since her earlier gaff.

Everyone in the neighbourhood would be talking about her, even those neighbours who were out at work would hear about it. She flicked through the channels with dissatisfaction. There was nothing for it, although it was barely nine on a Friday night, she was going to bed. How lame was her life?

Chapter Nine

The following morning his mother was horrified when she saw what he'd done. 'It's a navy suite. It'll show every bit of fluff. It'll be covered in stuff off the floor.'

'Why? Are your floors that dirty?' he asked. It was meant to be flippant, instead it came across as spiteful and childish.

'You always were the same,' his mother retorted, her voice warbling. 'Selfish and thoughtless.'

Felix hadn't been able to fit his large frame into the two-seater sofa, no matter how hard he tried. In desperation, in the early hours of the morning, he had made a bed on the floor with the cushions. It wasn't exactly comfortable, but it gave him the luxury of stretching out. He could try to explain, but he knew it wouldn't help. Not today. Instead he watched as she carried the cushions to the kitchen as if they were an endangered species.

'I'll just go over then with a damp cloth,' she mumbled, as she left.

Phoebe lay a hand on his arm. 'Emotions are bound to run high today,' she said.

'It happened to us all, not just her,' he spat back.

Phoebe nodded. 'I'll go and give her a hand.'

Felix, unable to sit in the living room now with the cushions gone, and not wanting to go into the kitchen, decided to go for a walk in search of the Saturday papers.

When he returned the cushions were back in their place, and he was instructed to sit opposite Phoebe at the kitchen table, while his mother served them breakfast. Felix forced her fry up into a heavy stomach, as she barked out the itinerary. This was going to be a long day.

Kate pulled her hand through her spiky hair as she walked along the street. It was a busy shopping area, full of estate agents and solicitors, interspersed with the occasional sandwich shop. A florist spilled out an array of colour over the pavement. Sam had told her the chiropractor's office was at the end of the street, near the mini roundabout, but Kate had been up and down twice already, and still couldn't find it. Perhaps it was on the *other* side of the street, she thought.

A blast of horn from a car made Kate spring back off the road, heart racing, she hadn't even looked. She stood still, breathing heavily, her blood racing through her body, and that's when she spotted a small brass plaque beside a peeling blue door.

No wonder she hadn't seen it, she thought as she walked the few feet. The small door was tucked back from the street, overshadowed by the colourful convenience store.

She tried the door but it was locked. She pushed the pristine new doorbell and waited. With its dirty peeling paint, and the weeds growing out of the wall, it didn't look very professional, and she was just beginning to have second thoughts, when the door opened.

A striking man, at least six foot tall, stood before her. He had dark unruly hair, chiselled cheekbones and a wide mouth. A pair of intelligent crystal eyes sat behind black rimmed glasses.

'Hi, you must be my eleven o'clock, Kate isn't it?' His voice had a bass drum tone, and as he held out his hand, he smiled. The dimple in his left cheek deepened and Kate smiled back, forgetting all previous concerns. 'Josh Evans, Chiropractor extraordinaire.'

His hand was hot, dry and soft. It felt good wrapped around hers, and she found herself holding into it longer than was customary.

Josh, recovering his hand, stepped back and opened the door wider. 'Are you coming in?' he asked, raising his eyebrows.

'Oh, yes, thank you,' she stepped into the hallway. It was small, cream, with parquet flooring. Two doors led off from it, one to the left and one to the right. On the wall opposite hung a picture of a human skeleton with a manic grin.

Kate pointed. 'Nice.'

'Yeah, possibly not the best welcome, especially after the door.'

Kate nodded then, realising she was agreeing with a negative, she tried to change her head direction. Realising she was in danger of looking as if her head was just lolling around on the top of her body, she stopped all movement.

'It gets better,' Josh told her. 'And the decorator is booked to come and do the outside next week.'

'Good,' she said, feeling she had to respond in some way, not trusting her head movements.

'Usually Suzanne's here, my receptionist, she's much better at this sort of thing,' he paused. 'Reception's through here,' he pointed to the door on their left with a sign that read 'Reception'.

He laughed. 'Obviously. Anyway, she phoned in sick this morning, so I have to make do. As it happens, I don't have many appointments for a Saturday, fortunately. You're my first. This is my office,' he opened the door to the right and entered, beckoning Kate to follow him.

'I'm a better chiropractor than a receptionist,' he said, laughing again as he took down the white coat hanging on the back of the door.

'Sit down please,' he said, one arm in his coat, and indicated a chair by the large mahogany desk.

Whilst Josh finished pulling on his white coat, Kate took the opportunity to look round his office. It was a larger room than she had expected. Light streamed through a large bay window at the back. A period fireplace dominated one wall, and in the alcoves on either side, shelves groaned under the weight of a multitude of books. In the centre, at odds with the rest of the room, stood a large narrow hydraulic bed with a lilac plastic cover. It was incongruous in this setting, as if beamed in from the future.

There were no voices today, and the absence of the electromagnetic field that could draw other people's thoughts into her head, like iron fillings to a magnet, meant she didn't need to be quite so vigilant.

All she had to worry about, was the competence or not, of the man who now sat in the leather chair in front of her. Her concern began to evaporate as he took her through the consultation. The awkward man that had greeted her in the hall, was replaced by someone with an air of authority and confidence. Kate sat back and began to loosen up.

They left the house around eleven-thirty in Phoebe's new oxford blue Mercedes. A thin fog had descended giving the proceedings a dour air. Mary insisted on sitting in the back. The car smelt of fresh leather and plastic, and Felix wondered how his nephews managed to be transported in such a car. The run in with his mother that morning over the sofa cushions swept over him. Did his nephews sit in this car in angst in case they made a mess?

He remembered a family holiday in Majorca when they had hired a white Polo for the day to explore the island. It was a beat up old thing, more rust than colour, but it went okay. Having no radio, his father had decided to entertain them by singing 'That's Amore', on the top of his voice, over and over again.

The only way to get him to stop was to take it in turns singing, they all joined in, under protest, but it was so much fun, it was often heralded later as one of their all-time holiday highlights. Felix shook his head. That was his father right through, always able to turn an event into a party, always so much fun.

He glanced over at his sister, her blonde hair looped over a delicate pink ear. Her usual pretty face was pinched and tight, as she focused on the road ahead. He smiled as he remembered her Buddha story from the day before. How she refused to accept the darts of criticism their mother sent out into the world, but she was looking tired this morning. There was weariness about her, and sadness crept into her eyes when she thought no one was looking.

'All right Phebs?' he asked.

She started and nodded, glancing at him and forcing a smile. He wasn't convinced, but decided not to pursue it for now. There would be time later on in this visit, he would make sure of it.

'Just relax,' Josh said.

Kate lay on her front, her face pushed through an oval hole in the bed. Josh had his hot hands on her shoulder blades. 'Breathe in and then as you breathe out, relax completely.' She did as he asked, and on her out breath he made a sharp movement. She heard a crack. It didn't hurt, but the sound made her jump.

'Okay?' Josh asked.

Kate couldn't see his face but thought she heard a smile in his voice.

'Bit of a surprise, the noise I mean,' she said.

'Yes.'

'Lay on your side please.'

He stood behind her and placed his hands one on her shoulder, one on her hip. The heat coming from both was tremendous. She knew what was coming this time, and although it hadn't hurt, she instinctively braced herself.

'Just relax,' he told her, and she tried to let go as he began to move her hips and shoulders in opposite directions, ringing her out like a dishcloth. She was beginning to enjoy the sensation of the stretch when he made another short sharp movement.

This crack was different. Louder, like a bullet going off in her body. It snapped like a neuron whip up her spine, creating synapse connections that flashed images of sun dappled leaves and the taste of strawberry ice-cream.

She could hear whispers, familiar voices, not her usual voices, these were real, indistinct but real. She followed, hoping to hear more clearly, but it was comparable to finding the end of a rainbow. Just when she thought she had arrived, they moved again. The room came back into focus.

'We need to go a little deeper with that one,' Josh said. When Kate tried to speak nothing happened. She felt Josh snap her limp body. There were no sounds this time, no crack. Instead a flash of lightening shot up her spine and exploded into her head. It wasn't painful, quite the opposite.

Her chest opened and she wanted to cry out from the joy of it. It was as if something had dislodged, a block cleared by a satisfying cough.

The room faded and images flashed before her. A blue scarf pulled through a man's hands. Something glinted and caught the light. She could smell iron. Saw a red flash quickly followed by a little girl's shoe. She heard something shatter. There was a musty smell. The flashes began again. A woman's mouth, red, a glint, a shattering, a girl's shoe; a carpet up close, pressed hard against her cheek, a red splash, a swinging light. The images spun faster and faster until she could no longer make them out.

'You okay?' Josh asked, and the words righted her, set her back in the room. She laid still, one hand gripping the side of the bed.

When Kate opened her eyes the room was a mass of particles. Nothing was solid. Something inside had changed, something fundamental. She had been broken down. Her body was strange, off balance, as if she had been given a third leg or grown a second head. She could feel herself sloshing around inside a physical body she didn't fit anymore. Her essence was splashing around in this casing. Liquid gold, she waited to solidify.

'You okay?' Josh asked again. 'That was a deep adjustment. It can take a moment to integrate, probably been out for a while.'

Kate thought he meant out of her body. She found her voice and asked, 'how long?'

'Hard to say, probably since childhood, a knock or fall.' He was washing his hands at a basin in the corner, his back to her.

Realising they had been talking at cross purposes, she adjusted her conversation to match his. 'Why hasn't it bothered me before?' The room was shifting, solidifying.

'Who knows?' he turned, drying his hands on a blue paper towel. 'When we get an injury it causes a tension in the body. Cleverly the body adjusts itself to accommodate that tension. That is, until it can't do it anymore,' he threw the paper towel in the bin and turned to face her. 'One day it presents us with some minor discomfort. If ignored the body continues to notch up the discomfort, until we have sufficient pain to prevent us from ignoring it any longer.' He walked towards the bed.

Feeling steadier Kate sat up slowly. Everything seemed in order again. The room and its contents were solid, her brain had stopped fizzing, the gold inside had solidified, and her body had regained its balance.

'You ready to stand up?' he put one hand out to steady her, as if she had aged a hundred years since getting on the bed.

'I'm fine,' she said as she stood up. The nagging pain, the drilling ache between her shoulder blades, and her headache, had all gone. There was a renewed sense of energy coursing through her body, as if she were a conduit of electricity.

'That's amazing,' she said.

'Another satisfied customer,' Josh said grinning. He licked his finger and drew a 1 in the air, making Kate laugh.

They pulled into the cemetery and drove slowly along the road, watching graves pass to their left and right. It was a huge place, with three car parks. They were heading for car park B. It made Felix think of amusement parks and airports, neither of which was really appropriate, so he forced himself to refocus.

It was unseasonably grey and cold for September. The trees were heavy with wet leaves turning in the early autumn air. As they emerged from the warmth of the car, Felix pulled his black overcoat tighter around him, feeling the damp tendrils grabbing at him and sending shivers through his body. Claustrophobia threatened, a feeling of oppression, despite the open space, as if the trees were marching in to close ranks on him. He shuddered as he followed Phoebe and his mother.

It had been twenty years today that his father had taken his own life, and Felix still missed him. He had resigned himself to the fact that he always would. Tom Shell had been a larger than life character, with a baritone voice to match. Wherever he was, whatever he was doing; building shelves; fixing the washing machine; driving a hire car on holiday, he would surround himself with his voice. Felix was convinced the man was ground down by the woman he lived with, why else would he have done what he did?

Felix was eleven when he lost his father. He remembered it well, unlike today it was hot, the sun baked the top of his head, and he could smell the shampoo on his hair from the previous night's bath. He remembered it well not only because he lost his father, but because it was the start of his black outs, and the trouble that was to follow. It was the day he killed a frog, and it opened a fissure for The Badness to get in. His illness had brought years of misery, as Phoebe had said the day before, for all of them.

He was alright now, had been for several years, but Phoebe was right, he did need to keep taking the pills. He could forget when he was feeling well, and he hadn't been taking them recently. Again, he wished he'd come clean when she'd asked.

The truth was, he hated that there was this thing wrong with his head, hated the drugs for reminding him. Without them he could pretend he was normal, but then, without them he wasn't. Without them he was dangerous and he knew that, so why had he stopped?

The line that mental illness was no different to a broken leg was crap, he decided. In his experience the moment people knew he had schizophrenia, they changed, treated him differently. With a broken leg people would help, but with a broken head they examined him as if he were a rare specimen. Even Phoebe did it sometimes. So he didn't tell people, and it helped that he didn't live with his mother anymore, she seemed to enjoy telling *everyone*. More proof that, despite what Phoebe said, she hated him. More proof that, despite what Phoebe said, she had driven his father to his death.

He watched his mother now, striding purposefully ahead of him and he filled with rage. Had he been given the choice of which parent he would lose, he would have chosen her. He remembered the beating he gave her before they took him away. She had deserved it, at least, he had thought that then. Who was he kidding, he still thought she had deserved it, would probably do it again if he thought he could get away with it.

Felix shook his head in despair, he didn't want to be this way, but it was her fault.   He was always like this around *her.* He held back, sure she could sense this malevolence in him, convinced it was as tangible as those damn cushions this morning.

Phoebe glanced back and Felix waved. A whitewash of guilt added to the emotions coursing through his body. He always did this, stood on the side lines and let Phoebe lead. He had done the same when they were kids. And it wasn't just at home, he hadn't joined in at school either, making few friends.

But he wasn't like that now, he reminded himself. Now he was part of a team at the Town Hall with Rose and Gina and John. He joined in, he participated. And there was Kate, the frustratingly beautiful, quirky, Kate.

No, it was different when he was young. He was shy then, unsure of his capabilities, but not anymore. He knew what he was capable of, knew the strength of his power, knew the depths of his badness, and it was under control now.

As if to prove it he jogged to close the gap between him and what was left of his family.

It happened outside the bank just after her appointment. The crushing pain had lifted, and whilst her neck was still sore, she hardly noticed it. She was free, light.

Kate stood outside the heavy studded doors at the top of the stone steps that led up from the high street to its entrance. She experienced a fuzzy feeling, she was a pencil sketch and her edges had been rubbed out. No, not rubbed out exactly, more softened, so she didn't have any definable areas of her own anymore.

As this feeling grew there was a deafening click, the kind a box brownie made to snap a picture, and she saw a little girl's shoe lying discarded on the road in front of her.

It looked ordinary apart from the pale blue haze that surrounded it; an electric Chernobyl glow. She closed her eyes and when she opened them it was gone, and all activity on the street had returned to normal. She had a sense that it meant something, but she didn't know what. What could a discarded shoe mean?

It was gone. Just as quickly as it had come. She felt dizzy and sat on one of the benches opposite to catch her breath. After a few minutes she regained her composure and began a slow walk home, unclear what she had just experienced, what she had seen, or what, if anything, it meant.

Paul passed Sam the plates from dinner as she loaded the dishwasher. It would have been quicker to do it herself, but he liked to help, and she enjoyed his quiet body radiating contentment beside her. He puffed out clouds of calm. It was one of the things that had attracted her to him originally. That steady rock quality.

'Jen next door found her cat,' she said, wanting to make conversation, get closer. Checking this solid tranquil mass was still hers.

'Good. She did get distraught about it.'

'She loved George.'

'I know, but I really don't understand the fuss people make over their pets,' he said this kindly, genuinely baffled by the phenomenon. 'I really can't understand it.'

Sam smiled. 'That's because you've never had one.'

He shrugged. 'Maybe.'

Sam stood up and shut the dishwasher door.

'I still don't believe I'd behave as if I'd lost my right arm or something,' he said. 'She was so upset, she couldn't go to work that day.' He shook his head. 'Amazing.'

Sam selected the program and pushed the start button. The machine jumped to life, gushing and growling. 'You think the dishwasher needs servicing?' she asked.

'Nah, it always makes that noise.'

She turned round and snaked her arms round Paul's waist to rest her head on his chest.

'You okay?' he asked, wrapping his arms round her and sitting his chin on the top of her head.

'Yes, why?'

'You've been a little…distracted recently, that's all.'

'Mmm,' Sam said into his chest. 'I've...I've been…' She had to say something at some point. 'Anne's offered me a promotion at work.'

Paul pulled away and held her at arm's length to look at her. 'What?'

Sam's insides tightened. 'She wants to retire and she wants me to be the new Managing Director. It's a great opportunity.'

'Sam!'

'I'm just thinking about it.'

'You're *thinking* about it?'

'What?'

'I thought we agreed, I thought we felt the same way?'

The cosy calm atmosphere she had enjoyed slid away. The steady rock from only moments ago, now stood in front of her as a solid impenetrable mountain.

'Paul, it's my life.'

'No Sam, not anymore, now it's our life and we made an agreement about the way we were moving forward. Didn't we?' Sam didn't respond. 'Or did I imagine that conversation?'

Resentment burned the back of Sam's throat. 'Can you let this go Paul?' She didn't want to have this conversation again, afraid of what she might say, afraid of what it might do to them.

'Let it go? Of course not. What a ridiculous thing to say.'

She swallowed hard. This wasn't going to be easy but then, she always knew that. 'Maybe it's not as important to me? Has that ever occurred to you?'

'Of course it occurred to me. That's why we talked about it.'

'Well, maybe I've changed my mind.' She heard the petulance in her voice. It wasn't the way she wanted to tell him.

Paul let go of her and stepped back, as if she had hit him. 'You don't want children?'

Why did he have to push these things? 'I'm not saying that,' she said quickly. 'It's just…' she sighed. How could she begin to explain when she didn't even understand it herself? Yes she wanted children, sometimes, but there was a bigger part of her that couldn't help feeling as if somehow it would be the end of something. She didn't know what, but it felt important; elusive, unknown, but important. She felt foolish saying all this until she could work out what this elusive thing might be. But perhaps it was time?

She looked at Paul and saw the tight line his jaw had taken. His blue eyes had darkened. His face set granite hard. No, she thought, not this time.

'I'm sorry,' she said instead, and she was.

'Why did you marry me?' he asked, growling out the words.

'Because you asked me,' she moved towards him smiling, hoping to bring him back to her. 'Over and over again, I seem to remember.'

He pulled away from her. 'Yes,' he said, the word hitting her. She braced herself for more, but he turned and walked from the kitchen without another word.

Kate picked through the reduced cold food section and found a lasagne for one, and some mozzarella cheese with today's sell by date. She would have an Italian theme tonight, maybe some Panini and olives, light a few candles and stick Puccini on full volume while she cooked. Have a private celebration that she was pain free.

Sam had bought Kate a Puccini CD last Christmas, which was bizarre considering Kate had neither listened to, nor expressed an interest in, opera. But something Kate 'heard' explained it. Sam had got it from a half price bin. It wasn't the first time. Still, this time it had paid off.

Kate paid the checkout girl and braced herself for the long walk home with her packed shopping.

NO! MAM! NO!

Kate woke with a pounding chest and a sinking feeling in her stomach; she knew who the voice belonged to. Was it a dream, or had she heard the child's plaintive voice for real?

She hoisted herself off the sofa, and in spite of the dream and her high emotion, found she was hungry. When she went into the kitchen to make dinner she was surprised to find very little in. Where was the lasagne? The Panini? Had she eaten it already? Had she left the bag behind in the shop?

She stood in the middle of her kitchen, her hand on her forehead, pressing the soles of her bare feet into the cold tiles, trying to grab the thread of a memory of the supermarket. Was it real?

As always the sounds gave it away; the piped music, the bleep of the scanning machine and the checkout girl's voice. She knew at once the shopping trip had been a dream. It hadn't happened at all. Sound, her tool to distinguish dreams from reality, had helped her make the realisation, but it was the absence of food that had finally convinced her.

What was reality anyway? Was this strange walking state she called her life really reality? Surely this existence full of other people's voices; their secrets and thoughts, dreams and desires, wasn't real. Voices calling to her from no-where, sometimes without warning. The ribbons of words that streamed from the unconscious minds of those around her, had slowly distorted her waking life, until it had a dream like quality, almost nightmarish, and her dreams of the mundane were becoming more real to her.

The shopping trips, walks by the river and the putting out of the bins that she dreamed about, seemed more like her real life than this.

And then there was Lucy. Little Lucy Newton. Wasn't she just obsessing about it all, to the point where she had begun to dream she was hearing things because she didn't in life? Assuming this waking *was* her real life...

She stood allowing the cold to soak into her feet and move into her ankles, cold as stone.

So where was the Panini? Where was the lasagne? The olives? Milk? Cheese?

The absence of these few tangible things she clung to. This was her proof of what was reality, what were her dreams. That, and the cold slowly creeping up her legs creating goose pimples, the pain in her chest and the tears on her cheeks.

It had started as such a good day, but so much weird stuff had happened since. Yes, she knew she should be used to weird by now, but this was new weird. The flash outside the bank, hearing Lucy's voice in her dream, those were new weirdness, and she wasn't sure she could cope with any more 'weird' in her life.

Finally, she turned and did the only thing she could do to stop her going mad, right there in the middle of her kitchen. She went to bed, pulled the duvet over her head, and waited for sleep to claim her.

The hands crawled round the clock face that Saturday night for Felix. Before dinner he had escaped the claustrophobia. He drove without direction and couldn't remember where he went, having suffered one of his black outs. He remembered listening to some of Women's Hour and PM on Radio 4, but other than that, nothing came back. They rarely affected him these days but, despite the gnawing worry that it had happened, he had to admit to feeling calmer than at any other point since arriving. Still, it was another reminder to resume his medication, and he resolved to do so when he returned home tomorrow.

Finally, at eleven, Mary bid her goodnights and made her way upstairs.

'You okay?' Phoebe asked, when their mother had left.

'No. I realised tonight there's no hell or heaven when you die, its right here on earth. This is my hell.' His previous calm had evaporated.

'God Felix, you're such a drama queen,' Phoebe rolled her eyes and giggled.

'It's not funny. I'm virtually brain dead from watching mindless television for four hours straight.'

'Stop exaggerating.'

'And now I've got to wedge myself into this sofa made for dwarfs, and try to get some sleep.'

'You can have my bed.'

Felix let the breath out of his body. 'No, thanks anyway.'

They sat in front of the television, the sound low.

'Where did you go before tea?'

'Just a drive, I needed to get away.'

'You seemed a bit…odd when you got back.'

'Did I?'

'Yeah.'

'Probably coming back here. I could easily drive home now.'

'I know, but I can't, and besides, it's not about you. It's about her. I'm here to support mum and you're here to support me.'

'Seriously, how does she not do your head in?' Felix said, his eyes glued to a game show where contestants got an electric shock if they pressed their buzzers.

'I told you, sometimes she does.'

'But you don't suffer like me.'

Phoebe laughed. 'Oh Felix, no one suffers like you.'

He turned to look at her. 'What d'you mean?'

'Nothing.'

'No. What?'

'You've always been the same,' she thought for a moment. 'Even as a little boy you were the sensitive one.'

'I'm not sensitive.'

Felix said nothing. He was young then, very young. People change. Circumstances require it sometimes, if you want to survive.

'And you didn't like joining in sports. It was all too rough for you.'

'You make me sound like a right girl.'

'Nothing wrong with girls,' Phoebe said.

'There is if you're a boy.'

She smiled. 'You were so different to my boys. You wouldn't have plaited those girl's hair, well, not together anyway.'

Felix didn't say anything, not wanting to spoil his sister's illusions of him. It was good to have someone think him noble. Phoebe shoved him gently. 'You'd have stopped my boys from doing it. Punched them on the nose.'

'So, not so much of a girl then?' he said finally.

'Like I said, sensitive. Not a wimp, sensitive.'

'Maybe,' he mumbled. He was beginning to feel anxious about his earlier blackout. What had he done? He pushed his mind to remember, even though he knew from efforts of the past, that it was futile. It would come back in its own time. Again he regretted not taking his drugs, especially on the run up to a visit to his mother's. Again he asked himself why he did it, but it was a mystery to him. Phoebe's next comment brought him back to the living room.

'Nothing ever survived though did it?'

'No,' he remembered the pets he had as a teenager.

Phoebe laughed. 'Don't look so glum. It wasn't your fault. You just looked after them a little too…vigorously. Smothered them with love so to speak.'

They were quiet for a few moments. It was tight and awkward. They turned back to the television.

'Those stairs are steep,' Phoebe said.

The contestants were now eating maggots.

'I guess.' He wondered what drove people to do the these things. Still, what drove anyone to do anything? 'I think they're fairly standard in these kinds of houses.'

He looked at Phoebe, her eyes full of worry. I am a bad person, he thought, not for the first time in his life. There she was, believing him to be sensitive and caring, when he couldn't care less if their mother fell down the stairs. In fact, if he was really honest, he knew there was a bit of him that would give her a push given half the chance.

'She'll be fine,' he said.

Phoebe nodded. 'I suppose.'

The stillness of the night enfolded them, the way it had done when they were children. Drawing them together like the threads in a weave, each depending on the other for its form and shape.

'Are you and David okay?' He noticed a slight shift in Phoebe's body.

She released a nervous laugh. 'Yes, why do you ask?'

'I've noticed things.'

'Like what?'

'New car, sad eyes, doesn't take a genius.'

'I'd better be careful in future. What does it mean if I buy a new pair of shoes? Or what if we move house?'

'Okay, okay,' he said. 'Just remember I'm here if you want to talk.'

'And you're sure *you're* okay?' she asked in return.

'Yes, fine,' there was a warning in his voice to back off.

She nodded and pointed at the screen. The contestants were now in their underwear being hosed down. 'Can you believe what some people will do to get on telly?'

They turned their attention back to the screen.

Chapter Ten

Felix woke at 6am and slowly unwound his stiff body. He had no idea how people overcame their body's physical requirements to break world records. Standing for sixteen days in a bucket of beans and that sort of thing, what possessed them? What gave them the idea they could mentally override their physical needs like that? One night on a cramped sofa told Felix, quite clearly, he couldn't.

A pewter light struggled through the curtains. He opened them but it didn't help. He pulled back the nets to look out. The view was bleak, nothing separated the house from the pavement and across the road, a row of identical terraced houses looked back at him.

What kind of people lived in the houses he was looking at? They seemed too small to house families, yet yesterday the street was filled with noisy children. He saw a flash of yesterdays drive, but it was too quick to catch. He let the net drop and went into the kitchen to make tea.

He flicked on the kettle and turned to look into the yard as he waited for it to boil. He could not understand why his mother had sold their home and bought this ugly little house. Such a cramped place, not just inside, but outside too. No garden for a start. His father had loved their garden. It didn't matter what the weather was like, he would be out there. If he closed his eyes he could still smell the straw hat his father always wore; a mixture of sweet hay and hair cream.

He poured boiling water over his teabag. Being locked away for two years at fifteen had been bad enough, but discovering the loss of their family house when he returned had been as hard as losing his father at eleven. It was as if his mother wanted to eradicate the memory of the man she'd spent most of her life with, and what had she done with all the money? This place couldn't have cost much. Still, it gave him the excuse to get away from her. It had spurred him on to find his own place in the world, and by the time he was nineteen he had left this crappy little house, and her.

'Hi.'

Felix jumped and turned to see Phoebe in the doorway, looking flushed from a warm bed.

'I couldn't sleep,' she said. She pulled her thick fisherman's cardigan tighter to her and shuffled in her Uggs to a chair at the table. 'It's a bit nippy isn't it?' She sat down.

'A bit. Tea?'

'Please.'

Felix pulled out another mug and scaled a second bag. After adding milk and a half sugar to his sister's tea, he brought the mugs over to the table and sat opposite her.

'Thanks.'

They sipped their tea in the hush, as the day stretched, ruffled its feathers and began to wake up; the pewter light giving way to a lighter pearl.

'How'd you sleep?'

'Badly. Squished up like a foetus in a womb.'

Phoebe nodded, but she didn't smile as he'd expected. 'You okay?' he asked.

'Sure.'

'Are you?'

'Am I what?'

'Sure?'

She shrugged.

'You do have a problem don't you?'

Phoebe stared at her tea.

'Tell me, trouble shared and all that.'

'It's a bit of a mess really.'

'What is?'

'I'm pregnant.'

Felix hesitated. 'But that's good isn't it?'

'I think David is having another affair.'

'Oh, shit.'

'Precisely.'

'But you don't know, I mean, for sure?'

Phoebe sipped her tea, then set her mug carefully on the table. 'I know I'm pregnant and I'm pretty sure David's having an affair.'

'What are you going to do?'

Tears filled her eyes. 'I don't know. That's the problem. The affair isn't the issue. You know what David's like. They never last. Usually it's not important. He's there when it matters, like the boys parent's evenings that sort of thing, but this time it does matter,' she cast out a half smile. 'Probably because I'm pregnant. Hormones get in the way of logic.'

'It should matter all the time.'

'Maybe, but it doesn't. Maybe I don't love him the way I should, but it doesn't matter. Well, usually it doesn't. He gets on with his thing and I do mine, and it works. Unconventional perhaps, but it works for us. We're a good team.'

Felix said nothing. He didn't know what to say. He disagreed with everything she had just said, but knew it wouldn't help to argue.

Phoebe reached out and placed her hand over Felix's. 'I knew before I married him Felix. It's the way he is. It's not as if he tricked me or anything, and I've saved myself a lot of pain by not thinking I could change him. I don't see it as a rejection of me, more a weakness in him. His being unfaithful isn't the issue here.'

'Then what is?'

'The pregnancy.'

'Will he leave you?'

She shook her head. 'God, no.'

'Then what?'

'I don't want it.'

'Oh.'

'This pregnancy isn't convenient. There's no reason for me not to have it. David would be delighted. It's me, not him.'

Felix bent his head low, unable to take in what she was saying, knowing that when he finally did, a small fissure would appear between them, and she would join the rest of the female sex, no longer exceptional in his mind. It seemed all woman had the capacity to destroy, and the disappointment shattered his heart.

Kate was making coffee when she had the feeling of being erased or softened around the edges, and then the loud click of the camera followed.

This time she heard noises; a low moan and a tinkle. It took her several moments to discern it. What she was actually listening to was the wind, and the sound of breaking glass. A gentle sound from far off. It lasted only moments, yet it felt significant.

What was going on? What was this thing that was happening to her? The voices had dimmed considerably since her visit to Josh yesterday morning, the memory of him sent a rush of excitement through her body but she forced her mind back to these…what were they? Flashbacks? Flash forwards? Or simply her brain resetting itself? And what about the strange dream of Lucy's voice yesterday afternoon? Did that fit in anywhere? Was it a dream, or had she really heard her? She shook her head, as if that would dislodge it all, nothing good had come of any action she had taken since hearing Ray in the corner shop ten days ago. She would simply have to put it out of her mind.

She picked up her coffee and retreated back to her Sims game. Jayne Shields was about to give birth to her third child, and Kate was keen to know whether she would have a boy or a girl. The couple wouldn't mind, she decided, and she already had name in mind. Lucy, the thought pleased her.

'Where's Felix?' Sam asked.

Kate and Sam were sat in the Red Lion on Sunday afternoon.

Kate tasted her G&T before replying. 'He's gone to visit his mum.'

Sam screwed up her nose. 'Urgh.'

Kate smiled, aware of how little Sam got on with her mother, reflecting on the irony that she was the only one of the three that enjoyed visiting her parents despite, or was it because, she was adopted.

'How's Paul?'

Sam shrugged. 'We are…a little strained at the moment. He's gone into his cave,' she rolled her eyes in exasperation.

Kate nodded. Sam had explained the whole Mars and Venus theory that she based her relationship on, and whilst she expected Paul to fully understand and honour her Venus traits, she appeared to find it rather more difficult to honour Paul's Mars.

'Have you talked to him?'

'I'm not sure 'talk' is the right expression. I've told him about the job offer, if that's what you mean.'

'So he hasn't taken it well then?'

'Kate, hello? He's not speaking to me at all, period. He's shut me out. He is so selfish at times, doesn't think how his reactions and behaviour will affect anyone else.'

The words kettle, pot and black sprang to mind, but Kate said nothing, enjoying the ability to have a conversation at face value, instead of having a background fear that at any moment her friend's thoughts would drop into her head. It was such a unique luxury. She could feel her body unbutton. Was this what it was like for other people?

Kate didn't understand why the voices had left her, but she was enjoying the freedom it afforded her, the freedom and the peace. Sam's voice brought her back to the moment.

'Oh, it's so easy for you,' Sam said airily. 'I envy you.'

'Me?'

'Yes, you. Such a simple life, no complications. You've got the right idea about men – stay well clear. They're a real pain. I'd have your life like a shot.'

Kate shook her head, amazed at her friend's lack of perception and chose not to mention the fact that, only a few days earlier, when they'd gone to the cinema together, Sam had tried to fix her up with Felix. She also chose to pass over her increasing preoccupation with Josh.

Chapter Eleven

The following morning, when Kate took her coffee onto the balcony, Felix was still breakfasting at his table in the yard.

'Care to join me,' he called up.

She was hesitant. The last thing she needed on top of everything else, was the lovesick Felix.

'Shouldn't you be at work by now?' she said, expecting him to leap up, swear and rush off.

'Day off. Needed the extra day to recover from the dreaded weekend visit.'

'That bad huh?' He did look drawn.

'As always,' his voice sounded lugubrious.

She felt sorry for him and perhaps, without the whispers, it would be all right, so with trepidation she agreed to join him.

Felix made fresh coffee and toast.

'You picked the perfect day for it. Can you believe the weather at the weekend?' she said, taking the spare chair.

'I was just thinking that myself. This is probably the last of the sun this year. Thought I might trot along to the seaside and take a walk along the beach.'

'Sounds lovely.'

'Want to come?' Felix's eyes held her.

What was he thinking? She sensed there was more to the invite, and she remembered Sam's comment. She didn't want to give him the wrong impression. She liked Felix but, well, not like that. If only he hadn't taken her underwear from the line...if only she didn't know he had. She tried to put it out of her mind, but somethings just sat there, squarely in front of you, she'd heard it referred to as "an elephant in the room", and her knickers, whilst not large, were very much elephant like in that respect.

Damn it, she wished she knew what was going on in his head, and suddenly against all odds, she found herself at a loss without the voices. It was as if, without them, she was more vulnerable, but this was what it was like for other people, and it was what she had always wanted. Besides, she

74

hadn't used the voices when she had them, in fact, she'd spent most of her life running away from them.

Felix dropped his eyes. 'Just a thought,' he said. His voice had that same lugubrious sound from earlier.

It pulled at her, what was her problem? 'Okay,' she said. Why not? What harm could it do? 'I'm looking forward to it,' she added.

Felix smiled at her and nodded in agreement.

Felix and Kate walked the length of the vast beach, empty apart from a couple of dog walkers in the distance. The tide was out, the sea a distant gleam. The wind tugged at them like an impatient child wanting attention, and for once Kate could ignore her.

'I like it here,' Felix said. 'It clears my head. I think it's the space, you know, even the sky seems higher.'

Kate looked up at the empty blue sky. He was right.

'Don't you like the town then?'

'It has its advantages, but on the whole, no.'

'So why live there?'

He shrugged. 'Work I suppose.'

'But it wouldn't take you long to commute from here.'

Felix shook his head and squinted out to sea. 'Hate rushed early mornings, sitting in traffic, that sort of thing.'

Kate laughed and they settled back into walking quietly side by side. She was melancholic walking like this, but didn't understand why. Perhaps it was the sound of defeat beneath Felix's words. Or was it defeat? Who could tell? For a moment she yearned again for the emotional tentacles she didn't realise she had always relied on.

The voices didn't drop into her head anymore, didn't act as signposts, and whist she had cursed them when she had them, she was discovering that life could be puzzling without them; or at least, people were.

A gust of wind whipped up strong, assaulted every sense, disorientating her; slapping her face and whipping her hair round. Laughter bubbled up inside her and forced itself out of her mouth, puzzling perhaps, but nice she decided.

They found a bench on the promenade to eat their fish and chips. The wind had dropped and the sun was warm.

'I haven't done this since I was a kid,' Kate said.

'You should get out more,' Felix told her.

'I know, you're right.'

'Can I ask you a question?'

Kate braced herself. 'Okay.'

'What do you do when you shut yourself up for days?'

Kate wondered how to answer. Should she tell the truth now, when it was all over? She'd had the secret for so long she forgot why she kept it in the first place.

'Sometimes,' she said, and then stopped, unsure how she was going to continue. Her hands dropped and she rested the fish and chips in her lap. She turned to him and took a breath. 'Sometimes I…well, you see…' she stopped, and looked at his face. It was an unusual face, lots of squares and angles that gave him an Eastern European look; it could easily have been cruel. It was saved by the softness and warmth in his eyes, Kate thought.

'You need space right?' Felix smiled, and Kate nodded. It was easier.

'It's nothing to be ashamed of. We all need that from time to time,' he laughed. 'You made it look like you were about to tell me some dark secret, as if you'd been up to something.'

She forced a smile. 'Tell me about your family,' she asked, wanting to move them away from the subject, now the moment to tell was lost.

'I have a sister who has two kids. Mum's still alive, as you know, but dad died when I was eleven. That's it. It was the anniversary of his death last weekend. That's why Phoebe and I went to visit my mother. I find it all a bit grim. It usually is when we go and see her, but this time was worse.'

'I'm sorry.'

They watched a woman, only a girl really, shout at her daughter. 'Kylie come 'ere will you.'

The child could only have been about three. The mother grabbed the child's arm and dragged her off down the road. The girl began to wail in protest. Kate bent her head and stared at her fish and chips, remembering Lucy's voice haunting her dream.

'No! Mam! No!'

'How did you get into planning?' she said, as the noise of the child faded into the distance.

'How does anyone get into planning? It isn't your childhood dream job. I had a dream of being an architect, I trained, realised I wasn't bright enough, and looked for a job, other than building, that was close to what I wanted to be. Fell into planning.'

'Really?'

'Pretty much. Had to switch my options.'

'How sad.'

'What?'

'Well, to have a dream and then,' she shrugged.

'It's called life, Kate.'

The idea that she didn't really know much about life weighed on her.

'What about you?'

'Huh?'

'You, Kate, you. What about you?'

'Nothing much. No siblings, that I know of anyway. Parents alive, well and still happily married, which I think is amazing.'

'Do you suspect your father played around?'

'What?' Kate looked at him and blinked, waiting to understand what Felix had just said.

'No sibling that I know of you said.'

She blinked again, then it dawned on her. 'Oh no, no,' she laughed. 'I'm adopted, so in theory I could have a sibling, or at least a half one somewhere.'

'Wow, I never knew you were adopted.'

'Why would you? I don't tend to introduce myself with it. You know, "hi I'm Kate and I'm adopted". It would be a bit strange,' she laughed.

'I've never met anyone who's been adopted. What's it like?'

'Don't know anything different. I had a normal happy childhood as far as I'm concerned.'

'How old were you?'

'Four, but I don't remember anything, and I've never felt the need to find out.' A swirl of emotion began to move, and she slammed the door on it.

'But aren't you even a bit curious?'

'Why would I be?'

'Just to see where you came from, you know, who you belong to.'

'My parents have given me everything I need. I belong to them. The others, well,' she shrugged. 'They just had a biological input.'

'You sound angry.'

'Do I?'

'Yes.'

Kate scrunched up her paper and stood. 'Well I'm not, but I don't like talking about it so, if you don't mind…'

'No sorry, of course, I was just curious.'

'I think we should be heading back now,' she looked up. 'It looks like it might rain.'

The sky didn't look any different from when they arrived. They drove back with individual blankets of silence wrapped round them.

'Thanks,' said Kate, when they got back home. The word split the air between them.

'It was nice,' said Felix.

They paused on the pavement. A car drove past. Kate tugged at her hair. Felix pulled at his jacket.

'Right then,' he said.

'Yes,' she said.

Kate and Felix caught each other's eye, Kate laughed.

'It was...good,' she said. 'Thank you,' and before Felix could respond, she turned and left.

In the early hours of the morning, Kate was woken by the sound of a car starting up. It sounded like the gravelly sound of Felix's VW Beetle. She dismissed the idea. What would Felix be doing driving around at, she glanced at the clock, three in the morning? As the car pulled away, Kate turned over and went back to sleep.

Chapter Twelve

Kate didn't read the paper or watch the news. It was all bad and she didn't need it. But even she couldn't ignore the headline on the local free paper as she picked it up the following morning with her post. Usually it went straight into the recycling box, but today it stopped her. Rooted in her hall, she read the words that poured lead into her veins, solidifying her blood. 'Girl aged 9, Missing.'

It was happening again. That blurring, then the click.

It was brief this time, just a glint of light, like a mirror catching the sun. Nothing more. Then it was gone, and Kate felt the familiar dizziness and exhaustion.

Kate knocked on Felix's door. There was no answer and she couldn't hear any movement inside so he must be out, strange then, she thought, that his car was outside.

Inside her flat she toyed with the idea of phoning her friend, but couldn't face Sam's self-absorption today. She needed someone to talk to, not someone talking at her. Besides, Sam would be at work and wouldn't necessarily have the time to talk.

Finally, she picked up the phone and dialled her mum.

'Hey sweetie, how are you? Haven't heard from you for a while, thought you'd dropped off the planet,' Jan Gregory's tone was light. There was no veiled criticism in the words.

'No gravity still working in my universe.'

Both women laughed.

'So, how are things?'

'Okay. Work's going well. Got lots of it so I must be doing something right.'

'That's good.' Kate was aware that her mum didn't know what to make of her work, or her lifestyle. As soon as she realised she was different, she kept it from her parents, afraid that she would once again be passed on, rejected.

'And dad?'

'I never see him love, to be honest. Always on the golf course. Not that I mind, gives me time to do my own thing.'

'So, what you been up to?'

'Had lunch with Sheila yesterday. We're going horse riding tomorrow.'

'Mum!'

'I know, I can't remember the last time I went riding. I'm so excited. It'll do me the world of good.'

'Sounds great,' Kate's voice came out flat.

'You sound a bit down. You okay? Something wrong?' Her mum always knew.

'Oh, you know. Something and nothing.'

Jan laughed. 'I know those days only too well. You need to get out more. Why don't you come tomorrow? It would be so nice to see you, and I know Sheila would love it. She's always asking after you.'

There was really no reason not to, now the voices had gone. It might even take her mind off everything, blow away a few cobwebs.

'Come on, how about it? I can book another place easily enough.'

'Okay, thanks mum.'

'Great, that's settled. You want to come over for dinner tonight?'

'No, thanks. It's not that bad, just needed to hear a friendly voice.'

They finalised the plans for the following day.

'Oh, I'm so glad you've decided to come. I haven't seen you for the longest time.'

Kate smiled. 'I'll see you tomorrow.'

'See you then sweetie, keep your chin up.'

She replaced the receiver and lolled back onto the sofa. Speaking to her mother had lifted her spirits a little, but she still had that gnawing feeling in her stomach, as if something were trying to devour her from the inside.

As she laid there, her arms stretched above her head, she thought she heard a voice. Faint and fleeting, much fainter than last time, yet still clear. Kate sat bolt upright to listen.

But it was gone. If it had ever been there in the first place. She jumped up and moved around, straining her ears, thinking she might catch it again.

Nothing. She threw up one of the sash windows in the living room and leaned out, if it was windy there might be something. But the air was still, only a slight breeze, and something told her she wouldn't hear it again. It was gone. Lost. They were gone. The voices.

It was something and nothing, Kate had told her mother. Now she knew it was something, more importantly, she had to take action, and she had an idea of who might be able to help her.

It was nearly teatime, Kate was flicking through the television schedule. She had been unable to get hold of Josh so her earlier plans were on hold, but she felt calmer now she had a plan.

She was trying to decide whether to have a quiet night in front of the television, or call Sam and suggest a night out. Without the voices she was finding that she could go out more. It felt strange and liberating, and she was reflecting on the internal turmoil she was experiencing at the loss of the voices, versus the subsequent opening of her life, when the doorbell rang.

Alarm filled her when she opened the door to the police on her doorstep, but after a few moments she realised why they were there, and, if she were honest, was surprised they hadn't been earlier.

She invited the two officers in, one male and one female, and as they sat down in her living room, their blue uniforms reassured her, despite the circumstances of their visit.

The blonde female officer, with her wide blue eyes and cherub face, looked too unseasoned to be involved in the disappearance of a child. Kate thought the police needed to be tough, but this one wasn't. She had a helplessness that made you feel protective, and Kate wondered if she was capable of throwing a man over her shoulders.

The male officer was more what Kate expected in an officer of the law, and as he removed his helmet she took a closer look. He was in his forties, with deep creases beginning to form in his face around the eyes, forehead and mouth. His lips were thick under his dark moustache, and his fat eyebrows met in the middle making him look cross. His chin had a blue sheen under the skin where the days growth was beginning to come through.

'I'm sure you've heard about the disappearance of one of the neighbour's children at the weekend,' he said. They had introduced themselves at the door, but Kate couldn't remember their names now.

'Lucy Newton? Yes.'

'We understand that a few days before the child went missing, there was an altercation involving you and the child?'

He made it sound as if Kate had behaved inappropriately; her heart skipped and her stomach tightened. She looked between the two officers before she spoke.

'I…well, there was a…an exchange of words between myself and Lucy's mum, Rachael, yes. Why?'

'Can you tell us what this 'exchange of words' was about exactly?'

He had his notebook out and was writing as she spoke. It unnerved her. Her mouth went dry as she realised there was more for her to worry about, than just Lucy Newton's safety.

'I was concerned for her.'

'Concerned Madam? In what way?'

Kate took a breath, unsure how to continue. What could she say? How could she explain her world to the two people in front of her who based their work around logic and fact? She doubted they ever got real life and dreams mixed up; they looked like they knew exactly what was real, and what was imaginary. She doubted they ever heard voices and other people's thoughts. Doubted they ever had images flash at them from nowhere. She might as well speak a different language to them for all the sense they would make of the 'facts' as she saw them.

'I had a…feeling that someone would hurt Lucy.' Was all she could manage, knowing how lame it sounded.

'And that someone would be who exactly?'

She wished he'd stop saying 'exactly' like he was in some bad cop show.

'Ray Mountford.'

'Ray Mountford your neighbour?' asked the female police officer. Her voice had an edge that belied her soft exterior. It was sharp and icy.

'Can I ask you Miss Gregory, what made you think that Mr. Mountford had an intention to hurt Lucy Newton?' asked the male officer.

Kate stared down into the gas fire. It was one of those that simulated a real fire. She had it fitted three years ago, and on windy nights she would light the fire, plug her ears with earphones to drown out the chaos, and watch the flames. The memory relaxed her.

'Miss Gregory?' the woman's cold voice dumped over her like a bucket of ice.

Kate jumped and look up at her. Her eyes, those that looked so soft before, now looked slate hard and probing.

'What made you believe that?' she said.

Kate took a breath and shrugged, trying to look relaxed as she answered.

'I'm not sure really. Just a hunch, women's intuition,' she smiled, but neither of them smiled back. Kate rushed on. 'I suppose it must have been the way he looked at her or something, I really can't pinpoint it.'

'Do you know Mr. Mountford well?' it was the man.

'Not really no.'

'And yet you've lived here,' he looked at his notes, 'seven years now. Is that correct?'

Kate nodded.

'Rather a long time to live next door to someone and not get to know them don't you think?'

Kate twitched an involuntarily smile, nervousness she supposed, because she'd never felt less like smiling in her life.

'I'm a bit of a loner, like to keep myself to myself.'

'So we understand.' It was her again.

The three words hung in the air like an accusation, and Kate was reminded of the police profile's she'd seen on TV. Being a loner was a definite no-no if you wanted to be left off the list of suspects. But surely they didn't suspect her?

'Where were you on Saturday between 4-5pm Miss Gregory?' the policeman asked.

They did! 'I'm not sure, here I suppose, I'm almost always here.'

'We've called on you on several occasions in the last two days, and until now, you have not been here.'

'I went to the beach yesterday,' Kate explained.

'Can you verify your whereabouts on Saturday?'

'What?'

'Can anyone substantiate your story? Did you call anyone? Did you have any visitors?'

'I don't know, I'm not sure,' Kate's heart was beating hard now. She didn't like the tone of the questions. She couldn't remember where she was on Saturday or Sunday. She was sure she hadn't gone anywhere but if they called...? Then she remembered.

'I was at the chiropractors on Saturday,' she said, relieved.

'And your appointment was between four and five?'

'No, it was at eleven in the morning.'

'So where were you between four and five on Saturday?'

'I was here, sleeping.'

'And no one was here? No one called in or called you?' he repeated.

'No. I was sleeping. Have you talked to Ray?' she asked, her voice tight.

'We're questioning everyone in the street.'

'Oh, thank goodness,' she said with relief, laughing. 'For a moment I thought you were suggesting that I might have had something to do with Lucy's disappearance.'

The two police officers looked at one another and then at Kate.

'It's too early for us to rule anyone out at this stage Miss Gregory,' he said.

Chapter Thirteen

'We haven't done anything together for an age, I'm so glad you decided to come along.'

'Me too Mum. This is just what I needed.'

Kate, her mother Jan and her friend Sheila Smith were hacking out across the fields behind a group of about a dozen women ranging in equestrian ability. Kate, although a reasonable horsewoman, was a novice compared to Jan and Sheila.

The air was thick with the damp smell of newly tilled fields, the earth turned in rich chocolate clumps. The sun warmed Kate's back.

'What are you up to these days Kate? Still the same?' It was Sheila. She and her mother had been friends since they met when they studied Law together at Newcastle University. Her mother now worked for a firm in Darlington, specialising in matrimonial law, whilst Sheila had stayed in Newcastle and was now in the criminal field.

'Transcribing? Yes,' said Kate.

'How's it going?'

'Good thanks. Plenty of work.'

'Too much,' Jan chided her daughter with a smile. 'I never see her these days Sheila.'

'I always consider that one of the joys of having grown up children. You don't have to see them as often,' she chuckled.

'You don't mean that,' Jan said, laughing too.

'No, you're right, but if I say it often enough, perhaps I'll start to believe it and stop missing them so much.'

Kate looked more closely at the woman she hadn't seen for years, but who had been a constant throughout her childhood. She was a tall elegant woman, with a long face and soft brown eyes. Her dark hair was now very grey, and refusing to obey convention, she usually wore it loose, spilling across her shoulders. Today, it was caught up in a ponytail and sat beneath her riding hat.

'Well ladies, do excuse me, but I'm off for a cantor.'

Kate looked up to see the rest of the group had gone ahead, cantering up the long hill in front of them.

'Care to join me?'

'In a minute Sheila, I want to talk to Kate for a moment.'

Sheila thundered off, her horse snorting in excitement. Kate and Jan had to hold back their horses as they made to follow.

'You okay?'

'I'm fine mum.'

'There's that word again.'

'I *am.*'

'I know you Kate, and I know when something's wrong. If you don't tell me I'll only fear the worst, so don't think you're sparing me anything.'

Kate shook her head in exasperation.

'Walk on,' her mother instructed her horse, Kate followed suit. The two women rode slowly side by side, Kate wondering frantically what she could say to placate her mother and put her mind at ease.

'It's that missing girl isn't it?'

Kate's body tensed and her horse, believing she was giving him the signal to cantor, lurched forward. She pulled in the reins to steady him and walk him by her mother's side again.

'She's from our street.' Kate said.

'Yes, it must be upsetting. Have the police been to question you yet?'

'Yesterday.'

'It's just a formality. Don't worry.'

'I had an…argument with the girl's mother, the day before the girl went missing.'

'An argument?' her mother glanced across to her. 'That's not like you.'

'It was more her shouting at me really.'

'Whatever happened?'

'I saw a man talking to Lucy and told her not to speak to him again. Apparently I frightened her. Her mother came to tell me off.'

'Did you tell the police?'

'Yes.'

Jan smiled at her daughter. 'Don't worry. It'll be fine.'

'Do you think I could be in trouble?'

Jan laughed. 'Of course not, but you might be able to help them find her if you know who the man is. Do you?'

'No,' Kate lied. Not wanting to prolong the conversation. Too tired to go into it all.

'Don't worry. If you need legal advice or representation,' she paused, 'I know a really good lawyer.' She nodded in Sheila's direction.

Kate forced herself to laugh. 'Thanks mum.'

'Anytime.'

'I do feel for Rachael though, that's the girl's mother. I saw her the other day and she looked so old. It must be awful losing a child like that.'

'I'm sure.'

'Makes you wonder.'

'Makes you wonder what?' Her mother's voice had a casual tone, but she knew better. Kate had wondered about her birth mother, and for a fleeting moment, considered discussing it with Jan, then dismissed it.

Instead she pointed up the hill and said, 'I do believe the group leader is requesting our presence,'

Her mother looked up. 'Good grief,' Jan said.

The group were small dots on the top of the hill and the hack out leader was waving her arms and shouting. Although they were too far away to hear the words, the meaning was clear. Everyone was waiting for them.

'Race you,' her mother said, and sped off.

'Hey! You cheat,' Kate shouted, and chased after her.

'So there you have it, another fucking disaster,' said Sam, pulling stringy mozzarella from her chin.

Kate and Sam sat in the pizza place on the high street. It was full of dense marble and polished chrome that escalated the noise levels and bounced them round the room. Harsh lighting drained everyone of colour. Cracked canvas paintings of sun faces hung on the walls as a testament to modern painting.

Kate's body was starting to seize up after the day's horse riding. She really needed to take more exercise. She brought her focus back to Sam.

'I'm sorry,' she said, for the lack of anything else to say.

'It's not your fault. Besides, we'll work it out, we always do.'

Kate nodded. Again the absence of voices left her stumbling. She didn't usually need to search through her mind like this; looking for appropriate words to comfort her friend, usually they just dropped out, but not anymore. It reminded her that she still hadn't managed to get hold of Josh. He was always in with a client when she rang, and she was reluctant to leave a message with his receptionist, she wanted to be ready when he called him, not caught unexpectedly. Besides, she was beginning to have second thoughts about her plan.

She picked up her glass and drank the remainder of her wine. 'So, you don't want to have children then?' she asked.

'Sometimes, when I see smiling mothers with their babies on the telly, but then I think of the reality, and I can't bring myself to face it.

'What is it you can't face? The birth?' Kate could understand that.

Sam shook her head. 'No, it's more complicated than that. It's like...' she stopped, her face screwed up with the effort of trying to add a logical argument to an illogical, but very real, emotion. 'Oh Kate, come on, help me,' she said. 'You always know exactly the right thing to say to sort me out. You can always put your finger on it.'

With the voices it was true, but tonight she was as unenlightened as Sam. A wave of grief and loss swept up, astounding her with its force. Behind it she recognised the familiar sensation and heard the click as her vision blurred.

When it came back she was focused on a light swinging, dancing from wall to floor to wall. Her jaw clenched as her teeth fused together. Deep in her throat a hard lump grew. Her pulse so fast she thought she would explode. Terror gripped her, invaded her, too colossal to be contained in her body. She was frozen, unable to do anything except watch the light swing. And blue, running blue, like water, solid yet flowing.

'Kate?'

Sam's voice was faint and distant, echoing down a long tunnel, but it was enough to pull her back to the present.

'Kate, are you okay?'

She saw Sam's freckled face with its halo of apricot hair, peering at her with concern across the table. The chrome and strip lighting came back into focus. The sounds of the restaurant returned.

Kate nodded. 'I'm fine, just went a little dizzy that's all.'

'You went really funny.'

'Oh?'

'Yeah. Your eyes, they went all starey, as if no-one was in. It was weird.'

Kate laughed. It sounded nervous to her. 'Thanks.'

'You okay now?'

Kate nodded again. 'I'm fine really. Absolutely fine.'

'God, you gave me the heeby jeebies then. You want some more wine?'

'No, thanks. I think...I think I should go home,' she said. She wanted to be alone.

Chapter Fourteen

Two days later, Kate woke naturally on Friday morning and stretched out fully in bed, splaying herself out into a star and enjoying the space. No whispers, no dreams, no visions and since her night out with Sam, a decision to put it all behind her. There was always a period of adjustment to change, she reasoned, and when she considered this monumental change, it was bound to create some mixed emotions from time to time, but now she had come to a decision.

Her body felt still. This was peace. This was the new person she had become and, for all its challenges, she basked in the stillness.

Lucy was missing and she feared for the little girl. But other than a single thought from Ray that may, or equally may not, have happened, she had no more role to play in the drama that was unfolding on her street than anyone else who lived there. In the interest of her sanity, she had made up her mind to consign it to her past, and abandon any plans she might have had.

She allowed her mind to wander, to idly flick through the filing cabinet of her mind, stopping to examine a file of thoughts here, before moving onto another there, nothing clicking or snagging her attention.

She skimmed across the lake of her mind like a flat stone, bouncing from one thing to another, until something that Josh said stopped her. She closed her eyes and squeezed them tight, trying to locate the cell that held the memory of their conversation.

She heard a loud click and found herself face down on a carpet. Her body throbbed with fear, terror pumping into her limbs, setting them rigid. Her mouth and lips cracked and dry, voice broke; a pulsing pain in her hip.

She heard screaming. Light and dark swayed intermittently. The carpet smelt dusty. She focused on it, not wanting to hear the screams. It was a swirl of red and blue, no discernible pattern, made of loops and scratchy on her skin. A man shouted and bellowed like a wounded cow, reminding Kate of a trip to the countryside with her mother. The screaming stopped, the hush that followed more terrifying.

Kate slammed back to the present, her body shaking uncontrollably. She began to cry. Was this a future vision? Was it something that was going to happen? But to who? When? Was this about Lucy? Why was this happening to her? What could she do with so little information? Why was it happening? It seemed that, regardless of any decision she had made to be involved with Lucy's disappearance or not, they were linked in some way. But how? Why?

Among the confusion and the questions she held onto one small fragment. A memory had come back to her of visiting the countryside with her mother. Not Jan, her birth mother. As she focused on it now, her breathing calmed and the memory grew in detail. Snatches at first, building into a montage of pictures, sounds and smells that, when put together, pulled the day to her from across the abyss of forgetting.

They caught a bus and played eye spy. They sat on grass and ate egg sandwiches from a plastic box that smelt like farts when it opened.

They saw a cow bellowing and her mother, a soft spoken willowy woman, said, 'it is calling for her calf. They must have taken it to market.' She held Kate tightly. Her blue silk scarf brushing Kate's face, soft and cool, like water. She smelt of roses. 'I would bellow too, if I were the cow,' she added.

She sang 'Strawberry Fair' as they walked down a long lane to catch the bus home, the sun so hot and bright it hurt her eyes.

Kate sat up, her face wet with tears. It was her first memory of her real mother. 'She loved me,' Kate whispered.

Chapter Fifteen

A week after Kate's original appointment with Josh she finally plucked up the courage to call in. His receptionist, a neat young girl so thin she looked like a cardboard cut-out when she stood sideways, told her he was busy with a patient, but he was free after that. Kate sat in reception and waited, determined not to put if off this time.

She watched the rainbow fish glide through the aquarium, so effortless. Now the voices had gone, she imagined her life would be like that. It should be effortless, but it wasn't. There were all sorts of challenges she had never faced before.

Like Monday with Felix at the beach, when she hadn't been able to read him, and Wednesday with Sam in the pizza place, when she hadn't been able to help her. When she had the voices she believed that life without them would be so much easier, but it wasn't. It was just different.

There were compensations of course. She didn't have to hide from the wind, she didn't hear lots of useless random whisperings in her ear in crowded places, and she no longer had to rein herself in and check whether she was supposed to know something or not, because she didn't know anything anymore.

But there were these visions...and of course, there was Lucy Newton. She was still missing, and given she had been missing for a week now with no news, quite probably dead. Kate shuddered at the thought. She believed knew who was responsible, but without the voices what could she do? She wasn't even sure she could do anything with them, but she had to try, regardless of what it cost her.

The police had been back again yesterday, asking the same questions, and they hadn't been as polite as the first time. Did the police really think she was involved in Lucy's disappearance? But wasn't she? If you do nothing when you know you should act, isn't that tantamount to guilt? It must be, there was a law against it; aiding and abetting or something.

She should have done more when she had the chance. If only she had spoken to Rachael properly, before the confrontation at her front door. That was the day before Lucy went missing. Kate cringed at the memory. What was the woman thinking now? Was it too late to help?

Last week she thought she heard Lucy's voice, but it was too faint to tell, besides, it was in her sleep, or as she was waking up. Either way, it wasn't clear. She had seen a child's shoe in one of those flashes, and they had found Lucy's sandle on the road. What did that mean? And what about the swinging light and the musty carpet, was that useful information to give to the police? The thought made her insides quail. She dreaded that look in their eyes that she knew from experience. They wouldn't believe her.

Josh's door clicked open and a tall gangly man with a bald head and large teeth emerged.

'So make an appointment for next week,' Josh said, as he followed the man into reception. 'Suzanne will do that for you. Okay?'

He spotted Kate and smiled. 'One minute,' he mouthed at her. He turned to the man, shook his hand and passed him onto the efficient, if effaced, Suzanne.

'Hello,' Josh said to Kate. 'Problem?'

'Sort of. I hope you don't mind me calling in on the off chance?'

'No, not at all. I'm pleased to see you.'

Her insides quivered. It was *pleased* to see her...

'I haven't got an appointment till after lunch now, so you're in luck. Come in.'

Kate crossed the hall, entered his office and sat down in the same chair as before. She realised she was trembling, and took a deep breath as Josh closed the door and joined her.

'So, what can I do for you?'

'It's a bit...complicated.'

'Okay.'

'I wondered if you could undo the adjustment you made.'

'Undo it?'

'Yes.'

Josh sat back into his chair and looked at her before he spoke. 'I've never had that request before. Is it worse? Sometimes an adjustment can be uncomfortable for a while after, until the body accommodates-'

'No, it's not that. It's fine. Not a jot of trouble since I came to see you,' she smiled. 'Well, not with the neck anyway.'

'Okay, I see,' he chewed his lip and then said. 'Actually, I don't. What exactly is the problem?' He smiled.

'I just want you to put it all back the way it was.'

'But why?'

'I can't explain.'

He was kind, but insistent. 'Try.' He smiled and his dimple deepened.

Kate took another deep breath, unsure of how much to say, trying to calm her jangled nerves as she looked up at him. He was focused on her, those deep brown eyes taking her in, and she was rapt, held in his gaze like this, the room fell away, and she lost the ability to breathe for a moment.

She understood if people had sat here and told him things they'd never told anyone else. She wanted to confide in him, to bring him into her covert world and wrap him up in her secrets.

'I've been having flashes,' she said, before she could stop herself. 'Pictures, sounds, that sort of thing. I get a loud click and then I see a picture in front of me. After a short time it clears and I see normally again.'

'Any dizziness?'

'No.'

'Problems sleeping?'

'None.'

'Do you have any other symptoms?'

'What sort of symptoms?'

Josh shook his head, his brow furrowed. With what, she wondered. Concern? Irritation?

'Is there…anything else I should know?'

Kate paused before shaking her head, his spell broken now she had spoken. She'd said enough.

'In that case,' Josh said, sitting forward over his desk and taking up a pen. 'I'm going to refer you to your GP. I'm concerned about these visual disturbances. And sounds you say?'

'Yes.'

Josh began to write. 'It may well be nothing, but I think we should be on the safe side.'

'What will my GP do?'

'Probably refer you to a specialist, a neurologist at the hospital for tests. Don't be alarmed, it's standard procedure, but it's better to be safe than sorry.'

Paralysis crept up Kate's body. Tests, hospital, a neurologist, she'd been here before. They would probe and prod, take blood and urine and any other body fluids her physical body excreted. They would intrude into her. The truth would come out at some point; she wouldn't be able to go through all that without cracking and telling someone.

She had kept her secret for this long because she had become good at hiding it. True, she got flustered from time to time, like when she'd made that mistake with Toby the courier, but she was usually able to cover it up. But with experts testing her…it was only a matter of time.

And then what? They would either submit her to more tests, like some freak of nature, or assign her to a psychriatic ward for observation. She had been there, done that, she wouldn't, couldn't go through all that again. And how would that help Lucy? That, after all, was what this was really about.

She watched Josh, his head bent as he wrote. Better to tell him here and now.

'There is something else.'

'Oh,' he looked up, and there was that look again, that spell of his that seemed to whisper, *'you can trust me,'* except of course, she didn't have the voices anymore, so it had to be her imagination.

'I haven't been totally honest with you,' she said.

Josh lay down his pen and turned, that look resting on her, again causing oscillations inside her.

'I used to have this…thing. I've had it since I can remember. And since the adjustment it's gone,' Kate stopped.

Josh waited, saying nothing, as if he had all the time in the world. She was forced to continue.

'I know you're going to think I'm mad but…I could hear people's thoughts. Not always clearly. They kind of dropped into my head. I learnt lots of ways to deal with it and tune it out, except when it was windy. Can't go out in the wind without music, and sometimes when I'm working I need the headphones then too, if there's going to be a lot of distraction. I know in the morning you see? I have this…had this…crackling feeling around me… like a magnetic attraction, and I know those are going to be bad days. Those and windy days.'

She could hear herself babbling but couldn't stop.

'But mostly I can manage. Makes living in the UK difficult sometimes. Do you know how many windy days we get?' she laughed. 'No, I don't suppose you do. I suppose, it's not something you'd notice unless it blew you off your feet. Anyway, I've always had this…what? Gift? Curse?

Whatever…and now it's gone. And I get these…visions instead now. And whilst I was pleased at first, I'm not so happy now.

'If you refer me to the specialist I know what'll happen. I went through all that when I was young. And there's this missing girl Lucy. If you refer me into that big specialist testing machine, I won't be able to help her.

'And maybe I'm being delusional thinking I could help. But I have to try. I'm sure I could hear her voice only a few days ago, just after she went missing, but I'm not sure. I'm not so upset about losing the voices, I could adjust to that, but it's the little girl, the lost voice. So if you could just put everything back the way it was, I'd be really grateful.' Kate stopped, held her breath, waiting.

'Wow,' said Josh. 'Are you serious?'

'Of course I'm serious,' her voice rose. 'You think I'd make this up for a laugh?'

'I'm sorry it's just…'

'You don't believe me.'

'It's not that.'

Kate's eyes strayed to a picture of a spinal column on the far wall, and traced down the 's' shape wondering if her spine followed the same curve. Josh stood up and walked across the room to a large filing cabinet. Kate watched as he drew out a manila folder and opened it, reading as he returned to his seat without looking up. It was a practised move, one carried out many times.

'I've lost the voices, and now I have these pictures that are just so confusing. And scary. And the girl that's gone missing, I heard her calling out.'

Josh looked up. 'Tell me about these visions.'

'There's nothing to tell, just random pictures and sounds.'

'Sounds too?'

It was the second time he'd asked. 'Yes, is that important?'

He shrugged. 'I don't know. It's just interesting,' he bent his head again to look at her notes.

'There's no rhyme or reason to any of it that I can see,' she offered.

'From your last visit we decided it could have been a childhood fall. Do you remember anything like that?'

'No, nothing. I had an idyllic childhood. My parents were wonderful.'

'Why did you say that?'

'What?'

'That you had an idyllic childhood?'

'Because I did.'

'I'm not talking about abuse here you know, I'm talking about accidents like...falling off a bike or...falling down stairs. Those sorts of things happen in every type of childhood.'

'I wasn't abused,' her tone was sharp.

'Okay but, what I'm saying is, you didn't have to be.' Josh went back to her notes. A phone rang out in reception and she could hear Suzanne's monotone voice, though she couldn't make out the words.

'I'm sorry,' she said, unsure why she was blurting out an apology. Her eyes stung with tears.

'It's okay. You've nothing to be sorry for.'

'I feel so...confused. Life, as you can imagine,' she snorted a laugh. 'has never been straight forward but, well, I managed. But now...I just don't know anything anymore. It just all goes round in my head, and the dreams, the flashes, everything, it's just all too confusing.'

'Do you do any relaxation? Pray or meditate?'

'Pray?' She was surprised by the apparent randomness of the question. Josh nodded.

'I'm not a religious person,' she said.

'You don't have to be religious to be spiritual and, unfortunately, vice versa.'

'What's the difference?' she asked, in spite of herself.

Josh settled back into his chair, an ankle resting on the opposite knee to form a triangular shelf, her file lay open across it. 'Well, the way I see it, religion is going to church, or the synagogue or whatever, and obeying all the outward rules of the spiritual text your religion subscribes too. Being spiritual on the other hand, is an understanding that the text, or life for that matter, isn't everything, that there's something greater. It's about endeavouring to connect with that. Now, if someone is both religious and spiritual, great things can happen. Like with Mother Teresa for instance.'

'Are you religious?'

'I'm a Christian.'

Kate nodded, suddenly feeling uncomfortable, and disappointed.

'I'm not trying to convert you,' he said quickly, and she smiled. 'All spiritual practices, whether they're religious or 'new age', encourage some form of daily meditation or prayer.'

'And you're suggesting I do this?'

'It may help.'

'So what would I do this for exactly?'

'It could help you in a number of ways. Give you some much needed time out from the mind chatter you're experiencing, a bit like a holiday from the self.'

She could do with that, she thought.

'But it might also help you understand these visions you're getting.'

'But I don't do either, never have,' she said. 'I wouldn't even know where to start.'

'It's easy, there's nothing to it. You just sit quietly for about twenty minutes or so, let your body and mind become relaxed and still, then listen for guidance.'

'Right,' Kate said.

'Seriously. It's incredibly calming.'

'I've never had the opportunity to be still, there's been a distinct lack of stillness for me to be still in.'

He laughed. 'Yes, I see that, but you could try it now. You can also ask for guidance, wisdom, strength, peace. Anything you want.'

'From whom…God?'

Josh shrugged. 'From whatever is meaningful for you.'

Kate nodded. A bit of stillness after all these years of chatter might be nice. Maybe Josh was right, maybe she should just enjoy the peace and quiet, but it didn't help Lucy.

'So there's nothing you can do? About reversing the adjustment?' she asked.

'We're not taught to undo the good work. Not much call for it,' he smiled.

'Suppose not.'

'Besides, something tells me you need to focus more on those images,' Josh said. 'When you're being still, ask what they mean, and ask what your neck has been trying to communicate to you too.'

'Huh? My neck?'

'There's a theory that pain in our body is an unheard message. The theory is that, when our lives are out of alignment with our true purpose, God's will, whatever you want to call it, the terminology is unimportant, when our lives are out of alignment, our physical body endeavours to communicate this by producing discomfort. If that isn't acknowledged, the discomfort becomes pain, dis-ease and finally, if it still isn't addressed, it will stop a person from moving around so they are forced to be still and observe. Unfortunately, it's often too late by then.'

'What d'you mean by out of alignment?' she asked after some thought.

'Anything that disconnects us from our true path, and therefore god, or all there is, that creative energy that surrounds us and flows through us.'

'I'm not sure I believe in that.'

'You think this is it?' he raised his arms to indicate his surroundings. 'You think we come here, we live, we die, end of story? With what you've experienced all your life with these...voices, you think what we know, is all there is?'

'No, I suppose not. I think there's something bigger than us, I'm just not sure what that is.'

'Good! Well that 'something bigger' you mention, is what I mean when I talk about God, but lots of people have a problem with that word, so substitute 'Universe' or 'Divinity' or 'Higher Self' instead. As I said earlier, the terminology isn't important. The main point to grasp is that, when we're unaligned we suffer, get ill, feel off balance.'

'Okay,' Kate said slowly. 'So what causes us to be 'unaligned'?'

'All sorts of things, but primarily negative beliefs about ourselves and others that force us into non-right action, make us become someone or something we're not. I mean, you were born unique, why die a copy right?'

Kate nodded, unsure. 'Give me an example.'

'Okay, an example...when we criticise others what we're really doing is criticising ourselves. Then we start to adjust our behaviours, bend ourselves into new shapes. I'm not talking about growing and changing and moving out of our comfort zone, I'm talking about distortion. We take a job with a high salary so we can buy stuff, or...we dampen down our dreams so hard and for so long, that we forget we ever had them. We become divided and alone. A lone soul is an unnatural state. We belong as one body.'

It was too much for Kate, all this talk of stillness, God and alignment. All part of one body, right. No matter how much 'aligning' she did she would never be, nor wanted to be, a part of anything that contained Ray! She had come here to get her voices back and help a little girl, but it was clearly a waste of time.

'What has any of this got to do with me?' she asked, wanting to end the conversation and leave.

'Perhaps you've lost these...'voices' because you weren't using the talent God gave you, you mentioned you heard this girl right?'

'Right.' She was interested now, maybe he could help her...

'Perhaps that's where you can help in the future, or perhaps they've been taken so you can concentrate on these images you've been getting. I don't know. But there'll be a reason. It will become clear in time. Just have patience. And practice being still. It could speed up the process of your understanding.'

Kate felt a hint of frustration. Time wasn't something she had.

Josh closed his file and stood up, indicating the end of the session. She stood up and held out her hand. Josh took it in both of his. 'Good luck,' he said, his eyes burning with genuine emotion.

Kate felt her face grow warm as her insides somersaulted. 'Thank you. I'll pay Suzanne right?'

'No. This is on me.'

'No, I couldn't, please let me pay.'

'Really, Kate, I find your whole...situation really interesting.'

'But I need to pay you something for your time,' she insisted.

Josh smiled. 'Alright I understand. I tell you what, buy me lunch some time, maybe next week, and then you can tell me more about these voices of yours, and how you're getting on. I'm intrigued.'

Kate shifted from one foot to another, she couldn't see how she could refuse without being rude, besides, though she hated to admit it, she was delighted that she could see him again.

'Okay,' she said at last, trying not to grin too hard as she left.

The shop had been busy today, as always on a Saturday, so Sam retreated to the office for a few minutes of peace and quiet during the usual three o' clock lull. It would start again in half an hour.

The girls were out on the shop floor tidying up the shelves and racks, preparing for the final rush of the day. The onslaught of posh middle aged women with bulging bank accounts desperate to buy back some of their youth.

Sam sat back and closed her eyes. It wasn't a bad life, she thought, although it was going through some difficulty at the moment. Paul was continuing to be unsupportive, having barely even grunted to her since their most recent spat.

She wondered, not for the first time, if she should just up and leave. The idea had some appeal. The thought of starting out again intrigued her and held some excitement. It was excitement that kept the blood pumping, the youthful blush to your skin. It was why these middle aged women spent so much on clothes, that rush. Sam loved well designed clothes, you only had to look in her wardrobe to see that, but it didn't bring a flush to her cheeks the way it did with her clientele, nevertheless, she understood the need for excitement in her shoppers as they pulled out their credit cards.

You needed excitement in your life, otherwise you lost yourself in drudgery. Take her parents. Married for over thirty years, mum a nurse, dad a taxi driver. Work, home and a two week holiday every year in the sun; another week's holiday at Christmas and Easter. That was their lot. No excitement, no change and it showed on their faces. They looked grey and old before their time. Just working and waiting to retire. To what, potter around the garden and wait for their two weeks in the sun?

She wanted more. So much more. What that 'more' was she wasn't sure yet, but she would know it when it came along. It might even be Anne's offer. And Paul? It seemed he wanted to follow that route to the elephant graveyard that was parenthood, and he wanted to drag her along with him. That's what changed it all; parenthood. That's when working, money, security and settling down became an imperative at the expensive of your life. That was when you resorted to buying four hundred pound skirts…if you were lucky. She wasn't prepared to let that happen.

She wanted, no needed, the freedom to be herself, and she was disappointed that Paul didn't know her well enough to understand that. Disappointed, and deeply hurt.

If he wasn't prepared to accept her the way she was, then maybe, maybe it was time to start a new chapter, not just in her career, but in her life. The thought stunned her with its implications.

Chapter Sixteen

Kate sat up in bed. It was four in the morning and it was happening again. She could predict when they were going to happen, these visions.

Now as she sat in bed she tried to piece these things together. The first one was easy; Lucy's shoe had been found on the road outside her home, the day she went missing. The very day, in fact, of Kate's first vision.

She was making coffee when the second one happened. That was hazy now and she couldn't remember very much about it. The tinkle of glass and a moan, like the wind. The third was light reflecting on something...a mirror or...a piece of jewellery or...the last thought caused her to tense, a knife? Her feelings of being rubbed out were increasing and she knew the click would occur soon, and another image would follow. She waited, her mouth dry, recalling the other visions while she still had the chance.

The next image was that swinging light and, running blue like...like solid water? It was also the one that had brought her the first memory of her birth mother, because of the bellowing sound, if she remembered correctly. And then there was the episode in the pizza place with Sam. What was that one now?

Before she could recall it there was the click and the bedroom faded. An image took its place that she couldn't make out at first. Slowly her eyes adjusted. It was something wooden, so close she could see the grain, a door maybe, or a piece of furniture? It was gone as quickly as it had arrived.

Kate shook her head. These strange pictures or visions or whatever they were, didn't make any sense. She lay back down on her bed and pulled the duvet up tight under her chin.

Inexplicably her heart raced, as it did after each of these experiences. Why? What was it about them that frightened her so much? She listed them again. There was: a child's shoe, the clinking breaking glass, a glint of light, a swinging light, flowing blue and a wooden door...or something. What did it mean? A struggle perhaps? Things breaking? But that only explained one or two things.

Could she be imagining it, making it into something when really it meant nothing? Maybe she didn't know anything about Lucy's disappearance. Maybe her head was just clearing after the adjustment?

The voices had gone, maybe her system was having a final clear out before she became like everyone else. She liked the idea that she might walk in the wind, like she had with Felix at the beach. Go to crowded places; bars, nightclubs, concerts, shopping at Christmas. Ride on a train, perhaps even go on holiday.

Kate had tried to see a piano concert at her local arts centre a couple of years ago, but she couldn't hear the piano properly over the voices. There were so many things she hadn't done because, if she locked out the world, she could lock out the voices.

Something Josh said to her returned now; something about misalignment and meditation. She couldn't claim to understand or agree with everything he said, but one thing that did stay with her, was her need for stillness. Letting her body relax and listen for guidance did have some appeal. He was talking about the visions at the time, but it could work for the voices too. Maybe she could hear something?

But what if they didn't come back? There was so much that she could experience. So many places she could go, so many things she could see, so many things she could do. She thought of Felix. No, definitely not Felix. Josh? Even thinking about him set her insides fluttering. But no, not Josh either, he knew her secret, and the best she could hope for was a friendship with him, but someone like Josh, who didn't know she used to be a freak.

With the voices gone, she could now consider the possibility of opening her life to someone. The idea gave her a shiver of excitement, something to look forward to.

The only thing that marred the excitement of a new life was Lucy. If only she was wrong about the whole thing, if only. But she knew as she drifted on the edge of sleep, that it wasn't over. Lucy Newton and Ray Mountford were unfinished business, and until the little girl was found, until Ray had paid for whatever he had done, she could not start a new life.

Chapter Seventeen

Sam drank her coffee ignoring the pile of paperwork on her desk. It would be there later, it wasn't going anywhere. More's the pity. She couldn't concentrate. Right now she needed to clear her head. She'd had another terrible weekend with Paul.

Since their argument over two weeks ago they had barely exchanged words, and some days she managed to get little more than a series of grunts from him. She knew it needed one of them to back down, one of them to apologise and break the stalemate. In the past it had always been Paul, crumbling after a few days. Sam would watch his initial solid resolve disappear like sugar in hot tea. All it usually needed was a little patience, but not this time. This time neither of them could back down because there was nowhere to go.

Paul had retreated so deep into his cave Sam couldn't even call out to him. He wouldn't look at her to initiate conversation, spent all his waking time in front of the television, and feigned tiredness to avoid sex. His warm blue eyes had taken on a permanent cold grey. He was was angry, his jaw set tight, holding back, his body hard. Like an over tightened guitar string, any moment he could snap. It frightened Sam, frightened and infuriated her.

Over the weekend she was tempted to apologise, try to find some compromise, but there wasn't want one. Besides, it wouldn't change anything and, she reminded herself, she wasn't in the wrong. What right did he have to be so unreasonable? So she didn't want babies, so what? Loads of women didn't these days. If she were a man no one would bat an eyelid. No, but because she was a woman he acted like she was the devil incarnate or something. Anger spiralled through her body and Sam plonked her mug down on the desk and coffee slopped over the invoices on her desk.

'Bugger!' she said, grabbing a handful of tissue and mopping up the liquid, turning them from a soft white to a soggy brown. She threw the sodden tissues at the bin in the corner, narrowly missing, and lit a cigarette.

Was it over between them? She wondered again, and blew out a plume of blue smoke. Could this be the end? She was still reeling from her thought on Saturday that she could start again, reinvent her life. Leave Paul. It was a big step, taking a marriage apart, but they certainly couldn't go on like this or, at least, she couldn't. And she was not going to apologise. She hadn't anything to apologise for!

She craned her neck and rotated it back and forth. It cracked audibly on one side, releasing some of the tension, but on the other side it wouldn't do the same. It was tight, as if there was some block to its full movement. It wasn't painful, or even unpleasant, but it wasn't right, and it gave her an idea.

Paul just wanted to punish her with this childish and petulant behaviour of his, well, two could play at that game. He needed a short sharp shock. She pulled out her mobile and flicked through to find the number of Paul's chiropractor. She could kill two birds with one stone, sort out the tension in her neck, and teach Paul a lesson.

Kate stood in the cobbled car park looking up at the tall grey building in front of her. A thick wooden door, studded in grey metal stood guard. She suddenly felt shy and out of place, a gate crasher at a wedding. She didn't belong here. This wasn't her place; her tribe. The people who came here were different to her, believed different things about how the world worked.

After another disturbed night's sleep, Kate had finally decided she had to at least give Josh's suggestion a try. She wasn't sure what had drawn her to the church. Something Josh had said about being quiet and listening came back to her. After all, where was quieter than a church? She had tried the library, but it was full of movement and rustling, bleeping, loud whispers and computer keyboards clicking. No. A church was the right place, she realised now.

She didn't know what she hoped to get from this place. All she knew was there was a piece missing inside her. Wasn't that what pulled everyone here; the hope of filling the gap inside them? Wasn't that what religion was for, along with drugs and alcohol, work and television, money and sex, gambling and shopping?

She stopped herself. She wasn't really giving it a chance.

It was cold, and the damp seeped into her bones. Kate pulled her coat tighter. There was something else, she thought. Hope. A small flicker of hope that here she would find the answers.

Pushing herself forward she walked up and placed a hand on the door. It was cold and the deep grain danced on her palm. She paused for a moment, heart jumping, throat swollen, took a deep breath and pushed.

The door was unlocked, and with a mixture of relief and fear, she entered the church. Her shoes clacked and echoed through the old building. Sound rippled and she stood, waiting for it to subside.

She closed the door and faced the alter. The air had a chill and smelt fusty, of damp wood and decades of mould; the way only an old church could smell. It reminded her of brownies; meetings in a chilled hall wearing her brownie dress and beret, comparing badges. They wore polo shirts and caps now, she remembered.

The church itself was small and gloomy, with dark mahogany pews on both sides and a pulpit to the left. Stone steps led to the alter, where a table was covered with a purple under sheet, and a white tablecloth. An unadorned wooden cross stood in the middle of the table, and Kate found that she was affected by the simplicity of the décor.

She sat down on the back pew and took a few deep breaths. Everything stopped here. Time stood still. Her breathing deepened and the blood moving through her body slowed. Her stomach gurgled like a contented baby. Something tiptoed through her body, softened the muscles, calmed the nerves, cleared the mind. Everything had led her to this point, to this moment.

Kate wasn't sure how long she sat there in the stillness. It could have been minutes or hours. Her mind was empty, her body relaxed. The sounds outside seemed to come from another world. It must have rained, the traffic tyres shushed as the cars drove by. She heard a clock chime; voices rose and fell as people walked past. Time passed.

Then she heard it. Her heart fluttered and in her excitement it was gone. She settled back down, trying to relax. As her breath deepened she heard it again, stronger this time. She tried to keep her emotions in check, but her heart scrambled in her chest and she lost it again.

The third time her control had improved, and she was calmer. The sound got clearer and clearer, until she knew she was not kidding herself, until she was certain. Yes, it was. It was the voices. Her chest flooded with heat and tears formed. It was the voices. They had come back. Familiar, comforting, it was like reuniting with a friend you thought you would never see again.

She noticed whenever she got emotional they slowly faded out, clouded by her emotional fog. Each time she slowed her breathing they would slip back, whispering in her ears like a long lost lover.

There were too many to make out individual words, but at least they were back, and what was more, there was a level of control to them. Even more important, she realised she might now be able to find Lucy.

Felix sat at his desk on his second cup of coffee when the call came through from Phoebe. She never called him at work.

'Phebs, you okay?'

'Yes, I'm fine. It's mum.'

'What about her?'

'She's had a fall, Felix, she's in hospital.'

'Is it bad?'

'I'm not sure, I got a call from the hospital about an hour ago. I'm on the road now. One of the neighbours found her this morning.' She began to cry.

'Phebs, she'll be alright. She's a tough old bird.'

'I know, it's just, oh, Felix, she fell down the stairs last night. She could have been lying there for hours. Can you imagine?'

Felix felt suddenly tired. 'It couldn't be helped. You warned her about those stairs.'

'I feel awful Felix.'

'I know, me too' he said, because it was expected. 'Where is she?'

'Ward 31, the Memorial. They're still assessing her at the moment.'

'Is she conscious?'

'Yes, but she's had a nasty bump on the head and they're waiting for the x-ray results.'

'Alright, I'll meet you there.'

'Oh, Felix, we should have done more for her.'

'I know Phebs, I know. Try not to fret. Let's just wait and see. I'll see you soon.'

Felix sat back in his chair, his inner turmoil etched across his face.

'Problem?' asked Rose.

'My mother, she's had a fall and been taken to hospital. I have to go. Can you call John and ask him to cover for me? And can you cancel my appointments this week, or reschedule them with John where you can?'

'No problem.'

Felix collected his things and slowly made his way to his car. He didn't want to go. He was angry at her foolishness. To buy that house with those ridiculous stairs, to sell their home, insist on having things her way and now look? Pulling him away from work when they were so busy, and worrying Phoebe when she had so much stress already. It was typical of his mother, always had been. Everything and everyone had to revolve round her.

Felix slammed the car door, started the engine and drove off towards the hospital with gritted teeth. His mind flicked to the remaining contents of the boot of his car, as if he didn't have enough on his plate right now. It was almost as if the bloody woman knew, damn her.

Kate walked through the church grounds towards the town centre. The church had a small graveyard that hadn't been used since the 1800's. Many of the tomb stones were cracked and lopsided, like bad teeth. All of them were covered in lichen and streaked with years of rain. She stepped through the gates and into the town centre.

Today was market day, and across the road from the church, the town square was filled with stalls selling everything from fudge to toilet cleaner. Kate stood and watched. A tall dark haired stall holder was calling to another and shaking a polystyrene cup. The older man gave him the thumbs up and turned back to the customer he was serving.

A mother and her truculent teenage daughter were at a clothing stand. The mother pointed out a pink dress and the girl shook her head violently. The mother threw her hands up in despair and turned to the girl. The girl pointed to a black ripped t-shirt and the mother strode off. A look of exasperation crossed the girl's face before she turned and flounced after her mother. Kate thought of the fraught shopping trips with her own mother years ago, cringing at the memory of her bad behaviour.

Kate turned down an alley away from all the noise and movement and headed off a longer, but quieter route home. She walked by the river and watched the ducks dipping up and down like awkward ballerinas. What if she couldn't hear the voices anywhere but the church?

The thought had bobbed under the surface of her consciousness since she left the church, but she had ignored it. Now as it surfaced it brought a raft of emotions with it. Not wanting to spoil her peaceful walk home, she boxed it up and put it away to be opened later.

Felix saw Phoebe as soon as he pushed his way through the double doors two hours later. She was sitting on a hard chair in the corridor under harsh lighting that bounced off the glossy green walls and drained everything of colour. She looked smaller than usual, and for a moment Felix lost his footing. This was his big sister, this small inconsequential looking woman sitting in the never ending corridor.

Her face was pale and had a worn aged look. For the briefest moment he saw shades of his mother in her face. 'Phoebe?'

A smile broke across her face wiping away the shadows as she stood up. 'Felix. I'm so glad you're here. Where have you been? I expected you to get here before me.'

'Sorry, I had to clear something up,' it wasn't a lie. 'Then I couldn't park. How is she?'

'She's conscious, but in pain. The doctor's with her now. From the little I've managed to gleam so far, they suspect a leg fracture, and perhaps some concussion.'

'Not too bad then,' he said with relief.

'No, it could have been worse. I just can't get over the idea of her lying at the bottom of those stairs all by herself.'

Felix rubbed his face with his hands, not wanting to meet her gaze.

'She won't be able to go back there you know?'

Felix glanced down either side of the corridor.

'Aren't you...overreacting a bit?' he said quietly.

'Felix! I told you about those stairs, and she's not getting any younger. She can't go back there.'

'No, I suppose not.'

Phoebe sat down and Felix joined her. They sat side by side, listening to squeaking shoes and rustling uniforms as nurses passed back and forth.

'She'll have to sell that house,' Phoebe said eventually.

Felix's stomach turned over. He did think she was overreacting, but said nothing more. Maybe she wasn't, maybe it was him.

'We need to put it on the market for her.'

'She won't like that,' Felix said quietly.

'We'll just have to persuade her. Next time she could kill herself.'

Felix sighed.

'Felix!'

'What?'

'Are you listening to me?'

'Of course.'

'Then say something.'

'What is there to say? What do you want me to say?'

'I want you to join in this conversation so I don't feel I'm having it on my own.'

Her voice was tight with emotion. He reached out and rubbed her shoulder.

'Okay, I'm sorry.'

'So what are we going to do with her?'

The blood slowed in his body. He opened his mouth but his throat closed and strangled the words. To his relief the doctor arrived.

'Miss Shell?'

Phoebe stood up. 'It's Mrs Wood, but I'm Mrs Shell's daughter and this,' she indicated Felix, 'is my brother.'

'I'm Mr Kwafi, your mother's consultant,' he was a tall dark man with wild hair and kind eyes.

'How is she?'

'She's a lucky lady. She does have some slight concussion so we'll be keeping her in for observation. We'll move her to a ward soon. Looking at her x-rays there's no break in the femur – it's just badly bruised. She's also suffered a minor sprain to her left wrist. We have her on a drip to hydrate her; the shock of the fall and the fact that she lay there for several hours hasn't helped her condition.'

'Will she be okay?' Phoebe asked. Felix stood watching.

'Given time, yes, there are no major injuries, but we are concerned about her recuperation period. She is going to need some care when she leaves hospital.'

'What kind of care?'

'No specialist treatment, simply someone to check on her. She won't be as agile as usual for a few weeks.'

'And stairs?'

The consultant shook his head. 'It's unlikely she'll be able to manage them either for a few weeks. Nothings broken, but she's been badly shaken up and bruised.'

'That's settled then. She can't possibly move back to her own home. The bathroom's upstairs.'

She turned to Felix. He faced Phoebe. She smiled as if coaxing a small animal out of its lair. With his insides on the spin cycle, Felix nodded. 'We'll sort something out,' he said.

Chapter Eighteen

Kate was giving her apartment a long overdue clean, but the vacuum had blocked. When she checked the bag it was so full, dust had backed up through the pipe. God, when was the last time she had emptied it? Before she could give it much thought the telephone rang. It was Josh and she instantly felt tongue tied and foolish.

'Suzanne said you called. I was with a patient.'

'That's okay. Sorry to bother you.'

Nothing further was said until Josh said, 'and you rang for…? I need a clue here.'

'Oh right yes. Well I needed to pick your brains again. A whole bunch of stuff has been happening recently. I'm not really sure what's going on so…I wondered if you'd give me another perspective?'

'Sure anytime. Let me just grab my diary.'

Kate heard the phone clatter onto the desk, mumbled words she couldn't make out, but assumed it was Josh asking Suzanne for his diary, and then he was back, breathless in that rushed way people have on the telephone.

'Got it. When were you thinking?'

'I hoped you'd have that lunch we talked about? I really don't want to take up anymore of your appointment time. Unless,' she added quickly, not wanting to give the wrong impression. 'You'd prefer that. It's just that last time you wouldn't let me pay, and I insisted and it got a bit…awkward, at least for me. Not that *you* made me feel awkward, I just did. That's just me. Anyway, I can hear myself babbling so I'm going to stop that now. Bottom line, lunch…or a paid appointment. Either is fine with me. Your call.' She held her breath, her insides squirming, what the hell was the matter with her?

Josh laughed. 'I think you managed the majority of those words in one breath. Very impressive.'

'Thanks,' she relaxed. 'You should see me underwater. I can hold my breath for days.'

Another laugh. 'Lunch would be great. I've been waiting for you to call.'

He'd been waiting for her to call. He'd been waiting for her to call? What did that mean? Looking forward to it or dreading it? She reminded herself not to get too excited, because even if it was the former, it would only be out of professional curiosity.   He'd be wondering about the latest insane occurrence, what obscure event was going on in the life of the town freak. She didn't think he'd be disappointed either.

They set a time and date and Kate rang off. Despite the echoes of failed love in the past, despite the memories of disappointment and rejection snapping at her heels, despite the voice warning her his interest was purely professional, she really couldn't help but feel a little excited at the thought of seeing him again.

'You know you'll have to sell that house mum,' Phoebe said to her mother the following day. She and Felix had decided not to broach it immediately, wanting their mother to recover from the shock of the fall first.

'I know nothing of the sort. Stop fussing.'

'Look at the state of you. You could have died.'

Felix heard the emphasis Phoebe placed on the last word.

'Well I didn't,' his mother replied crossly, patting the sheet with her hands. 'Let's get a little perspective here. I sprained my wrist.'

Phoebe looked over at him. 'Felix?'

He attempted to step closer to the bed and his mother, but the space between them pushed against him so hard he stayed where he was. 'Phoebe's right,' he said.

'I'm absolutely fine.'

'No, you aren't mum,' Phoebe insisted. 'The doctor says you won't be able to manage stairs for a few weeks, and even when you're recovered, those stairs are just too steep. Even I struggled and I'm half your age.'

'Oh do what you like,' she snapped. 'You two always did anyways.'

'It's for your benefit mum,' Phoebe reminded her.

Disgust congealed in his stomach as he watched his mother fight back the self-pitying tears.

'I knew this would happen. I knew it.'

'Knew what would happen?' Felix asked.

'Mum, stop this, that's enough,' Phoebe said quickly. Her voice was harsh initially, but then it softened and thickened as she continued. 'Please don't do this. We're not trying to take over; we just care about you, that's all.'

His mother's hands lay blue against the white of the sheet, giving her a vulnerable look Felix wasn't used to in his mother.

'And you?' she fixed Felix with a cool stare that penetrated him, skewering him to the spot. He raised his head and met her eye to eye, quivering inside. The vulnerability he had seen in her moments ago, gone.

'Do you care?' she demanded.

Looking into her eyes Felix saw past her challenge. He remembered, she hadn't always been this way. The crisp hard shell had developed over the years, and he knew deep down that he was a part of the reason. When he was small she had been soft, warm and funny. Her smell, as he nuzzled into her lap, flooded back to him now. The songs she sang, the stories she read, her patience as they made pizzas or baked bread or painted hand print pictures. And later, when he was a teenager that towered over her, he would bend down and kiss the top of her head. Enchanted by how her hair caught the sun, and she would laugh with pleasure. That was all before his illness, before he started to pull what was left of their family apart. She would never forgive him for it, she would keep making him pay, never let him forget it.

'Well?' the word bounced around the room and brought Felix back to the sour faced stranger in the bed in front of him. For a moment he forgot what she was asking, who she was, where he was and then it tumbled back on him.

'Course,' he said, pushing the word out, trying to hold onto what this woman had once been to him.

'Humph, you could sound like you mean it,' she grumbled.

Phoebe laughed, icing over the tension. 'Okay mum, so Felix and I will sort it out and get it on the market.'

'You will do no such thing!'

'Mum!'

'I mean it Phoebe. That's my home and that's where I intend to live until I say different. We had an agreement, remember?'

Phoebe sighed. 'Well, regardless of anything else you can't go there when you're discharged. Doctor's orders.'

'So where will I go in the meantime?'

Felix caught a tinge of thinly disguised fear and saw her shrink before him, suddenly small and broken again. He hated her dominance of him, but he didn't want to see his mother broken up. Seeing her helpless like this made him scared. Made him want to get close to her, to protect her. Yet he couldn't afford to get close again. He had to stay away, for his own protection and, now that he remembered what happened the afternoon he'd blacked out, for everyone else's too.

Phoebe patted her veined hand. 'Don't worry mum, we'll sort something out, won't we Felix?'

His body tightened with resentment. He always ended up doing what they wanted. It had always been like that.

'Felix?'

His chest clenched so hard he thought he'd pass out, he pulled air into his lungs and the tightness eased.

'Yes, he said,' he nodded, and pushed the corners of his mouth up in what he hoped resembled a smile. A black boulder sat in his stomach, fear of what Phoebe had in mind, but even more so, what he might do as a result. His mind on the edge of the abyss.

Sam knew Josh was dishy but she had forgotten how much. His soft eyes and gentle voice contrasted starkly with her experiences at home at the moment. If Paul had been more attentive, if he had been more affectionate, well, she wouldn't be here. She was glad she'd worn her Ghost dress; it clung in all the right places, and showed off her cleavage to its best advantage.

'Hello,' Sam said, and gave him her sexist smile as she entered his office, wondering, not for the first time, just what she hoped to gain from this.

Josh said nothing and pointed her to the seat next to his desk. He tugged at his white coat, pulling it round him as if to fend her off. He looked shy, and Sam smiled to herself as she watched him take the chair at his desk.

'Thank you for seeing me so quickly, I didn't think I'd get an appointment the next day!'

'We aim to please,' he said, as he consulted his notes. 'So, Sam. What seems to be the trouble?' Finally, he looked at her.

She moved her head to one side and pulled her hair back exposing her elegant neck. 'My neck.'

Josh lowered his eyes to his notes. 'Just the one side?'

She nodded.

'Have you recently had any kind of accident or strain that you can remember?'

'I don't remember anything,' her voice was coy and soft.

He asked her a number of questions and she answered in a slow, deliberate way.

'Okay, if you could go behind the screen and change into the gown there, then hop onto the plinth for me.'

'Plinth?'

He signalled with his pen,' the couch.'

'Oh, the bed.' Sam giggled. 'That's the best offer I've had all day.'

Josh smiled, it appeared to be the first genuine one since she had walked in the office, and she trilled with delight.

'How's Paul?' he asked, as she rose to change behind the screen.

They both knew it was deliberate. 'Fine thanks,' she said crossing the room.

She was undetered. Getting your own way was a little like cleaning brass, she thought, as she got undressed. You had to rub and rub and rub until eventually, with enough patience, the brass shone through. 'Actually,' she said from behind the screen, deciding to try a different tack. 'Things have been a little…strained between us recently.'

'Oh?'

Sam thought she could here interest in his voice. 'It's been tough for both of us. I think,' she said emerging from behind the screen and getting onto the bed, 'it's exacerbated by the fact that neither of us talk to other people about it.'

'Face down,' he said, and began to manipulate her neck gently.

'Mmm, that feels good.' She wriggled suggestively.

'Hold still and relax,' he said, moving to her upper back. After a few minutes he pushed on her upper shoulder and something cracked loudly.

'Okay?' he asked.

'Fine thanks,' her answer was muffled, but she decided to try again. 'Except for my relationship with my husband.'

'Have you thought about counselling?'

'No, counselling's out of the question, Paul wouldn't do it.'

'That's a shame, it can be really helpful. Turn on your side for me'

'I know, but it's pointless going on my own,' as she turned over, she deliberately stuck out her hip in a provocative manner.

'Not really.'

'You seem to know a lot about it.'

116

'I trained as a counsellor.' Josh twisted her body gently, rolling it back and forth. 'Thought I wanted to do that with my life.'

'Wow. What changed your mind?'

'I couldn't detach myself from the suffering people brought me.'

His response was a little...pious for her, but he was cute and, she decided, she was only having a bit of fun. 'So you retrained?'

'Yep.'

'Impressive.'

'Expensive.'

They laughed and Sam saw the chink; a little glimmer of the brass underneath. A little persistence was all it took.

She stayed quiet, allowing Josh to crack, crunch and stretch where he needed to, while she worked out what her next move should be.

'I think you're right,' she said.

'About what?'

'Counselling.'

'I use it.'

'You do?'

'Sure.'

'You don't look like you need it.'

Josh laughed. 'You can get dressed now.' He went over to the sink in the corner and washed his hands.

'Seriously,' Sam said, as she stood up and moved her neck from side to side. It was looser. 'You look…'

'Normal?'

'Yeah, I suppose.'

Josh pulled out a blue paper towel from the dispenser on the wall and dried his hands. 'Don't have to be a basket case to see a counsellor. It helps me get some perspective. Sort my thoughts out. Could help you and Paul too.'

'You think so?' Sam smiled shyly.

'Sure. There's no stigma, not these days,' he indicated the screen. 'You can put your clothes back on now.'

'How would I convince Paul?' she asked, when she emerged dressed.

Josh shrugged. 'You know him best. Take a seat.'

They sat at the desk and Sam watched as Josh wrote up her notes. When she thought it was the right moment she said, 'could we meet, talk some more? I'd really appreciate your input, and I'm sure you could give me some pointers.'

'Erm, I…'

'Please? It would really help.'

'I told you, I don't practice counselling anymore.'

'I realise that but, I thought you might be able to at least give me some basic advice?'

'Really, seriously, it's not my thing. I'm not the right-'

'It could save my marriage.'

He paused, 'that bad huh?'

'That bad,' she said.

Josh paused for a long time before saying 'okay. Check with Suzanne at the desk to see when I have an appointment-'

'Oh no, I wouldn't dream of a counselling session with you, not after what you said earlier. I just want to get some friendly advice, a few pointers. That's all. Let me take you out for a drink.'

'I don't drink.'

'Lunch then.'

'That won't be necessary.'

'Please, my treat? My way of saying thank you. Pleeeease?' She watched as Josh struggled with her proposal. 'It would make all the difference to me. I don't know what I'll do otherwise. How I'll convince Paul.'

She waited.

'Okay, lunch. But it will have to be quick. I'll bring along my address book, then I can give you some names and numbers of colleagues who might be able to help.'

'Oh that's brilliant. Thank you.'

They set up a date and time for that Thursday and Sam left. She felt light on her feet and bounced down the road. As she skipped down the street, a cab driver whistled at her. Sam beamed. She still had it.

'Kate, I think I'm in love.' This was Sam's response later that afternoon to Kate's story about being questioned by the police.

Sam and Kate sat in their usual café. It was Tuesday so it was quiet, and they'd been able to bag the large comfy armchairs.

Kate smiled in resignation, knowing Sam had not heard a word, and waited for her friend to continue.

'Don't look like that, I'm serious.'

'Well of course you are, you're married aren't you?'

Sam looked irritated at Kate's response.

'Okay, who, or should I say, with what?'

'No, this is serious; I've never felt like this before.'

Kate put her mug down, sensing the conversation demanded her full attention. 'Who?'

Kate's stomach lurched when the answer came.

'That chiropractor guy, Josh. We're having lunch together.'

'I'm having lunch with him,' Kate said quickly, wanting to stake a claim, but the moment she said it she felt foolish.

Clearly lunch meant nothing; it appeared he regularly had lunch with clients. Besides, when she compared them there was no contest, if indeed there ever was one, which there wasn't, she reminded herself. But if there was...well, she was all gangly, thin and angular, whilst Sam was all...voluptuous and...womanly.

'Is it a date?' Sam asked.

'No, of course it's not a date.' There was irritation in Kate's voice.

Sam raised one neatly shaped apricot eyebrow.

'Really,' insisted Kate. 'He helped me out but when I offered to pay he refused, so we agreed I'd buy him lunch instead.'

Sam leaned forward, her eyes wide. 'Who instigated the lunch?'

Kate didn't want to discuss this with Sam. 'I can't remember.'

'Kate!'

'Well, I can't.'

'Did you ask him to lunch?'

'No!'

'Then he must have asked you.'

'I suppose so. But it wasn't like that,' she added hastily. 'It kind of evolved during our conversation. No one asked anyone 'out'.'

'Oh my God, he must fancy you,' she wailed. 'I had to prise a lunch out of him.'

'You did?' she said, her heart skipped.

'Yes, damn it – he fancies you.'

'He does not, besides, he's a Christian.'

Sam leaned back and roared with laughter.

'What? What are you laughing at?'

'You! Just because he's a Christian doesn't mean he's cut off from the waist down.'

'Don't be so crude.' Kate could feel herself blush.

'I'm not, but I'm sure being a Christian doesn't mean you don't fancy someone. It probably just means he won't try and get his hands down your jumper on the first date.'

'It's not a date!'

Sam shrugged and smiled. 'Okay, if you say so. *He's just a nice guy who likes to help people.*'

Kate's insides began to churn. Was Sam right? Did Josh fancy her? A pang of fear sprang up and yet, she was pleased too. She was certainly looking forward to seeing him on Friday.

'So, when are you two having lunch?' Kate asked.

'Thursday. You?'

'Friday,' said Kate.

A taunt quiet fell between them, spiked with unsaid words. For the first time in their relationship Kate wanted to dampen Sam's enthusiasm and smother her zest for life, if even just for a moment.

She picked up her mug and sat back in her chair. 'How's Paul?' she asked.

Sam shot her a glance. 'He's fine.' Her voice was hard; the words short and sharp.

The two women eyed each other for a few moments. The coffee machine hissed in the background.

Sam leaned forward and played with a condensation ring on the table. 'You don't have a…thing about Josh do you, Kate?'

'Me? No, of course not,' Kate heard the high tone of her voice and hoped Sam wouldn't.

Of course she had a thing about Josh, but there was no point in going down that route. His interest in her was of a professional nature. She was a specimen to him, something of technical interest, nothing more. And if she were beginning to have feelings for him well, she could deal with that easily enough. It wasn't the first time.

'Only, well, I wouldn't want us to fall out over a man.'

Kate laughed. 'You're not serious…' she stopped and looked at her friend. 'Are you?'

Sam shrugged but didn't look up, focusing instead on the pattern she was making on the table.

'Sam, you're married!'

'Ur, dur, I know that.'

'You know what I mean.'

'Paul hasn't spoken to me in over two weeks. I'm fed up with it. I'm trapped, I'd be mad if I didn't take this job, but if I do...well, Paul and me, we may as well call it quits. It's so unfair! What a choice, and Paul is pushing me to choose between him and my career.'

Until recently Kate didn't know Sam had a career, or even a desire for one. Anger bubbled in her.

'My whole life feels like it's going down the pan. This isn't how my life was supposed to be, Kate.'

Kate imagined bouncing her friend's self-absorbed head off the table, repeatedly, but instead took a deep breath and said, 'I know, but all relationships have rough patches.'

'This is more than that.'

'I'm sorry.'

'It's not your fault,' Sam always said this as if on some level, someone other than herself was to blame. 'This thing with Josh, I know I only saw him for half an hour, but there just seemed this...connection between us, you know?'

Kate nodded, she knew, but it hurt that it wasn't something unique to her, she pushed the stab of disappointment to one side and focused on her friend. 'But Sam, think for a moment, isn't that what he's supposed to do, connect with his clients?'

'This was different,' Sam said, dismissing Kate with a wave of her hand. 'There was a connection; we got on so well, had loads in common. I left feeling on cloud nine. I haven't felt that good in ages now.'

'And you're sure you're not misreading what is simply his bedside manner?' As soon as the words left Kate's mouth she regretted it.

Sam snorted. 'Wouldn't mind a bit more of his bedside manner.'

Kate fought the urge to slap Sam.

'Anyway, I asked him out for a drink.'

'You did?'

'Don't sound so surprised, I made out it was just a friendly gesture.'

'What did he say?' Kate's body strained forward.

'He said he didn't drink, that's why he settled on lunch.'

Kate regretted she had arranged to meet him now. She nodded at Sam and forced herself to smile, but all her breath and energy had escaped her.

'Kate, you okay?'

She nodded again. 'Fine, just a bit tired.'

Sam smiled. 'Don't worry, I won't corrupt your little Christian friend.'

'I'm sure you won't. Just be careful Sam. Paul's a good bloke.'

Sam snorted, and it made the anger spiral inside Kate again, pushing on her brain.

'He is,' Kate repeated in earnest. 'I know you're going through a tough time at the moment, but don't do anything you might regret.'

'Maybe I won't regret it,' Sam said, with a smile.

It was too much, Kate couldn't hold it in any longer. 'God, you are the most selfish self-absorbed person I have ever met,' she said.

Sam looked as if she had been slapped. 'Pardon?'

Once she had started, the dam on her anger broke. 'You heard me. You waltz around thinking of no-one but yourself. You think the world revolves round you, and give no thought to the people around you who, against all the odds, love and care about you!'

'Are you alright?'

Kate stood up. 'No, I'm not, but you'd know that if you listened for once. A little girl has gone missing; I've been questioned by the police. I'm scared Sam, and all you can do is talk about your bloody love life. A love life you shouldn't even *have*, because you have a perfectly decent man at home who loves you.'

Kate attempted to throw her paper napkin down, but it stuck to the palm of her hand. She shook it off and it fluttered lamely onto the table.

Sam watched with her mouth open.

'I've got to go,' Kate said, regretting her outburst. What was happening to her? 'I'm sorry...it's...I'm...sorry.'

She left Sam sitting in the café, only later realising she hadn't paid her half of the bill.

Chapter Nineteen

The following day as Felix tried to concentrate on the case papers in front of him, his thoughts turned to Kate. He hadn't seen her at all this week; he hoped she was thinking about him. He had thought they had a chance together, the day at the beach, that was of course, until the discovery he made in the boot of his car.

He pushed the image of what he'd done to the back of his mind, and ran his hands through his hair in a subconscious effort to straighten out his thoughts and refocus his attention.

His phone rang and he jumped. Could this be Kate? Picking up his thoughts on the ether? Were they synchronising after all? He took a deep breath and picked up the phone. He couldn't hide his disappointment at hearing it was Phoebe.

'Oh, it's you.'

'Oh hello to you too,' she said.

'I'm sorry I thought you were someone else.'

'Someone special?'

'Yes and no. I don't want to talk about it.'

Felix, suddenly exhausted, pushed the papers to one side to concentrate on the phone call. 'To what do I owe this pleasure?'

She took a deep breath and Felix felt his stomach tighten. He knew what was coming next.

'We need to talk about mum.' Felix groaned. 'I know, I know but we must. You haven't been to see her recently.'

'I've been busy.'

'So have I. That's no excuse. And there's something else.'

'Oh?'

'She'll be out soon and we don't have a plan.'

'I thought she was coming to you.'

'When did I say that?'

'At the hospital.'

'I did no such thing Felix, you just assumed. Like you always do. You always assume I'll take care of mum, and it's not on, not this time.'

'I can't.'

'Why not?'

'You know why.'

'No, Felix, that's unfair. You can't have it both ways. One minute saying you don't want your condition to define you, the next using it as an excuse to get out of looking after mum.'

He ignored her. 'I'm out at work all day.'

'She needs a place to stay, not twenty-four hour nursing.'

'But it makes sense if you take her.'

'Why? I have two hyperactive boys, I'm pregnant and David and I are at a critical stage in our relationship. We don't need the strain of anyone, least of all mum, staying with us right now.'

'You have Gertie.'

'Well, that's a whole other story.'

'Oh?'

Pheobe sighed. 'She's the one.'

'The one what?'

'The one David's been having an affair with.'

'And you haven't sacked her yet?'

'Not exactly. David had a word and she's leaving at the end of this week.'

'You're keeping her in the house?'

'Felix, it's not her fault, she's young. David is...David. She's lost her job, her home and he's probably broken her heart. The least I can do, is let her stay on until the end of the week so she can get herself sorted.'

'God Phoebe, you really are a fucking saint!'

'Felix!'

'Sorry.'

'Anyways, that's off topic. I phoned to talk about mum.'

Silence fell between them. Finally Felix spoke, 'I'm sorry, but I can't have her staying with me. It'd be a nightmare. She'd have a relapse within twenty-four hours...or I would. '

'This isn't funny Felix, I'm serious.'

'I'm not joking!'

'And I'm not baling you out, not this time. There's no reason why you shouldn't face your responsibilities, and like it or not, mum is one of those.'

'Where would she sleep? I've only got one bedroom.'

'We don't have a spare room either. We'd have exactly the same problem.'

'What about Gertie's old room?'

'We're interviewing this week for her replacement.'

'That explains it.'

'Stop it!'

Felix fumed.

'So neither of us have a spare room,' she continued. 'But you have a futon.'

Felix didn't answer.

'Felix?'

'What?'

'I said-'

'I heard what you said.'

'There you are then, you might not have a spare room, but you have a spare bed, which is more than we have, besides our bathrooms upstairs. Yours is all on the same level. You heard the doctor, no stairs.'

'Seriously Phoebe, I can't.'

'Seriously Felix, you'll have to.'

The stalemate hummed down the phone.

'Felix,' said Phoebe, her voice softer now. 'I can't do it anymore, not all of it. David and I are sorting out the house sale, you have to do your bit.'

'Then I'll take over the house sale.'

'It's in the hands of the estate agents now, besides that's not what I mean,' she sighed. 'Don't you think it's time you two sorted out your differences? Don't you think this would be an ideal opportunity to get to know each other?'

'We do know each other, and we don't like each other.'

'That's not true. Mum loves you, it's the illness that convinced you otherwise. She's wary of you, but given what you did, don't you think that's understandable?'

'I suppose,' he pushed the memories away. He was different then, or was he?

'Felix, this is your opportunity to get to know mum properly.'

'It's easy for you,' he said sulking. 'She likes you.'

Phoebe laughed. 'She likes you too. She *loves* you. You just don't give her a chance. Look, I'll make a deal with you. You have her for the first week or so, and if things don't work out by then, well, we'll review it. Okay?'

Felix didn't see how he could refuse, with resignation he agreed.

125

Kate wasn't sure what had happened. Maybe it was the stress she'd been under recently, maybe it was a build-up of frustration about her friend's behaviour over the years, or maybe it was as simple and childish as jealousy about Josh. It was probably a combination of all three, screwed up tight in the bullet Kate had hit Sam with.

But that incident, and the fact that Lucy Newton was still missing, convinced Kate that she had to explore the voices, she had to know, one way or the other, if the church on Monday had been a fluke, a one off.

Her breath short, she sat on the sofa. The blood pumped hard in her chest and her throat was swollen tight. No more procrastination, this was it.

She tried to slow her breathing the way she had at church, but her nerves danced and jangled, interrupting the stillness she knew she needed. Her heart beat a tattoo on her eardrums.

She stood up and strode around the room in frustration, stomping and huffing like a toddler in a tantrum. This was ridiculous. There was nothing to be nervous about. What was the worst that could happen? Nothing. Nothing happening that's what…and what was so bad about that?

Kate sighed and slumped back down. Who was she kidding? Nothing would be awful. Nothing would be the end, all hope extinguished. And when all was said and done, what were we without hope?

Kate shook her head, she couldn't do it. It was too much. Tears filled her eyes and slipped down her face. It was too much. She ached inside, and became painfully aware of the emptiness around her, the loneliness that was her life.

She lay back on the sofa clutching a cushion tight as if it were a life buoy, and allowed the emotions she had battened down over the years, to come up and wash over her. The feelings of loss and rejection she thought she had left behind long ago, resurfaced. The deeply buried pain of being rejected by the very people who shared your blood and DNA, tugged at her body, pulling her into a vortex of black and blue. Kate broke down into sobs, washing away a lifetime of disappointment, rejection and self-loathing.

Some interminable time later she lay quiet, washed up drift wood after a storm. Her in-breath hiccupped with the rhythm of a train, and with each out-breath her body softened and relaxed. And then it happened.

She thought she'd imagined it at first and sat bolt upright, then it disappeared. But when she lay back down and allowed herself to relax, it returned. Soft words, undefined, but definitely there.

Her heart fluttered, chasing the words away like nervous birds. She soothed her body, and the words crept back, slowly, softly at first. They were scrambled and made little sense.

I can't believe...she would say...apricots...had to get...porridge for breakfast...maybe this will...could I?...I'm not so...Stan said...jury service... bollocks...a fore and...work was...sure you didn't...why is it...did she know?...what time...the beer's awful...pick it up...tell her I'm sorry...

On and on it rolled. Nonsense ramblings, a collection of disjointed thoughts in a myriad of voices, picked up on the breeze and carried around like dandelion seeds waiting to be deposited. And now Kate could hear them again.

She began to experiment. When she sat up they disappeared, but if she sat back, closed her eyes and took a deep breath, they came creeping back. Slow, quiet, timid, but there they were. She stood up and they disappeared. She stopped, closed her eyes and took a deep breath, and there they were again. Quicker this time. Clearer too.

She plonked herself on the sofa and grinned. Not only had they returned, but she had some control over them. All she needed now, was to be able to distinguish between them better. Unravel the jumble of words so they were discernible.

She sat up straight, closed her eyes and welcomed the words in a way she had never before in her life. They tumbled over her, around her, through her, and when Kate felt fully enveloped she began to probe. She wasn't sure what she was doing, just reaching out with her mind, exploring, playing, the way she had when she was a child. There was a catch on her mind, a slight tug. Her father used to take her fishing when she was younger, and it reminded her of the feeling of the line when the fish took a bite.

She waited, feeling the tug, unsure what to do next. Then, remembering how they reeled in the fish, she slowly tugged her mind, the way her father had taught her, not too quickly, not too slowly, nice and gentle, but she got excited and when she knew it was close she speeded up. Her mind snapped back and she lost it.

She cast her mind out again, like her father had shown her with the line, and probed, waited for the tug, and once again began to draw it back, her father's words in her ear. "Gently Kate, not too quickly now, not too slowly, nice and gentle".

This time she listened to him, and this time, when her mind snapped back it brought with it a single stream of words from one voice. There it was, definable words, a dialogue she could understand. So unlike her past experiences of the voices, which had been random thoughts dropped into her head, or a cacophony of noise.

'Was I unreasonable? Did I overreact? No. No definitely not. He came in late, woke me up and didn't even apologise. Where'd he been anyway? He didn't say. He started it. He was the one stomping around. Anyway, he never did tell me...beef, that'll be good for Sunday. Jean's coming. Oh god, we'd better get this sorted before then. She can sniff trouble a mile off. I'll have it out with him tonight, tell him we need to get it sorted before his mother comes over. Yogurts, I need yogurts. Will Hannah eat beef? Is she vegetarian this week? I must talk to her about her basket ball kit tonight.'

Kate shook her head and the dialogue ceased, like clearing an etch-a-sketch board. She stretched out her mind and probed again. Again there was the slight tug, the slow reel back and the pop as her mind snapped back into place.

'Red really isn't her colour. Do I say? How do I say? She looks so happy. It's bought now. I'll tell her the truth and she'll hate me, and wear it anyway, now she's bought it. Should have said something before, in the shop? Why didn't I? If I tell her I love it what's the harm, who's to know? But what if-'

Kate shook her head and it stopped. Again she probed, already it felt familiar, already her confidence had grown.

'What did she want? Flowers were lame. I'd get flowers for mum not Shirley, not for her birthday. God, it is so hard. She might like some jewellery but what kind? Oh shit, there's Jack, I don't want to see him after last week, shit I think he's spotted me -'

Kate sat up and massaged her neck and the words ceased. She sat perfectly still, looking down at her hand, focusing on the crumpled skin around her knuckles, barely breathing from shock and delight; she could hear them. All of them, except one. She knew what she had to do next, but she was afraid.

Afraid for Lucy, and afraid for herself.

Around six Kate sat bolt upright. Her chest squeezed, her throat tight with the screams she was unable to voice in her sleep. She peered into the familiar room that emerged from the dim light, her bedroom, and began to relax. 'It was a dream,' she murmured, 'just a dream.' She could barely hold onto it now she was awake, but it had terrified her moments ago.

She was small. There was a man's voice, shouting. Kate couldn't remember much more. She couldn't see the man clearly, it was blurred. He was shouting and flailing his arms around. Then she heard a woman screaming over and over again. She saw nothing, only heard them. Everything was blurred and colourless. But the woman's screams terrified her, even now as she recalled it, goose pimples rose on her arms.

There was something else too. Some hollow place deep inside that never seemed to be filled. She thought about Josh, how full he seemed, full and content and assured. Was that was what came of believing God was on your side?

She took a deep breath and the turbulent emotions began to subside, eventually she thought she might be able to fall back to sleep. She lay down and thought about Josh.

She wanted to see him again, whatever the risks, and she was glad they were meeting for lunch. She pushed all thoughts of Sam to one side. Kate was no match, she knew that, but this was not a competition. If it had been, she wouldn't have entered it in the first place.

The weighed of what Sam might be doing dragged on her, until she reasoned that whether Sam's behaviour was right or wrong, was up to Sam to decide. Whatever happened, Kate could still enjoy his company, and there is was again, the flicker of hope that maybe, just maybe, she was more than a professional interest to him.

Chapter Twenty

Kate was heating up tomato soup, absently stirring the red liquid. Last night's dream hung around her, wisps of a suggestion. As usual she was no closer to remembering it now, let alone figuring out what it meant, all she knew was that she felt disturbed by it.

As she lifted the pan off the stove it slipped and clattered to the floor. Soup splattered across the kitchen, blood red. The sight made Kate's chest constrict, her knees buckled and she fell.

It had been a while since the last time, but she recognised the familiar click when she heard it. Her face was in the musky carpet again, the light dancing across her in a slow rhythm. It was silent except for a horse heavy breath behind her, she didn't know if it was animal or human. Her heart clenched and pumped, clenched and pumped, in her chest, her throat as tight as wire. She opened her eyes and across from her, directly in her eye line, the wall was splattered, a vivid red, lit up periodically as the light swung by. She stared at it for a long time.

It was tomato soup on her kitchen floor, Kate reminded herself as she came round, her cheek resting on the cold hard tiles. Shaking she sat up, unable to comprehend what was happening to her, asking the same questions. What were these flashes? Flashbacks? Flash forwards? Where *was* Lucy? Kate was sure these...things, whatever they were, involved the little girl somehow. But how?

She had lunch scheduled with Josh tomorrow, perhaps he could help her make sense of all this. Perhaps...

Sam and Josh had agreed to meet in the cellar café, a coffee house situated, as its name suggested, in the bowels of a large department store in town, about five minutes walk from Sam's boutique. The walls had a rough plaster finish with coffee quotes painted in a black border around the top. Coffee was a serious business here, with a menu that boasted twenty-two varieties, as well as homemade carrot cake and panini's.

Sam couldn't remember the last time she had been so nervous. 'Nervous' wasn't something she usually did. It had taken her hours in the shop that morning to decide what to wear. She had finally decided on her jade channel dress, tight fitting with a scalloped neck, a white fitted jacket and killer heels. As she stood in the doorway to the café, she ran her hands over her hips where the dress hugged her figure, she couldn't have looked better.

Josh hadn't arrived, but she was fifteen minutes early, so she ordered a Java coffee and a panini of brie and walnut, and took her red flag marked "order 29" to one of the seats in the alcoves to wait. She had to admit she was disappointed. This wasn't how she envisaged the start of the date, but when she saw Josh she forgot her disappointment and stood up to wave.

As she watched him meander through the tables towards her, she wondered again what she was doing. There was no doubt that Josh was an attractive man, but she'd met many attractive men during her five years of marriage to Paul; none of them had effected her like this. Why now? Why Josh?

'You ordered?' he said, when he reached the table pointing to the flag. Sam nodded. 'I'll just be a sec,' and he went off to the counter.

Were things so bad in her marriage? Paul was still giving her the silent treatment, and she found it hard and lonely living with him. They were at an impasse. He wanted children, she didn't, no compromise. No matter how much he pushed or she sulked, neither was likely to change their mind.

He couldn't expect her to make a decision like that under pressure, and yet, there he was, piling it on. Anger and frustration built up in her chest, creating a hard knot. Why couldn't he see how unreasonable he was being? He, she decided, was driving her to this. Whatever 'this' was.

'Mum?'

She turned from her locker. 'Hello Felix, I'm nearly ready.'

'Here, let me get that stuff for you.'

'I can do it Felix,' she snapped.

Felix stood back and shook his head, his teeth tight against the words. He released a breath slowly as he sat on the end of the bed to wait.

'Don't sit on the bed!' Felix leapt up. 'The nurse just made that this morning for someone else.'

He stood, moving his weight from one foot to another as he watched his mother packing her bag in slow motion.

'Mum, please let me help you. My parking runs out in twenty minutes.'

'Stop fussing Felix, I'll be done in a few minutes.'

Felix chewed his lips in the hope that, by occupying his mouth, he wouldn't say something he would regret. Why did this always happen? And why was it always him that bit back the words? He was in his thirties, a grown man, and yet she still treat him like a child.

'There, all done,' she said, smiling at him.

He took the bag and turned quickly to leave.

'Wait on Felix. I'm not that young anymore you know, and I've been injured.'

How he wasn't going to add to her injuries whilst she stayed with him was beyond his imagination, but he slowed down to allow her to catch up with him.

'Aren't you supposed to have a wheelchair to the car park?' he asked.

His mother's laugh played on his nerves, finger nails down a blackboard. His shoulders tightened further.

'That's only on the way in silly boy. On the way out you're on your own.'

He wished he was.

They drove in silence and just as Felix was taking the opportunity to let go of some of his tension his mother began to speak.

'I know you're angry with me, Felix,' she said. Her voice was gentle, and Felix glanced at her before focusing back on the road. 'About a lot of things, but…I had my reasons for doing what I did, selling the house while you were away, for example.'

Felix swallowed before responding. 'And the reason was?'

'I don't want to go into that. It's not important. It's history. I just wanted you to know it wasn't an easy decision.'

'It's important to me,' he said, an edge to his voice.

Felix's mother sighed. 'Let's leave it at that, Felix.'

'I want to know.'

'And I don't want to talk about it.'

Then why bring it up, he thought. They drove for a few minutes before she added, 'your father was a good man.'

'I know that,' he said, confused by the statement.

They continued in isolation.

'Is the house on the market?' she asked.

'Yes. Phoebe and David sorted it out.'

'Any viewers?'

'I don't know, I haven't spoken to her about it.'

It had started to rain and Felix flicked on the wipers. They thudded rhythmically across the screen as they drove. The tyres hissed.

'It was stupid to stay in that house so long,' she said.

Felix nodded, but didn't look at her.

'I only thought that last year.'

'So why didn't you move?' He indicated right and waited in the centre of the road for a break in the traffic. The clicking filled the quiet of the car.

'It's difficult to explain.'

Felix said nothing.

'I just want to tell you I'm sorry if I've upset you. I always seem to upset you, and I don't mean to son.'

'Forget it,' he said, and the silence pulled them apart as he turned the car through a gap in the traffic.

'You've hardly touched that,' Josh said.

Sam shrugged. 'Wasn't as hungry as I thought.'

He smiled and Sam's stomach liquefied. What was this effect he had on her? Surely this was special?

'You okay?' he asked.

Sam nodded.

'You seem…preoccupied.'

'I was just thinking?'

'About?'

Sam shook her head, she couldn't tell him. She was tongue tied, like some love-struck teenager. It had been years since she felt this way. The pleasure-pain of yearning to touch someone, kiss them, the electricity humming in the air. Did he feel it to? How could he not?

His hand lay on the table. She stretched out her fingers and touched him. Sparks of lust shot through her finger tips, ripping through her body.

'How's Paul?' he said, removing his hand. 'I haven't seen him for a while so I'm guessing he's well.'' His words doused her fire with a cool bucket of reality. 'What does he do again?'

'He's an architect.'

'Oh yes. That must be really interesting?'

'Not really. He designs shopping centres. It's very dull.'

'Does he enjoy it?'

'I think so.'

'You don't know?'

'He…he's not a great conversationalist, and he doesn't like talking about his work.'

'Sounds like he doesn't enjoy it then.'

'Why?'

'Well, usually if someone enjoys what they do, it tends to spill out into other things, whether they mean it to or not. When you're passionate about things it's inevitable.'

'I suppose. What about you, are you passionate about your work?' Sam asked, wanting to move the conversation away from her husband.

'Yes, I suppose I am. I get excited when I wake up in the morning. There is the occasional patient who I'd rather not see, but that's more about me than them.'

'What d'you mean?'

'I believe that when you point the finger at someone else in judgement, what you're really doing is judging something inside yourself, something you refuse to accept is there.'

Sam thought about this for a moment and then said, 'I don't believe that.'

'Makes no odds to me,' Josh smiled. It was an amicable rebuff.

This time, instead of Sam's stomach liquefying at his smile it set hard with anger. He was making fun of her. She leaned forward, tapping her words out with her finger.

'What you're saying,' she said with care. 'As an example, is that if I criticise Paul for his lack of communication and attention to me, I'm guilty of the same thing? That doesn't make sense.'

'It makes sense if you don't want those attributes. And didn't you just tell me you didn't know if Paul was happy in his work?'

'So?'

'That suggests to me a lack of communication and attention on your part.'

'Rubbish!'

'Is it?'

'Yes,' she played with the crumbs on her plate.

Josh shrugged. 'Okay, give me another example of when my belief isn't true.'

She thought for a moment. 'What about child molestation,' she said triumphantly. 'We all judge someone for that, but you're surely not suggesting we all have child abuse tendencies?'

Josh sat back in his chair, his eyes softened and he spoke so quietly Sam had to strain forward to hear him.

'Have you ever abused your power over someone smaller and weaker than you?'

Sam snapped back into her chair. 'Never!'

Josh leant his elbows on the table. 'You mean you've never made fun of someone at school, another pupil or a teacher perhaps? You've never stood on a spider, swatted a fly or tormented some creature smaller than you? As an adult, you've never made an unkind comment to a friend or colleague?'

'Yes, of course, but that's not the same thing at all.'

'Why?'

'Why what?

'Why isn't it the same?'

'It just isn't.'

'Because there's some general consensus of opinion that insects don't matter, that children will be cruel, that everyone makes judgements on everyone else?'

'Exactly.'

'Do you think the slave trade is acceptable?'

'Of course not!'

'Less than a hundred years ago, the general consensus would have disagreed with you.'

'But we've evolved since then, we know better.'

'How did we evolve?'

Sam shrugged. This lunch wasn't going the way she envisaged at all.

'We evolved because people broke away from the general consensus,' he continued. 'They decided for themselves what kind of person they wanted to be, what kind of actions they wanted to take, and what kind of society they wanted to live in.'

'Isn't that judgement too? They're judging someone else's opinion as wrong, bad even. We need judgements to make sure we know right from wrong.'

'It doesn't mean you have to point the finger. When you make the choice, when you follow your own voice, you don't need to point out the "faults" of others, because you know they exist in you too.'

'So you just let people hurt others and stand by and say "oh that's okay"?'

'No. You can discern right from wrong actions, you can take steps to protect people if you feel it's necessary, but you don't have to apportion blame. You don't have to do it from anger and a sense of righteousness. You don't have to do it from a place of vengeance. You do have to take care of those most vulnerable, but you don't have to crucify someone in the process. Often the perpetrator is as much a victim as the victim themselves.'

'Try telling that to the parents of some abused kid, or the parents of that missing kid. Would they agree? I don't think so.' She was beginning to rethink her attraction to this man.

'Is it? I agree we need to protect our children. I agree that we need to ensure those who are likely to hurt or damage anyone, need to be taken out of society. But I don't believe we need to destroy them and demonise them in the process.'

'They need to be punished if they hurt others.'

'Without exception?'

Sam thought for a moment then nodded. 'Without exception.'

'Regardless of how big or small the hurt they inflict?'

'Yes, but appropriate punishment for the appropriate level of hurt inflicted. It's how things work now isn't it?'

Josh ignored her question. 'So what about you? We're supposed to be here to discuss your marriage, yes?'

'Yes,' Sam smiled.

'Okay, so let's start with that. Don't you think you might be hurting Paul by having lunch with me?'

'It's only lunch.'

'Is it?'

Sam looked around the café, suddenly uncomfortable.

'No, it isn't,' he continued. 'We both know that. You just used that as an excuse.'

'Well, I can't deny I find you attractive, and my marriage is…struggling.'

'So, I repeat my question, don't you think you might hurt Paul with what you're doing?.'

Sam didn't like where this conversation was heading. 'Possibly. A bit.'

'So, don't you think you should you be punished? Possibly, a bit?'

He was mimicking her! How dare he? He didn't know anything about her, or Paul for that matter. Sam stood up.

'Screw you,' she said, and left as quickly as her killer heels could manage, her bag clasped tightly to her side.

Kate checked her bank balance at the machine on the high street, crossed the road designated for buses only, and headed for the covered market to buy fruit and vegetables. It was crowded. The smell was ripe, a mixture of dank vegetables, heavy cheeses and fresh meat. The noises buffeted her; a banging butcher's cleaver, the trill of the tills and the bubbling conversation. It was a luxury to hear it all. Life. Right here and right now. She moved slowly, working her way through the people towards her new regular grocer situated in the centre of the market.

A familiar movement caught her eye. Her heart hiccupped as she searched the crowd. Was it possible? Was it her? Kate strained forward, pushing now.

'Hey?' a large woman turned and glared at Kate, her face red with effort or anger.

'Sorry, I'm trying to catch up with my friend.'

'Then have some bloody manners and people might let you through.'

'Yes, sorry.' Kate escaped the woman and peered through the crowd. There she was, she was sure of it. Tiny in the crowd, but real and alive. Lucy!

She pushed forward, excusing herself this time, winding her way through the people, all the time keeping one eye on the girl ahead. She had stopped at the bookstall and was only ten feet away now. Kate was close enough to call out but, remembering the last time they had met, she didn't want to shout and scare the girl.

Then suddenly Lucy turned and exited through one of the doors leading to the street. Kate pushed forward hard, but by the time she reached the door and followed, there was no sign of her at all, and Kate was left wondering if she had imagined her.

She sighed and returned to the bookstall hoping for some clue. After a few moments Kate realised that she was wasting her time. She didn't know what she was looking for, and now she wasn't even sure it was Lucy. It could have been any little blonde waif. But she couldn't let it go, not yet.

The owner, a large hairy man with a soft belly, sat on a stool by the till reading The Sun newspaper. People milled around the stall, but seemed unsure about disturbing him with a purchase. Kate approached him, and smiled as the man looked up. He folded his paper and stood beside her. He smelt of old sweat and vegetable soup.

'What can I do for you pet?'

Other customers began to press forward, seeing an opportunity to pay for what they wanted.

'That girl who was just here, do you know her?'

'Can't say that I do.'

'Did she buy anything?'

The large man scratched his stubble creating a rasping reminiscent of tics and lice.

'No, haven't made a sale in the past fifteen minutes. Kids never buy anything anyways.'

'What was she looking at?'

'I've no idea,' his voice became hard. 'Who are you anyway? The police?'

'No, no I just thought I recognised her that's all.'

'She was rummaging in that box over there,' he said. 'Now move aside pet, I've got customers.'

The man turned away.

'Thank you,' Kate said.

She went to the box he indicated and began to search through it, unsure what she was looking for. It was full of self-help books. What peddled garbage, she thought, the man had made a mistake, there was no way a child would bother to look at this sort of thing.

I'm wasting my time here, she thought, and was about to leave when she spotted an old hard backed book that looked out of place among the bright paperbacks. It was deep blue, the spine was cracked in a couple of places, but the title etched in tarnished gold could still be read. *'METAPHYSICS: A Study of the Mind'*.

She opened the cover to release a musty smell. Pasted on the reverse of the front cover was a map of the brain, and on the opposite page there was a hand written inscription in faded blue ink. All the air left her as she read it:

"In Rama was there a voice heard,
Lamentation and weeping and great
Mourning. Rachael weeping for
Her children, and would not be comforted, because they are not"

Kate's stomach turned over. Rachael? Lucy's mother was called Rachael. A coincidence, thought Kate, it had to be. The air round her stilled, the noises, smells, the jostling of the people, faded into the distance. She stood in a silent vacuum.

What was happening to her? Since her first visit to Josh and the arrival of these…visions she was having, since the disappearance of Lucy, she couldn't help but feel she was somehow inextricably linked with the girl. And now she, or a girl just like her, had led her here, to this book, with this inscription. Was Lucy trying to tell her something?

'Weeping for her children,' Kate shuddered at the possible meaning. She bought the book and hurried home, forgetting the fruit and vegetables.

'It's small Felix. Nice, but small.'

Felix gritted his teeth and flicked on the kettle. 'It's enough for me,' he said, his voice tight.

'I dare say, but where am I going to sleep?'

'You take the bedroom, of course.'

'You can't be sleeping on a couch for any length of time.'

Felix wondered how long she would be staying. 'It's okay mum, I don't have a couch, I have a futon.'

'A foo-what?'

'A futon. It's…like a fold out sofa bed.'

His mother shook her head. 'Why you just can't call it a sofa bed is beyond me.'

'It's Japanese. It has a special slatted base, low to the ground with an unusual mattress.'

'Oh,' she was looking round the kitchen with interest.

He watched her eyes scanning everything, making comparisons, judging. Felt her slit into his life and open it wide, as neatly as a paper knife on an envelope. He wanted to stand in front of her and shield his home. He couldn't feel more embarrassed, vulnerable and violated, than if she'd caught him naked. He wanted to put his hand over her mouth and smoother her. A flash of Lucy came to mind and he shook his head.

'Do you want tea?' he asked, desperate to pull her away from her prying.

'Love one.'

'Okay,' he stood before the open cupboard. 'I've got Redbush, green, lapsang, souchong, pepperm-'

'Don't you just have regular tea?'

He turned. 'What kind?'

'You know, Tetley or PG?'

'No, sorry, but I can go and get some.'

'Don't bother on my account.'

Felix picked up his keys from the counter, elated at the thought of escaping for a while. 'It's no bother, I've got to pick up some bits and pieces anyway.' And he retreated fast, before she could stop him or suggest she join him.

At the door guilt swam over him and he stopped. 'Make yourself at home, ' he said, and then left.

How dare he? Sam thought as she slammed the dishwasher door. It had been another strained meal. Paul's face set tight across the table. Over the last three weeks they had got into the habit of switching on the television during meal times to drown out the lack of conversation. It didn't help. It was like spraying perfume on a decaying body, the odour still managed to filter through and clog the nostrils.

Paul had retreated to the living room to watch a makeover project where people bought a property to develop, and the host of the show criticised every decision they made. Sam had watched it, in the old days when they were speaking, but couldn't bring herself to do anything with him when he oozed such distain.

She wasn't really sure who she was angry with right now; Paul or Josh. Both had let her down in their own way. Maybe that was men. Maybe they couldn't help it. A genetic default inherent in the male Homo sapien. The thought brought a smile on her face as she climbed the stairs to run herself a bath.

Cruelty, that's what it boiled down to. They were just mean. Take Paul, no woman could refrain from speaking to another human being for this long, it was insane! And Josh, turning on her like that. Pretending to be her friend, and all the time he was just waiting for some way of winning the upper hand. Such an ego. They have to win at any cost. And he talked such rot!

She poured a generous quantity of foam bath into the running water and watched the bubbles form. Well, that was it, sod them, sod the lot of them, including Kate. She was another one, just went off like a Catherine wheel. What was up with her? She sighed, it was no good, even Sam couldn't ignore that a pattern was forming.

Kate had accused her of…what was it? Being self-absorbed and selfish. Kate, her best friend! Her only real friend when it came down to it. Didn't that say something? And Josh today, what was all that about?

Sam bent down to push the mounting bubbles to the back of the bath and test the temperature. She noticed a discomfort in her solar plexus, the type she got when she was a child and she'd done something wrong. Did she take the people in her life for granted? Maybe a little, but didn't everyone?

As she straightened up and dried her hands she thought of her parents and the discomfort deepened. They had worked so hard, given her anything she needed, and she barely kept in touch with them now. She wracked her brain trying to remember the last time she had called them.

And this business with Josh, she knew Kate liked him, even if Kate wouldn't admit it, it was obvious, but still she had carried on regardless. No wonder Kate was angry.

The room began to fill with jasmine fragrant steam, misting up the mirrors and window. Sam leaned over the sink and drew a love heart on the window pane.

And Paul? Was he really so wrong to want to have a family? It was what most people did when they got married. If she didn't want one, was that any reason for them to be so angry with each other?

Her body began to close up and she thought she would cry. There was a creak of floorboards on the landing and Paul appeared in the doorway as Sam turned off the taps.

'Programme's finished,' he said.

Sam held her breath.

'Want a cuppa?

She turned and smiled. 'Please.'

Paul smiled back and Sam's body skipped.

'You okay?' he asked.

'I'm okay. You?'

'I'm okay.'

Sam noted that neither had asked the question 'are we okay?' but at least they were talking again. As Paul went back to the kitchen, Sam closed the bathroom door, and let out tears of relief as she undressed for her bath.

Chapter Twenty-One

Felix woke on Friday morning knowing that Kate was having lunch with Josh that day. It was there, in the forefront of his mind all morning. He lost track of the points being made in meetings, requested telephone callers to repeat what they said, reread one planning request five times, and Rosie had to ask him three times if he wanted a coffee before he heard her.

To add to his troubles he'd woken on the futon in the living room, reminding him that his mother lay sleeping in his bed. He had left before she was up and about. He knew it was wrong not to check if she needed anything, but he couldn't face her, not on top of everything else today. Besides, it was only a sprain, everything she could possibly need was in the flat. As he sneaked away he promised he'd ring her at lunchtime.

Instead he called Kate's flat, knowing she would have already left, just to create some noise, just to create evidence that he could disturb some element of her life; scraping 'Felix was 'ere' on the sound waves of her home.

He replaced the receiver and decided it must be love. Felix didn't usually equate being in love with this gnawing feeling inside him, a feeling of being eaten from the inside. But then, Kate wasn't the usual kind of woman. Or maybe, just maybe, this was the real thing. Perhaps love wasn't singing in the rain and riding on cloud nine and all the other clichès he'd heard growing up, and as he didn't have any real experience how would he know?

What if real love was painful and difficult and confusing? What if it felt as if your insides were being ripped out, that your heart was too big for your chest and you'd never be able to function properly again? What if real love was a bone crushing daily disappointment, the fight between wanting to see your love and the dread of doing so? What if it was misery, despondency and desperation?

He ran his hands through his hair then rested his head on them, elbows propped on his desk. He didn't see the overflowing in-tray, the scraps of paper littering his desk, the cold mug of coffee forming a deep brown skin as a defence. Instead he was wrapped up in his own thoughts. Why hadn't he said something to Kate on the beach that day? He shook his head, because he wasn't sure how he felt then.

His mind turned to his mother. He couldn't conceive of her living with him like this for long. He couldn't even bring himself to ring her to check she was alright. Truth was, he didn't care. This was ludicrous, he'd have to ring Phoebe and tell her.

Anger flared up. Why were women so difficult? All his angst in life was created by them: Kate, Phoebe, his mother, even that child, Lucy. It wasn't fair. They tormented him. He had to do something, take action, and show them once and for all that they couldn't push him around like this. He was a grown man, they couldn't treat him like this anymore. Pushing him around, forcing him into doing things he didn't want to do. Ignoring him, ignoring his needs. Action was needed, he needed to reclaim his life from them, from them all.

Just as an idea was forming John interrupted him to ask about a case. Felix pushed it all aside. Something would come to him, it always did.

Kate sat at the table wondering if this was where Josh had met Sam the previous day. She was dying to know what had happened, but Sam had not contacted her since their argument, and she could hardly ask Josh.

He returned to their table with the coffees. 'Sorry I was so long, they're really busy today,' he said. He put the flag on the table and nodded at it. 'They'll be along with the food order soon.'

'Thanks,' she said, as she pulled the cup and saucer across the table towards her.

'So, what's new?' he asked, as he sat down.

Kate wasn't sure where to start. A sticky silence stretched like chewing gum between them.

'Why the invite?' Josh said, eventually.

'I couldn't sleep one night and told God that I'd invite you to lunch if I could just get some sleep,' she smiled. 'I dropped into a deep sleep and didn't wake up till morning.'

Josh laughed. 'I thought you didn't believe in God.'

'I'm not sure I do, but a deal's a deal.'

'So, you're here under sufferance?'

She smiled. 'No, not quite.'

He smiled back, 'thank you.'

Her insides quivered and she focused on her coffee. 'Seriously,' she said, when she had composed herself sufficiently to look at him. 'Do you remember I told you about the voices?'

Josh nodded.

'They're back.'

'Is that good?'

'Yes. I have control over them now.'

'What kind of control?'

'Before all I got was a lot of hissing, loads of voices all talking at the same time, nothing really made sense except the occasional clear message dropping through. I couldn't switch it off, and had no control, some days it was there, banging in my head, driving me insane, and other days there was nothing but a faint hiss, whispers. Now I can, switch it on and off I mean, and I can kind of...how do I explain it? Move the frequency up and down.'

'Like tuning a radio?'

Kate stopped. 'Yes, I hadn't thought about it like that, but that's exactly what it's like.'

'So where are these voices or whatever coming from?'

'I don't know for sure, but I think I'm tapping into people's conscious thoughts, it may even be their sub-conscious ones sometimes, it's too early to tell. But if I had to, I'd guess it was people's everyday thoughts.'

'Wow! Are you...now...' he cocked his head at her.

Kate shook her head. 'Funny thing is, now I have control over it I don't use it, except to practise at home and check I've still got it. The rest of the time it's switched off. If it's what I think it is, it's just too intrusive to use.'

Josh smiled.

'What?'

'I'm just thinking that maybe that's why you have this gift, because of your level of integrity.'

'Maybe.'

Kate looked at him, this man with wide clear eyes and an open smile. She found him both a reassuring presence, and an incredible distraction.

The waitress brought their food and they were quiet for a while.

'There's something else,' Kate said. 'Remember the flashes? They're still happening, and I'm still having dreams that seem...real. I've always got a bit...mixed up between dreams and real life, I...' she stopped.

'What?'

She wanted to tell him how she wasn't always sure what was real and what was a dream, but she knew it sounded weird, and she didn't want this man to think her any weirder than necessary.

She shook her head. 'Nothing.'

'Tell me,' he said, and something about the way he said it made Kate relax and she found herself doing exactly that.

'You know what I mean?' she asked, when she'd finished using the butter dish dream as an example. She waited for his reaction, expecting the worse.

'Of course, none of us really know what's reality, especially if we have very vivid dreams.'

'Right, exactly,' she almost jumped out of her chair with excitement. Encouraged she continued. 'I've had that problem in the past, but now with these visions during the day too, well, I think I'm losing it. Just the other day, in the indoor market I swore I saw Lucy,' she saw Josh's puzzled expression. 'The missing girl? Lucy Newton?' He nodded in understanding.

'I swear I saw her just ahead of me in the crowd. I followed her, but just when I nearly got to her she just seemed to…vanish. The bookshop guy said she'd been looking in a box of new age books. I wasn't sure myself, but as I was looking I spotted this one.' She pulled the hard backed book out of her bag and pushed it across the table.

'Metaphysics: A Study of the Mind,' he read out loud.

'I've only just started it. Anyway, what's even more weird is the inscription inside. Rachael is the name of the missing girl's mother.'

Josh opened the book, read the inscription and whistled.

'I know spooky huh?'

He put the book back on the table. 'I've been thinking about the adjustment I made.'

'Oh?'

'Yes, remember I said it could have been caused by a childhood trauma?'

'Yes.'

'You were very...tetchy about it at the time, so I'm nervous about bringing it up, but…'

'You think there's a link to that and,' she raised her arms in a sweeping motion. 'Everything that's going on.'

He shrugged. 'I don't know, maybe.'

Kate played with the crumbs on her plate for a few moments whilst she gathered the courage to confide in this man.

146

'Josh, I'm adopted. My mother and father have cared and loved me for all my life. They have never done anything to me, nor have I suffered any 'trauma'.'

'That you remember.'

'That I remember,' she agreed reluctantly.

'What about your birth family?'

'I don't know who my birth family is.'

'You can find out you know.'

She knew it wouldn't take long. It rarely took anyone long to start down this track. 'I know, but I don't want to. The way I figure it, it's their loss. I'm okay.' She braced herself for an argument.

Josh watched her for a few moments then, to her relief and surprise, he turned his attention back to the book. 'This looks interesting, what d'you think?'

'I've read a little. It is...interesting.'

'But?'

'But it's not really my cup of tea.' Kate took a bite from the remainder of her sandwich.

Josh laughed. 'What don't you like about it?'

Kate swallowed quickly. 'Sorry,' she brushed the crumbs from around her mouth and pointed at the book. 'The title put me off straight away!' Josh laughed again and Kate smiled. 'I'm serious.'

'I know, I'm sorry, I shouldn't laugh.'

'You know Josh, I've always thought I was a bit weird, and I was okay with that, well, to a point, I'd learned to live with it put it that way. But now, now I'm genuinely concerned about my sanity.'

'Your sanity is fine.'

'How d'you know? Think about it. Hearing voices; unable to differentiate between dreams and reality; seeing a girl who's been missing for weeks? You were going to send me for tests, remember?'

'That was different. I didn't think you were insane.'

'No?'

'No. I have a responsibility to refer patients displaying symptoms beyond my professional capability. My referral didn't mean you were, or are, mentally unstable. I thought there could be some neurological problem. That was before you told me of your...ability.'

'Then what's going on? Why does my brain feel even more scrambled than ever? Why these flashes; the dreams; why do I feel so attached to Lucy? I barely knew her.'

Josh leaned forward and placed his hand over Kate's. It was big and hot and engulfed hers. She liked it and left her hand there.

'I don't know, but there *will* be an explanation. You'll see.'

'There's more.'

Josh waited.

'When Lucy first went missing, I think I heard her, calling for her mother, but now, no matter how hard I try I can't hear her and it frightens me. That's why I followed that girl in the market.'

'You think she might be dead?'

Kate hung her head. Stung and shrunk by Josh's words, a thought she had not been able to acknowledge, even though it had been in the back of her mind. 'Maybe,' she muttered. 'Which means the girl I followed in the market was a ghost, and adds to the long list of reasons why I might be going insane.'

'You don't know for sure it was her.'

'True, but it really really looked like her.'

Josh sat back, removing his hand, and sipped his coffee for a few moments. Kate's hand felt cold and exposed.

'How far does your radar go?'

'My what?'

'How far can you pick up people's thoughts?'

'I don't know. Why?'

'It could give you an idea of how far away she might have been when you heard her.'

'I never thought of that. And she could have been close then, and have been moved since? She might be still alive just out of my…radar.'

'And someone must know something. You might be able to pick that up.'

Kate heaved a sigh. 'But what will I do if I find out something? How would I explain it? The police have been to question me twice now. I'm sure they suspect me of having something to do with her disappearance.'

'We can deal with that if, and when, it happens. Let's take it one step at a time.'

Kate nodded and liked the 'we' in his statement.

'There is this neighbour who I was convinced had something to do with it, at least at first.'

'What changed your mind?'

'The police haven't arrested him, so maybe I'm wrong,' she shrugged. 'I'm not sure of anything anymore.'

'It is all for a reason, everything is.'

She looked at him, her eyes shiny with unshed tears. 'How? What possible reason is there for a little girl missing, maybe even dead?'

'I don't know. But you have some very special gifts that you now have to use. The challenge we all face, is to find out who we are, what we're here to do, and then be that person, do our thing so to speak, with grace. You've found yours. We're all unique, and we all have a job to do in our lifetime, but some are a little more…unique than others.'

Kate smiled feebly. She didn't want to be unique; she didn't want special gifts or tasks. She was strapped to a sledge, hurtling down the side of a mountain, and she was convinced it was only a matter of time before she hit something, and if she was right, it was really going to hurt.

Sam and Paul cleared the dishes and loaded the dishwasher, their familiar routine comforting her after their recent turmoil, and her unsuccessful flurry into illicit relations. Paul had returned from whatever silent pilgrimage he had deemed was necessary, and whilst Sam would usually flail him alive for his recent behaviour, she didn't. It was ignored, swept aside, by them both. No harm done. Everything the way it should be.

She watched her husband cleaning the hob, stooped and focused on the task. He looked different now. Less the hunky rogue she had met seven years and more…well, older somehow. She couldn't put her finger on it. He looked like…someone's dad. Only he wasn't, and wasn't likely to be, if they stayed together.

She turned away and picked up the wooden salt and pepper grinders they had bought on holiday in Cornwall. He wanted it so bad it was pouring out of him. He would be a good dad. She could see that. He wasn't the problem, it was her, she would have to make too many sacrifices, and surely, if she were calling them sacrifices, that said it all?

Paul looked settled in his life, whilst she was…what? What was she? Definitely not settled, that was for sure. She wanted more. What that more was she still didn't know, but it wasn't a baby. Her's was a more that had

149

freedom and adventure, not nappies and cracked nipples. She was not mother material, why couldn't he see that? There was nothing maternal about her. She was too selfish, she knew that now. Did that make her a bad person? Probably, she thought with misery.

She returned the condiments to the cupboard and rinsed out a cloth to wipe down the table. There was always more mess at Paul's place. Food and crumbs and splashes of whatever sauce or gravy or cream they had eaten. Her stomach turned over before she had a chance to stop herself.

She scrubbed at the table where Paul had sat. Hard, over and over again, clearing away all evidence he had sat there. Josh's words filtered back to her, cutting deep. She would have hurt Paul, given the chance, and she hated Josh for telling her that, hated that he saw her like that, hated that she was like that.

I didn't *do* anything, she reminded herself, but the words rattled empty. The only reason she didn't do anything, was because Josh had made it clear he wasn't interested. Her face reddened at the thought, and she rubbed harder, until she was out of breath, then stood listening to the pans rattling behind her.

Where did it leave her now? There existed a truth she hadn't been aware of before. She wanted someone else, and it had been exciting, an adventure of wonder and electricity. There was a saying that an affair of the mind was as treacherous as an affair of the body.

She turned and watched Paul at the sink, his back to her, bent over the pans and, as she looked at him whistling and cleaning, she knew the saying was true. Now, when she looked at her husband, he looked tarnished and dull. Such a good man, and this was how she now saw him, not because of anything he had done, but because of her. He deserved more. He deserved a wife who thought he was a hero, and wanted to have his children. He deserved so much more.

For the first time in her life she was ashamed of who she was, she wanted to be a better person, wanted to be more than this selfish, self-absorbed, greedy little woman she had become, but she didn't know how. How do you become something else? She stood, the dishcloth in her hand, pondering her future.

One thing she could do, she realised, was the right thing. The only trouble was, despite all her good intentions, she wasn't sure she was brave enough.

Chapter Twenty-Two

Saturday morning was a crisp autumn day and the sunlight streamed through the windows in the flat. Mary had declared that she was going to 'take some fresh air' and had left about ten minutes ago, much to Felix's relief.

It was time to put his plan in place. It was so simple he couldn't believe he hadn't thought of it before. He had a course of action now and relief spread through his body. He was going to knock on Kate's door and tell her. Just tell her. Simple, to the point, that was his plan. That was why things hadn't worked out, she didn't know how he felt. As soon as she did, well...

So why was he so nervous? He was a grown man and look at him, striding round the house unable to settle, prowling like a lion. There was a knock at the door and Felix leapt at the sound. He laughed at himself, a skittish deer was nearer the mark. It would be his mother he thought with despair, as he made his way to the door. He only hoped that she had forgotten something and would be going back out. When he opened it, Kate stood in the door frame.

'Hi!' her face broke into a wide smile, her eyes gleamed like buttons. 'Was beginning to think you'd died in here.' She breezed in, oblivious of her effect on him.

Felix closed the door, swallowed hard and followed her into the lounge. Kate slumped into the sofa and Felix lowered himself into the chair opposite.

'How's your mum doing?'

'She's okay. She's gone out for a walk.'

'Oh that's good. It's lovely out there. You okay?'

Felix nodded, amazed that he really could hear the pounding of his heart in his ears, stunned that she couldn't hear it too.

'Is it really awful? Having her here?'

'No, it's not so bad..,yet.'

Nothing stirred.

'I'm sorry,' he said. He wasn't prepared, hadn't finalised his speech, got into the right frame of mind, it wasn't supposed to happen like this. His scrambled brain tried to find purchase on something so he could interact with her.

'You sure you're okay?'

Felix nodded.

'Good. Look, I haven't got long, I just popped by to ask you something.'

'Coffee? Tea?' Felix didn't want her to leave now she was here. As tortuous as it was, he wanted to keep her close, keep her here. If he could, he'd carry her in his pocket all day.

She hesitated.

'It won't take long,' he added.

'Okay. Coffee would be great,' as usual she padded behind him into the kitchen, but for once Felix wished she hadn't. He needed some space, some time. He felt crowded, was convinced he was going to make a fool of himself. His head felt scrambled, the words a jumble, a senseless noise clashing around.

'What have you been up to?' Kate asked.

He focused and dipped in, found a few words he could toss out, hoped they made sense. 'Nothing much. Work mainly. You?'

Kate shrugged. 'Had lunch with Josh yesterday.'

If she'd punched him in the stomach it would have been easier to deal with, but the red rage that now started to burn through his brain cleared his thoughts. 'How was it?' He forced the question through his clenched teeth.

'Interesting.'

'You two got a thing going then?'

Kate laughed. 'I...I don't know.' Her face went a little pink.

Felix felt his breath shorten. 'He's not your type then? Actually,' he asked, handing Kate a mug of coffee and hoping she hadn't noticed his hand shaking. 'What is your type?' He hoped this could be an opening for him, it backfired.

'Oh, I'm not sure, I've never thought about it before but, well...Josh is in lots of ways I guess. Now I come to think of it.'

Damn! Then don't, Felix thought *don't think about it.* 'Oh?' he said, trying to buy some time while he figured out what his next move could be. This wasn't going to plan at all. His head started to fill with confusion again.

'Yeah, I can talk to him. He's going to be a good friend, he's good looking, has his own successful business. My parents would approve,' she laughed, her face was glowing. She wasn't in love with this man surely?

152

Felix became more confused and less sure of himself as each moment passed. There was a heavy pause.

'You got any biccies?' Kate asked.

Relieved at having something to do, Felix went into the cupboard behind him and pulled out an old tin.

'Thanks,' Kate said, when he took the lid off and gave it to her. His insides liquified as he watched her peer into the tin, carefully making her selection, her eyes wide like a child's. He could watch her all day. Finally, she picked a custard cream, put the tin down and turned to him.

'You must be the only single man on the planet with a biscuit tin,' she said.

'Am I?' he asked, unsure if it was a good thing or not.

'Probably. Anyway, I just popped in to ask you when the next recycling is due for collection. I've got out of kilter with it the last couple of weeks, and I missed it last time. It's starting to build up.'

'So is there a spark between you two then?' he persisted. It was reminiscent of picking at a painful scab, and he wasn't sure why he felt compelled to do it.

'I don't know, Felix.'

She seemed reluctant to talk about it, looked a little cross even, but he had to know. Had to.

'Do you love him?'

'Felix!'

'Well?'

'I've never been in love so I wouldn't know.'

'Never?'

Kate shook her head. 'I have no idea of what is and isn't love. How long is your mum staying with you?'

He ignored her question. 'Even people in love can't explain it,' he said.

She sighed. 'I guess not.' They listened to the fridge humming. Finally Kate asked, 'so, the recycling?'

Felix had run into a brick wall. Why was she so obsessed with bloody recycling!

'I've been in love,' he persisted. 'A long time ago, she never knew.'

'Oh, how come?'

'I never told her,' he smiled. 'It's an unfortunate habit of mine.'

'Ah.'

'I was afraid,' he continued. 'I was shy. We were friends.'

'That's a shame. So how long is your mum staying?'

She kept wanting to talk about either recycling or his mother. What was wrong with the woman? Here he was, trying to tell her something, trying to figure out a way of telling her he loved her, and all she could do was keep asking about his bloody mother.   Christ! The woman got in the way of his life even when she wasn't bloody there.

He pressed on, more determined. 'If someone were in love with you would you want them to tell you?'

Kate looked uncomfortable by the question. 'I don't know.   It would depend.'

'On who they were?'

'I suppose.'

'We were friends. I didn't want to spoil anything.'

'Yes, I can see how that could be awkward.'

The words strung between them, pearls on a wire, heavy with expectation. They sat and looked at each other. He watched Kate, her struggle apparent. Her mouth opened and closed, but nothing came out. It was Felix who broke the silence. Her face told him everything he needed to know, and the crushing disappointment bit down deep inside him.

'You needn't look so worried,' he rallied. 'You're quite safe.' His jaw tightened, and his eyes took on a cold sad look.

She turned and put her cup on the side. 'I have to go now,' she said. 'I'm meeting Sam, she's got the day off so we're going shopping.'

'Sure, catch you soon,' he said, his voice casual. The air shifted between them. His moment gone. If there had ever been a moment that is. He edged a step closer to the black hole.

Kate and Sam slumped into the chairs at the coffee house; their arms aching from the bags they carried. They had brushed over their argument, Kate had apologised and Sam waved it off.   Both were relieved to have it behind them.

Previously, Kate would have done anything to avoid a shopping trip with Sam on a Saturday. On the rare occasions she was unsuccessful, it had been a tortuous experience, a battering of voices and noise from start to finish. Now, as she relaxed into the chair she couldn't take the smile off her face. She had done it, and it felt wonderful.

'Fantastic,' Sam said. 'There's something so precious about these rare Saturdays off.'

Kate laughed. 'You said it.'

'What?'

Kate rolled her eyes. 'It's because they're rare that they're so precious.'

'I suppose so, I'd never really thought about it.'

'We having lunch? I'm starving.'

The two women selected pasta from the menu and ordered coffee, then sat back again.

'I love those crocodile-snake boots,' Sam said, pulling her unruly hair from her face.

'They are striking.'

'Don't you like them?'

Kate nodded. 'On you, yes.'

Sam smiled. 'Honestly Kate, you're so unadventurous.'

If only you knew, Kate thought. 'I like what I like,' she said. 'Besides, I've never been as comfortable around clothes as you.'

The waitress brought their coffees.

'I am good at putting things together,' Sam said. 'Wish I hadn't messed around at school so much. I could have been a designer or something.'

'Is it too late?'

Sam sipped her coffee. 'Much.'

'So if you like clothes so much, why did you want to leave the boutique?'

Sam laid her cup down carefully. 'That wasn't really the problem. It's me.'

Kate knew that. 'I thought things had settled down? I thought that Josh thing was just a mad moment?'

'That's just it,' Sam said. 'I don't think Josh was a mad moment, I don't think it was anything really. It certainly wasn't the problem either.'

'You've been doing a lot of uncharacteristic thinking lately,' Kate quipped.

'Wouldn't you?'

Kate nodded.

'I've been blaming anything I could think of to avoid the truth.'

Sam looked out of the window. Kate waited, watching the harried shoppers pass by, their faces drawn and creased. No one looked happy these days, just frantic and exhausted. Or was that just her?

The book she'd found in the market said everything we saw, how we viewed the world, was simply a reflection of us, a mirror of our own beliefs and experiences. Perhaps there was some truth in it, because today, the frantic and exhausted faces that passed by the window, really did reflect how she was feeling.

The coffee with Felix this morning had disturbed her. He had been acting strangely for several weeks now. Ever since he'd visited his mother, the same weekend Lucy went missing. A thought skittered through her mind, freezing the blood in her veins, she dismissed it instantly. It was ludicrous.

The pasta arrived and as they started to eat Sam looked at Kate. 'I have come to realise that I don't like who I am.'

Kate laughed with her mouthful. 'What d'you mean?' she said, when she had swallowed her food.

'You know, selfish, self-absorbed, all those things you said the other day.'

Kate shook her head. 'I'm sorry-'

Sam held up her hand. 'Don't Kate, I needed to hear it. You didn't say anything that wasn't true, and you were a good friend to say it.'

Kate smiled, she had never seen Sam like this, reflective, self-castigating. She wondered, unfairly perhaps, if it was just another one of Sam's little games.

'But self centred or not, I'm just not ready to settle down and have children. The thought terrifies me. I can't understand why anyone would want them, and I know that may make me sound like a bad person, but there you have it. They disrupt your life, cost a fortune, and then turn round when they're old enough and give you the finger. Why would I want to do that to myself? Why would anyone?'

'I think other people may have a different perspective on it.'

'Exactly. That's exactly what I'm talking about. But it isn't just the kids issue Kate. It's the whole package. It's the dullness of marriage, the sameness, the lack of excitement.'

'Again I think some people find sharing the day to day with someone special makes it all worthwhile, makes sense of life-'

'So why is the divorce rate so pigging high?' Sam interjected.

Kate shrugged. 'Wrong choices, lack of commitment, fear, who knows?'

'I'm just afraid I'm missing out on something. I can't believe this is all there is. Paul deserves more.'

'You don't think perhaps everyone hits stale periods in their relationship?'

'Sure, but if you're with the right one it shouldn't be this hard, this...dull!'

'I don't know Sam, I'm not sure love conquers all. Sometimes I think it might just need a bit of grit and determination.'

'But that's just it – I don't think I have that.'

'Really?'

'And there's something else about that Josh episode. What kind of person does it make me, Kate? Paul's a good man, he deserves a better person than me.'

'Paul chose you and besides, I don't think you should end your marriage to punish yourself.'

'It's not about punishing me, it's about letting Paul off the hook.'

'He may not see himself *on* a hook.' Kate said.

'You know what I mean.'

'I do, but I don't see any point in ending your marriage when you didn't actually *do* anything.'

'That was just fortuitous. It wasn't anything to do with me. And anyway, it's not just about that, it's about everything. My whole attitude stinks.'

'Look Sam, it's good to reflect on your behaviour, it's good that you have discovered a conscience, but don't beat yourself into oblivion with it.'

'But I can't believe how...self-centred I've been.'

'Well, none of us is perfect; it's just that you're a little late in discovering that,' Kate smiled at her friend. 'Just don't rush into anything Sam, that's all I'm saying. Give yourself time to adjust to this...this...new you.'

Sam nodded, but Kate would be surprised if she took any notice.

That night Kate woke with a start. She wasn't sure what had woken her, a loud noise perhaps, a bang somewhere off in the distance. She glanced at the clock. The red neon glow spelt out 4:05. She groaned as she lay back down.

She stared into the darkness, watching her familiar room emerge. She was wide awake with the gnawing feeling that there was something she had to do. It was Sunday. She dismissed work. She was on target with all her transcripts, a little ahead if anything.

Kate reflected on the day. Felix was odd, but then so was Sam. What was happening to her friends? Sam had come over all Mother Teresa today. Had she genuinely had an epiphany, or was it, as Kate thought earlier, some new adventure she was embarking on? And if it was the latter, what damage would she wreak before she was satisfied.

And Felix, she knew he was going to tell her he loved her today. She was glad he hadn't. She cringed at the memory of the awkwardness of the whole experience. No more coffees, no more breakfasts, possibly no more friendship.

He hadn't been the same since his visit to his mother's. No, that wasn't true. She remembered their trip to the beach the day after. He'd been fine then. Maybe it was his mother's accident. That would upset anyone, despite the fact that he insisted he disliked his mother. No one really disliked their mother.

Kate hadn't had another memory of her own mother, but that wasn't surprising. What was surprising was that she'd had one in the first place. It had made her wonder what her mother was like, and, if the memory was true, why would she have left her? It didn't make sense. Why would you leave a little girl you loved?

Not wanting to pursue that train of thought, Kate turned to Lucy Newton instead. Where was that little girl? Who had taken her? What had they done with her? And what were the visions trying to tell her? She was sure they were to do with Lucy, that's when they started, the day she disappeared.

But she'd been over them a hundred times on nights like this. They didn't make sense, just fragments. It was like having the pieces of a jigsaw puzzle without the full picture, and she wasn't even sure she had all the pieces.

She had thought she was going insane on more than one occasion recently, but talking to Josh helped. Her feelings for him went much deeper than she cared to admit, and it frightened her. She hadn't felt like this about anyone before, and certainly didn't want to feel like this now. It wasn't convenient. But then it would never be convenient to feel this…what? Out of control? Excited? Confused? Alive? She thought any of those adjectives would suffice. Thinking of him now caused something to move inside her, stone grinding against stone, tectonic plates sliding, rusted over emotions shifting. The dust clogged her thoughts, stopped her words, stopped her brain.

All she wanted, was to reach out and bury into him. Drink in his smell, soak in his essence, feel his arms round her, but there was too much in her life to contend with now.

There were too many fragments, too many pieces that didn't fit. Folding into him now would be too difficult. She couldn't do it. Besides, he didn't feel the same way. She had shared the confusion inside her, and now he saw her as an interesting test case, something to be studied, instead of the woman she was.

Kate turned on her side and closed her eyes in the hope that feigning sleep would bring her the real thing. Her blood pulsed in her ear; a comfortable regular beat that soothed. Her breathing slowed and her body softened into the mattress. Eventually sleep took her away.

Chapter Twenty-Three

Felix moved with stealth around his kitchen, holding his breath. Everything seemed to clatter and thunder around him, and he was convinced he would disturb his mother with all the noise. It had been two days and things were easier between them, they had reached an unspoken truce, but he would still be pleased to have the place to himself again.

A few minutes later she appeared in the kitchen dressed in a pink dressing gown that drowned her. She looked small and pale.

'You okay? Did I wake you?'

'No, it was the pain.'

Felix opened a cupboard and pulled out an old ice-cream tub he used as a first aid box. 'I put some paracetamol by your bedside yesterday.'

'I've used all them.'

'But that was a box of 24!'

'Your point being?'

He took a deep breath; everyone is cranky when they're in pain, he thought.

'You've taken too many.'

'I'm still upright son.'

'Mum, you've exceeded the stated dose.'

'So shoot me. It's not my fault they're crap.'

'Maybe you need to visit the doctor's, get it checked out, get something stronger for the pain at least.'

'Felix, doubling the dose *is* taking something stronger.'

'But you need to do it properly.'

'I'm fine, stop fussing. It's probably just the walk yesterday, over did it.'

'I'm not sure. I think you-'

'Oh, do shut up. I haven't the energy to argue.' She shuffled to a stool and dropped onto it heavily. 'Make me a cuppa will you?'

The kitchen was hushed save for the noise Felix made as he prepared the tea. When it was ready they drank it without speaking.

Finally, Felix plucked up the courage to speak. 'Mum I really think you should get it checked out again, just to be on the safe side.'

'I'm fine Felix,' she said, 'Besides, you're a right one to talk about dosages and doctors. Are you?'

'Am I what?'

'Taking your medication? Seeing Dr. Carmichael?'

'This isn't about me.'

'You're acting up. I know the signs, lived with it long enough,' she sighed. 'You're getting all...confused and twitchy again, aren't you?'

'Mum!'

'Well, aren't you? You'll end up doing something you'll regret Felix.'

'I'm sick of being typecast,' he spat.

'Then stop acting like a clichè.'

The air pulsed with agitation.

Felix spoke, quietly breaking the crust of tension that had developed between them. 'I'm a grown man, I can take care of myself.'

'Ditto,' she said, and took her tea into the bedroom.

Felix sighed with relief.

The idea came to her quite by accident as she was cleaning the toilet. It just dropped in fully formed and, like most good ideas, Kate couldn't believe she hadn't thought of it before. It was so simple, so obvious.

After washing her hands she settled on the sofa in the living room and immediately began to probe. She picked up a woman deciding what to wear, a teenage boy listening to music and flicking through a comic book, and a man planning his garden chores for the winter; all fascinating in their own way, but not what she was looking for.

She persevered, endeavouring to keep it light, trying not to get too intense because she knew it would cease altogether if she did.

After a few more moments her blood slowed in her body and her heart thrummed. Thoughts, like voices, could be very distinctive, and Kate would recognise Ray Mountford's gravelly tone anywhere. Her high emotional reaction caused her to lose the connection momentarily, but she was soon reconnected.

She wasn't sure what she hoped to hear, perhaps a clue as to where Lucy was, or what he had done with her, anything to help. Even then, she wasn't confident about what she would do with the information once she had it, an anonymous call to the police perhaps? A 'tip off' maybe? It wasn't important at this stage. As Josh had said, they could cross that bridge if and when. For now she just wanted…what? What did she want? To reassure herself she was right about Ray? Possibly, because there was still a chance this had all been a figment of her imagination…except the little girl had been missing over two weeks now. That was evidence enough surely?

Kate brought her attention to Ray's voice and listened, trying to stay calm and keep her emotions in check. It was difficult, he crawled through her veins, but although she kept losing him, she had enough of a connection to make out what he was thinking, more or less.

'This is gonna be tricky…How to tackle it?'

He seemed absorbed in some task. Kate knew this by the quiet gaps in his thought processes. That, or he was very slow, either was possible. The answer came as she listened. He was definitely absorbed in some task. But what? She continued, hoping to find out more.

'No one comes, it's not a bad thing…I'll visit her soon…That's better, tighter. No chance of anything getting out of that…nothing…tight as fuck. Peachy.'

It was the last word Kate heard that made her jump up and ran down the stairs, pulling open her front door. She'd been here before, heart racing, running through the house on account of Ray Mountford. It had ended in disaster then, and she was aware it could turn out the same again, but she didn't care. She had to do something.

She pounded on Ray's door with her fists, shouting, her chest heaving. She wasn't sure if she was out of breath from the running, the shouting or the sheer raw adrenaline pumping through her body. When he didn't open the door immediately, she began to slam the door knocker hard over and over again. The noise reverberated through the street and echoed off the bricks, drawing people from their homes.

Kate spun round to face them, wanting them to help her, wanting them to know what she knew. She saw Rachael Newton come out and stand on her doorstep, her arms folded across her chest. She leant against the doorframe, not in a nonchalant manner, but more as if she couldn't stand up alone. She was watching Kate.

Felix emerged from their shared entrance looking bewildered. 'Kate?'

Before she had a chance to say anything to Felix the door opened and Kate spun back to face Ray. He appeared, squinting at Kate as if he'd emerged from a mine. He seemed even bigger than usual, and for a moment Kate wondered if this was wise. Still, she had no choice.

'Kate!' he seemed mystified, and Kate took advantage of this to push her way into his home.

'What have you done with her?' she said, as she stormed down the hall. The smell hit her hard, choking her. 'Jesus! What is that?'

Ray did not follow her, instead he stood out on the steps of his home, waiting.

It didn't take Kate long to discover what the smell was. A piece of rancid meat sat on the draining board in the back kitchen, and the sink was full of moulding pots. The stench was so bad Kate retched several times before she was able to back out of the room and close the door.

Her eyes streaming she moved to the front room. It was dark, the curtains closed, but even if they had been open the room would still have had a dismal air. It was damp and unlived in, the wallpaper peeling away from the walls, and it smelt stale and dirty.

Kate made her way upstairs, passing Ray who still stood on the front step. Felix and a number of the neighbours had joined him. There was a murmur of conversation from the small crowd that had gathered, Kate ignored them.

The upstairs rooms were no cleaner or inviting. The smell of meat downstairs had begun to permeate the upstairs rooms. In Ray's bedroom the bed sat unmade, greying sheets crumpled, reeking of stale sweat.

The second bedroom at the back was full of junk. Old pieces of furniture piled up on top of one another, stacked cardboard boxes from the supermarket, rolled up rugs, all stored higgledy piggledy. Kate's eyes swept over it all, unsure what she was looking for, a hand maybe, or a pair of eyes, Lucy's little blonde head peeping over something.

'It's my mother's stuff,' Kate jumped and swivelled round. Ray loomed behind her on the landing. She hadn't heard him come up the stairs.

'She went into a nursing home last year and I haven't had the heart to get rid of it.'

'Where's Lucy?' Kate asked, her voice sounded calmer than she felt.

Ray smiled and shrugged. 'I wish I knew. I'm very fond of Lucy. This is all a mistake. I don't know, really I don't.'

'What were you doing when I knocked on the door?'

He sighed, 'Tightening the u-bend under the sink, it got blocked.'

'You have rancid meat in the kitchen.'

'So?.'

'It stinks.'

'It's none of your business.'

Kate realised he was right. There was no evidence here of what she was accusing Ray of, and they both knew it. Once again she had gone off half-cock and made of fool of herself.

Her whole body sank into itself, the adrenaline quit her body rapidly and left her with a headache and a sore neck.

'I'm sorry I…' she what? What explanation could she give?

'Kate, I'm not sure why you think I've hurt little Lucy, but I can assure you I have not.'

Kate nodded and tears threatened. He sounded so calm, was it possible he was telling the truth? She had no evidence to point to him except that lascivious thought in the corner shop. It seemed like years ago now.

'Can I ask you something?'

'It depends,' he didn't sound very friendly and Kate couldn't blame him. He sighed and added, 'if it can clear this misunderstanding up I'll try to answer it.'

'You use the word…peachy don't you?'

Ray nodded. 'Sometimes.'

'What do you mean by it?'

He pulled his mouth down thoughtfully. 'Well, it depends, but probably that it's good, it's right, it's…nice I suppose. My dad used to use it when I was a lad and I'd done something right. Why?'

She shook her head. 'It doesn't matter.'

'Hello? Mr Mountford?' an authoritative male voice travelled up from the front door. 'Mr Mountford, it's the police.'

'Oh god, that's all I need!' said Kate, as she twisted her neck from one side to the other in an effort to ease the pain, unable to believe this nightmare that was her life.

'I'm up here officer, I'm fine.'

'Can we ask you and Miss Gregory to come down here please, sir?'

They knew her name. That was bad. She was in trouble now. Ray smiled at her and Kate wasn't sure if he was being smug, friendly or forgiving. She couldn't criticise him for the former.

'It seems he thinks I may be in danger,' he said with amusement. 'After you,' he indicated the stairs with an imperceptible bow and Kate hesitated, sure for a moment that he would shove her down them. She couldn't exactly blame him; after all, she had accused him of child abduction, molestation and possibly murder; she had accosted him both in the street, and in his own home, with no evidence that he'd done anything wrong.

'Thank you,' she said, trying to sound gracious. She descended the stairs with trepidation but reached the bottom unharmed. Two policemen were stood in the hall, the crowd of neighbours had been dispersed.

Ray explained to the officers that there was nothing for them to be concerned about. That there had been a misunderstanding between two neighbours which had now been resolved, once and for all.

'Isn't that right Kate?' he looked at her pointedly, making sure she understood his meaning.

She nodded.

The police officer investigated the stench, and when he was satisfied that Ray did not have a rotting corpse under his floor boards, he left.

'Thank you,' Kate said, as she walked down the hall to leave.

'That's quite alright,' he paused at the front door. 'I believe I will not be seeing or hearing from you again.' His tone had grown cold and Kate glanced at him. 'And in case I haven't made myself clear, let me spell it out for you. I haven't, nor would I wish to, harm Lucy or anyone else. I'm sorry if you don't believe me but frankly, that's your problem. I have been more than patient because,' he stopped to compose himself. 'Well, it's been an upsetting business, Lucy and…anyway. If you should accost me again I *will* press charges. Do you understand?'

Kate nodded and left quickly. Her eyes slipped surreptitiously to the Newton's home, but Rachael had gone back in. Kate felt tired and sick to the stomach as she closed her door to her flat. Moments later she heard a knocking and knew it was Felix, and chose to ignore him. She didn't want to see or speak to anyone at the moment, least of all him.

She flopped on the sofa. She was back to square one. No Lucy, no idea who had taken her, what they had done with her or where she was now. But if Ray was to be believed, didn't that let her off the hook? It made that thought in the corner shop, the one which had started Kate off on all of this, an innocent remark. She hadn't let the girl down.

So why did she still feel so responsible? Why did she now have a greater need to find the girl? And if it wasn't Ray…who had taken Lucy Newton and what had they done with her?

Sam sat on the sofa flicking through 'Hello' magazine and surreptitiously sneaking a look at Paul. He was watching another house design programme and occasionally clicking his tongue in disapproval.

Glancing down at the page she took in the photos of the latest 'Z' list celebrity wedding. They all looked so fresh and clean and dynamic; so keen for their life to begin. She looked up at their wedding photo on top of the television. She and Paul had been the same on their wedding day, fizzing like freshly popped champagne. Now they were as flat as yesterday's San Pellegrino.

She still hadn't talked to Paul properly about the job offer and what it might mean to them, nor had she discussed how she felt, nor had she done anything about her recent epiphany, instead she was trapped in limbo. What was she waiting for? Kate's words had stopped her, she thought, but if she was truthful she wasn't sure it wasn't just downright cowardice. No, her epiphany was still being assimilated, she reasoned, but she needed to do something.

'Fancy popping out for a drink?' she asked.

Paul barely looked her way. 'No thanks love.'

'I thought we -'

Paul held up his hand without looking at her. 'Want to watch this. Let's talk about it later.'

Sam's face flushed with anger at the dismissal. Since their recent fall out, he had been much more assertive with her, and she didn't like it.

'Paul!'

He looked at her with a coldness in his blue eyes that frightened her. 'I said,' he said slowly. 'I'm watching this. When it's finished, we can talk.'

He turned back to the programme and left Sam rooted to the sofa, stunned. In all of her turmoil and angst, she hadn't thought about how Paul might feel, how it might be affecting him.

It was in that moment that an idea struck her, one so far-fetched it took her a moment to comprehend. When she did it caused tiny tremors through her body, like aftershocks from an earthquake. Was it was possible, just possible, that Paul was falling out of love with *her*?

166

That Sunday evening Kate lay on her bed staring at the ceiling, trying to get her thoughts in some sort of order. The memory of her latest catastrophic flare-up with Ray earlier that day sat heavily on her. The mortification of her second spectacle in front of the neighbours, coupled with what she could only describe as misery at not being any further forward with Lucy, made it difficult to see any way forward and, despite hours of pondering, she still had no ideas.

In addition, her recent encounters with both Sam and Felix had left her feeling unsettled. What sort of friend was she turning into? Although she and Sam had put Kate's outburst behind them, she was still surprised at her own behaviour.

And Felix, where to begin? What sort of friend was she to imagine he had taken a child? True, it was only a fleeting idea, but even so...plus he had witnessed her outburst. It was all too humiliating.

Unable to speak to her two best friends Kate was more adrift than usual. There was Josh of course, but she was reluctant to call him, he would ask about Lucy and she wouldn't know what to say. The frustration of it all was only alleviated by the fact that, apart from Josh, no one knew of her failure, even if most of the street were questioning her sanity.

And then there was the memory of her birth mother. Kate rose, sat at her dressing table and stared at her reflection in the mirror. When she was younger people would say she looked like her mother, not knowing Jan and she were not related.

There was a resemblance, both had high cheek bones and long noses, but there were differences too. Kate's mother was blonde with blue eyes and an hour glass figure, whereas Kate had dark eyes, dark hair and a long athletic body. The difference had never bothered her. When she looked at her girlfriends at school, many of them had only a fleeting echo of their mother's faces.

As she looked at her face now she tried to remember what the woman from her memory looked like. It was sketchy; long dark hair swept up, lots of jewellery and scarves, but no detail. The memory was hazy, just a few scraps of information, but nothing concrete, nothing *real*. Story of her life, she thought.

Then there were these visions, flashbacks or whatever they were. They didn't make sense. Random images that didn't piece together in any meaningful way, and yet she was convinced they should.

She sighed and turned away from the mirror. She didn't want to do this anymore. She didn't want her thoughts to oscillate between these visions and the missing child, churning up thoughts of her own mother who, rightly or wrongly, had long ago abandoned her.

She pushed her hands through her short hair and rubbed her head. It was no good, she needed to get away. Needed a break. Then it occurred to her...she would take a holiday! She could now, it was now possible. She could take a break away from Sam and Felix and Josh and the neighbours, but most of all from the haunting absence and worse, the silence, of Lucy Newton.

Chapter Twenty-Four

'There you go,' said Rose plonking a mug of coffee onto Felix's desk.

'Thanks. Where's John today?' he asked, looking at the empty desk on the other side of the office.

Rose rolled her eyes. 'He's on holiday. Remember?'

'Oh yeah. Again? He's never bloody here these days.'

'Not much of a holiday if you ask me,' said Gina, coming in with the post. 'He's decorating his living room.'

Rose and Gina chuckled at the foolishness of the thirty-something's.

'And Brian?' Felix asked.

'Went to see the James' property. They'll appeal and he wanted to talk to them...' she shrugged. Felix nodded.

'Did you put sugar in this?' Gina asked Rose.

'Can't remember. Try it.'

Gina sipped her coffee, pulled a face and headed out towards the kitchen next door with her mug.

Rose sat down at her desk opposite Felix. 'So?' she said.

'So what?'

'So, how you doing?'

'I'm okay. Any reason for asking?'

'I've just noticed you haven't exactly been yourself recently.'

'I'm fine thanks.'

'Suit yourself,' she picked up her notebook. 'You've got to ring Mr. Jensen, he wants an update on the planning application he put in last month; Janet Freeman of Freeman's Furnishings wants some advice on the big expansion programme they're planning, and Godfrey Davis rang to say he can't make lunch this week, but suggests Wednesday of next. Oh, and have you checked the press releases ready for Hayley on the new hospital development? Apparently, the Echo is doing a feature and they want our input. Hayley's put a press release together and just needs someone to give it the okay. She wants to get it off ASAP.'

'Okay,' he held out his hand with a sigh. 'Give me the list and I'll sort it.'

Gina came back into the office. 'Felix there's a query on an appeal from Justine Faulkes. They claim we've misunderstood them on something.'

'And have we?'

Gina shrugged. 'I don't know.'

'Then can I suggest you take a look and come back to me when you've got all the facts?' He heard the cold slap of his voice and saw the girls exchange a glance but he didn't care. They took advantage of him in the office, these bloody women, as did Phoebe and his mother. And then there was Kate. She had refused to open the door yesterday.

He turned to the window and looked across the cemetery to the river below. The trees were blushed now with red and yellow leaves. One blustery day and they'd be bare.

He thought he deserved better. That was women for you. Always let you down. He couldn't recall one in his life that hadn't caused him some grief somewhere. He sighed, his jaw relaxing and the tension in his shoulders eased.

He looked over at Rose and Gina. Silent now, heads down, their jollity that usually filled the office stifled by him. The thought weighed on him, along with everything else.

In the few days of his mother being with him he had gone from feeling everything was going his way, to someone who had lost the path and was fighting through undergrowth.

He shook his head. Even if Kate agreed to see him, they would have lost that comfortable ease of being with one another. Instead of the soft blanket that pulled them together, there would be spikes of uncomfortable silences, things unsaid. They had lost something, and no matter what he did, it was irretrievable.

He sat back down at his desk. 'Sorry,' he said to the girls.

They both looked up. 'You sure you're okay?' asked Rose.

He nodded. 'Sure,' he smiled as he stretched out to pick up the ringing phone on his desk.

'Felix, it's Pheobe. You have to get to the hospital quick.'

'What's happened?'

'It's mum.'

Kate was in the airport waiting to board her flight to Barcelona. She had surfed the net and picked up a last minute flight. It was a place she had never visited before, would never have even thought of until the flight flashed up for £50 return. £50! She would have flown to Beirut for a break for £50.

She knew how it might look with the police, but she was only going for a couple of days. With any luck she'd be back before anyone missed her.

Kate was bursting with excitement. To be here among all these people, flying to a strange city. She had flown before, with her parents, never by choice, and always plugged into her music. This was an entirely different experience. It was amazing how open her life was now, compared with just a few short weeks ago.

Kate took in her surroundings. In the bar opposite were a flock of men in a uniform of black and white football shirts. Loud and raucous, the Magpies' holiday already begun.

A couple were looking pensive. The man talking, his jaw jutting out as he spoke, the woman looking distracted, tearing a tissue into small pieces. Kate tuned in.

'He doesn't have a clue. How do I tell him? How can I? He'll be devastated. Devastated. I just can't...'

A woman with two children, all smiles and stress, sat down opposite Kate. The children were blonde with blue eyes. The girl, a teenager, slumped into the seat next to her mother, determined to be unimpressed with the world. Kate smiled, she remembered that feeling. The boy chattered incessantly. The mother tried to look as if she was listening.

The flight was called for boarding, and before she knew it she was sat by the window in the plane watching the terrain beneath slip away. The last time Kate had been on a plane it had been hell. A confined space crammed full of people, people with heads bursting with words. She had barely been able to breathe. This time it was different, this time she could switch in and out. She laid a hand on her iPod in her pocket for reassurance, just in case.

When they ascended she peered down into the land below. It all looked so different from up there; circuit board cities and molten silver rivers. Still. Without turmoil. The idea of a couple of days away from everyone and everything eased, the last remaining tension from her limbs, and she settled herself into her seat. All that remained was a small tug on her heart for the missing girl.

Sam rummaged round the cold shelf of Marks and Spencer looking for something she could pass off as a meal that evening. She only had forty-five minutes, and twenty of those had passed already.

Dinner was always a challenge. She envied Paul's ease in the kitchen, she would sit back with a glass of wine, as if preparing to watch a show.

Paul changed colour when he cooked. He went from a cool blue to a roaring red. He didn't pour the olive oil into the pan, he cascaded it from a great height, creating a golden waterfall, then he swiped the bottle aside and stood it upright with a flourish.

He chopped and threw the food at the pan, never missing. He whistled and clattered and shook pans vigorously, quite out of character to the calm placid being he was at any other time.

He glided round the kitchen, demanding the spotlight, as dramatic and daring as an ice skater. Sam watched him with a tight breath, waiting for the spill, the slip, the fall. The knife to draw blood, the pan to catch fire, Paul's skin to sizzle against something hot, some disaster to befall this haphazard performance that was Paul's cooking. But to her delight and amazement he always pulled it off, defying the odds to produce something spectacular.

In the kitchen Paul commanded attention and Sam loved it. She only wished he was more like that in everyday life.

In contrast Sam followed the recipe to the letter, painstakingly cutting and chopping, measuring and stirring, peering and cautiously adding. It was all so utterly depressing when she turned out an insipid dish which, whilst edible, had about as much appeal as limp lettuce on a snowy evening. So now she had these brief sorties into M&S, knowing that whatever she chose would be an improvement on what she could produce in the kitchen.

In haste Sam settled on lasagne, grabbed a head of broccoli, a packet of two film wrapped jacket potatoes, and a chicken tikka sandwich to eat at her desk.

Walking back to the boutique Ann's offer weighed heavier than the shopping she carried. Despite Paul's olive branch there was naturally still an undercurrent between them, things left unsaid. Whenever she tried to approach it he bristled, taking a deep breath and holding it, as if it made him bigger, more intimidating. A warning to keep away.

It did the trick and she was happy to put it off, for now, but they were only deferring the inevitable. They would have to broach the subject sometime. Anne wouldn't wait forever.

When they were first married there was an old sycamore growing beside their next door neighbour's house. Whilst it didn't appear very big to look at, it began to destabilise the building. The discussion they were putting off would have the same effect on their marriage. This wouldn't be some tiff they could weather. This was deep-rooted and at the core of their marriage, and whilst she had made up her mind what she would do, she found actually doing it difficult. She opened her mouth and nothing came out, she meant it to, it just didn't.

By mentioning the promotion two weeks ago, Sam had shown her hand and reaffirmed clearly her desire not to have children, not only now, but for the foreseeable future, and that was just the start of it, at least for her.

The realisation that she wanted something or someone else, and that quite possibly, so did Paul, was gut wrenching, but her further realisation that she wanted to be someone better, clouded an already hazy picture.

Sam was hesitating because she knew the conversation would force them both to make a decision, she knew what her's was, and she had a strong suspicion that Paul had reached the same conclusion. So what was stopping her?

No one could tell Felix anything and Phoebe hadn't arrived. So he sat in the same seat in the same corridor that he had the previous week. Waiting. All he knew was what Phoebe had been able to tell him on the phone. His mother had developed some 'complications' as a result of the fall, and had been taken back into hospital.

Felix wondered what sort of complications could result from a fall. Surely they hadn't missed a broken bone or something had they? He remembered the vast quantity of paracetamol his mother had been taking. Was it that? Had she overdosed? God, he had been so stupid, he should of insisted she return to the doctor. But she wasn't a woman you could push around, well, not one that Felix could push around anyway, and he had tried. As she said, she was a grown woman.

He wondered what his father would have done. Nothing, he realised, he would have done no more than Felix had. Not with her. No one could do anything with her. Not even his dad. Look what had happened to him, and look what Felix had done after spending only one night in her proxy little house, she was poison.

The day his father died was the same afternoon the first frog crawled from their pond and sang its croaky song.

Felix was enthralled; observing its small knobbly back and wide wet eyes. It seemed to have been magically made from water. He had been waiting weeks for this, watching the tadpoles that he and his father caught, as they changed and morphed.

That day it was hot and the afternoon seemed to stretch into forever as Felix waited for his father. Six thirty eventually arrived, but his father didn't. At seven his mother insisted they eat.

'I'm starving,' she announced. 'If he can't get himself home he can do without.'

Felix was anxious, if his father wasn't home soon it would be too late to show him the frog. Bursting to share it with someone he told his mother.

'Bloody dirty slimy creatures,' she said, with a shudder. 'Go and wash your hands.'

'It's not dirty mum, it crawled out of the pond, so it's clean.' As she dished up the sausage, mash and peas he tried to explain to her the evolution of the frog from tadpole.

She picked up the jug of gravy. 'I don't have time for this, go on now, go and wash your hands.'

Felix trudged upstairs, his heart smarting at her lack of enthusiasm. His dad would have understood.

It was late when they finally ate their meal, his mother's anger hanging over them, grinding them into their seats, snuffing out any hope of conversation. The food grew in his mouth and congealed in his stomach, but he didn't dare leave any, not when she was in this mood.

The doorbell rang as Felix and Phoebe were finishing the washing up. It had been his turn to wash and he was chasing the suds round the sink with the water nozzle, imagining it was a great tidal wave and the small bubbles were groups of people rushing to the safety of the plughole. A deep rumble of male voice drew his attention from his game. It wasn't his father's voice.

Felix and Phoebe exchanged glances, then simultaneously moved to the kitchen door, crouching out of sight they peered through the gap at the hinge of the door. A policeman stood in the doorway.

After, when his mother told them, he had gone out, pulled that frog out of the water in the dark, and crushed it with his hands. It had been so easy, it was easy, to snuff out life, even if you didn't mean to. He thought of Lucy again. He hadn't meant to, not like the frog. No, Lucy had been an accident.

'Felix?'

He jumped at his name and looked up. 'Phoebe,' he stood.

'Any news?'

'Nothing yet.'

'I don't understand it. How was she this morning?'

'Fine. Okay, I think. She'd been taking more pain killers than she should.'

'And you let her?'

'I could hardly stop her could I? I did suggest she went to the doctors.'

'Suggest…suggest!'

'Phoebe stop it. This isn't my fault!'

They stood glaring at each other until Phoebe let her shoulders sink. 'I'm sorry,' she said. 'You're right. It's not your fault.' She sat down and Felix sat next to her.

'I've been trying to figure out what sort of complications you can get with a fall,' he asked. 'Any ideas?'

'No, but it didn't sound good.'

It was mid afternoon by the time Kate arrived at her hotel and checked in. Hungry, she decided to set off into the sunshine to look for coffee and food.

The sun baked the road and as she stepped out, Kate felt the air thick in her nostrils, the heat soaked into her shoulders and her eyes squinted into the bright day. As she put on her sunglasses the tension in her shoulders loosened, and her body began to relax.

The road was busy, and it took Kate a moment or two to fathom the road system, and remember that everyone drove on the 'wrong' side of the road here. If she were to survive for the next couple of days, it would be important for her to remember to look the right way when she crossed the road.

When she had finally figured it out, and had crossed safely, Kate's thoughts naturally flitted back home. It was all there, waiting for her return. Sam and her failing marriage, the awkwardness with her friend Felix, her unreciprocated feelings for Josh, the neighbours sidelong glances and whispers, and finally, there was Lucy. It all crowded her head and a heavy weight sat on her chest. She stopped walking, reminded herself that she was here to take a break, leave it all behind, just for a couple of days. She had to be firm, otherwise this was a waste of time and money.

Decision made, her step became lighter, and she went in search of a quick sandwich and coffee at one of the pavement cafés. Once that was done she intended to take a cab to the place all the guide books said was not to be missed: Los Ramblas.

Los Ramblas was made up of a long wide strip of pavement, with a one-way road running up one side and down the other. Off to the left and right ran narrow shaded streets crammed with shops, bars and cafés.

Down the Los Ramblas strip itself was a cacophony of sights and sounds that assaulted the senses, and it took Kate a few minutes to adjust. Once she had, she found herself transported and delighted by the throng of street entertainers. Men and women dressed up with painted faces holding statue poses that amazed Kate with the stamina and control needed, especially in the afternoon heat. When a member of the crowd dropped a coin in the tin in front of them, these statues would come to life and act out some mini-play, or be frightening, or funny, or quirky or entertaining in some way. The ingenuity of these individuals delighted Kate.

One man was covered entirely with plastic fruit, naked but for the fruit. A couple further down had set up a scene where they were decorating, but had fallen over and become entangled in themselves, holding an awkward statue pose.

Kate stopped to watch a man standing on a box in a long dark cloak that covered his face. When a coin went into his tin his hand appeared from under the cloak holding out a piece of paper. A young boy of about ten years old came forward with some trepidation to take it. The boy stretched out his hand, not wanting to get too close, and just as he had almost reached it, the man whipped back the cloak's hood to reveal a hideously painted face. The boy jumped in fear, and those surrounding him jumped too, including Kate. A burst of nervous laughter rippled through the crowd.

Kate walked on, passed a set up that was obviously supposed to be the invisible man, and she smiled at a group of Japanese tourists who were crowding round and photographing it. She couldn't understand what they were saying, but from their expressions it was clear that they were highly impressed by this exhibit. What they failed to realise was that the man wasn't there at all. Kate wondered if he'd just nipped to get some food, or if it was the intension that it would be without a person. Either way, it made her chuckle from time to time throughout the day as she travelled round the city, taking in the sites, soaking it all in, enjoying the freedom a life without the voices afforded her.

Chapter Twenty-Five

They returned to the hospital from Felix's flat early the next day. Felix had slept well on the futon, but he noted that his sister, despite having taken the bed, looked like she hadn't slept at all. Dark circles had formed under her eyes, and she had an unhealthy pallor. They drove in silence to the hospital.

Their mother had suffered a blood clot as a result of the fall. The pain she had been suffering, which both Felix and Mary had largely dismissed, had been an early indication.

'She could die,' Phoebe said, when they were travelling in the lift to the haematology ward.

'She'll be fine,' he said.

'But she could,' she insisted.

'I know,' he said finally, 'but let's deal with that if it comes to it eh?'

Phoebe nodded.

Felix had started on his drugs again, as if that would eradicate the fight he and his mother had on Sunday. So far it hadn't made a difference, but he knew it would take some time. He'd been foolish to stop. It pained him to admit it, but as his mother said, as long as he behaved like a clichè, he'd be typecast. He hoped it wasn't too late for him to change that. He could start again, no one knew.

When they reached the ward they were asked to wait. The doctor was with their mother now. The nurse looked grave under her surface smile, and Felix wondered if something had happened in the night.

Eventually the doctor appeared and they stood up in unison to greet him.

'It's not good news I'm afraid. The medication we have given her to try to break down the blood clot hasn't had the effect we had hoped. We're going to have to operate.'

'Operate!' said Phoebe.

The doctor nodded. 'We can't allow the clot to remain. If it starts to move it could be fatal. We're preparing her for surgery now.'

'Can we see her?'

'For a few moments, yes. She's already had a pre-med so she might be a little drowsy and confused. Don't worry about that.'

Felix followed Phoebe into the room. She walked up to the bed and took her mother's hand. 'Mum? It's Phoebe.'

Felix stood at the bottom of the bed watching.

Mary opened her eyes. 'Hello love.'

'How you feeling?'

'I've been better I can't lie, but they've given me something for the pain.'

'You're in good hands.'

Mary nodded, but said nothing further.

'Felix is here too,' Phoebe said.

Mary looked at her son and Felix felt himself shrivel under her gaze.

'Hello son,' she said.

He waited for something more, some sting, some rebuke, but nothing came. They stayed like this, the three of them, until they came to take Mary away.

'Sam? It's Mrs. Fletcher on the phone for you.'

'Thanks Tracey,' Sam said, and made her way in to the back office.

'Anne, hi.'

'Hello Sam. I just thought I'd call to see if you'd been able to give my proposition some thought?'

Sam sat down. 'Anne, I'm sorry I haven't come to a decision yet. There's a lot to think about.'

'I realised you would need some time to think, but it's been over three weeks now, Sam. I don't want to pressure you, but it seems rather straight-forward to me, either you want the position or you don't. And I really need an answer. If you don't want it I'll need to start thinking about recruitment.'

Sam held the phone to her ear unsure of what to say. Should she explain her predicament? Should she tell Anne that by taking the position she could lose her husband? One thing she knew for sure, she hated the idea of someone else doing the job.

'Sam?'

'Anne, yes, I'm still here. Just give me a couple more days.'

'Alright, but then I'll need an answer.'

'Yes. Thanks.'

Sam replaced the receiver and sat back in her chair. Now what?

Kate had explored the city relentlessly the day before and had fallen into her hotel bed exhausted and happy. Today it was cooler, but still considerably hotter than she was used to. Over a quick breakfast of coffee and pastry, she decided to return to Las Ramblas, this time to explore the areas off the main drag, before catching her plane home later that day.

As lunchtime approached she found herself meandering down an avenue which led into a large square with buildings on all four sides. On closer inspection Kate noticed the square could be accessed from all four corners, as well as the avenue she had passed through.

The lower part of the buildings held dirty sandstone arches, under which the café's nestled, their chairs spilling out beneath outstretched parasols. She selected one of the café's, ordered a coffee and rested in the soft autumn sunshine, taking in her surroundings.

The mustard yellow and ecru buildings towered above, dressed with tall dark wood shutters covering elegant windows with ornate balconies. The square was dotted with tall palm trees, and small black lamp posts with filigree detail.

She breathed in and caught the smell of cooling hot stone, coffee, and the underlying muted cooking smells of tomatoes and fried potatoes. The air buzzed with pockets of conversation, occasionally a noise rose above the bustle: a child's shriek, the tenor of male laughter, or a single voice. Crockery slammed together and cutlery danced tinkling like colliding stars. Kate loved it. Loved to hear it all.

She watched the world pass her by as she sipped the strong fragrant coffee. A small group of pigeons pecking and strutting became disturbed by the bell of a thin man riding a bicycle across the square. A round man in a trilby tipped his hat as he passed, his little dog, equally rotund, waddled alongside him. A bell chimed far off. Ripples of groups moved through the square, passing through with a guide. Birds chirped beneath the conversation. Occasionally the rumble of a car, or the shout of one of the street entertainers and the responding crowd, swept through the square from Las Ramblas.

Kate closed her eyes. Her mind stretched out, probed and found an English train of thought moving through the air. A woman's.

'Hope Sean's okay. Maybe I should have frozen more dinners for him. Shouldn't have bought a new carpet, he's bound to have a party. I'll phone Sarah, ask her to check, he'll hate that but hey ho, he'll just have to lump it. I was hoping-'

Kate smiled as she listened. She sensed someone sit down at her table and the whispers receded. She opened her eyes to see a heavily made-up woman sitting opposite her.

'I hope you don't mind me joining you,' she said. Her speech was heavily accented. 'It is very busy today and we two are single yes?'

'Yes, I mean no, I don't mind.'

'I'm Colette-Maria,' the woman said as she sat down. 'Colette my mother called me and Maria my father so I call myself Colette-Maria to avoid taking the sides,' her voice modulated up and down, in a sing-song manner that was pleasant to listen to.

'Kate.' It was all Kate could say, unaccustomed as she was to meeting and talking with strangers.

The woman had jet hair piled on top of her head, dark kohl eyes surrounded by thick lashes and sensuous red lips. She was in her fifties, and breathtakingly beautiful. The waiter approached and Colette-Maria ordered in a rolling of quick-fire Spanish.

'My mother was French, my father Spanish. A poor combination, both stubborn and passionate. It was a difficult house to grow up in,' she smiled and took in the scenery.

'That must have been strange, having two names.'

The woman turned and looked at her. 'It was strange,' she said, the words rolling around her mouth. 'Like being two people. Strange, but delicious. I love being different don't you? Don't you love being different?' Colette-Maria didn't wait for a response. 'Great things come to those who are different. We are born unique, don't die a copy, eh?'

She wore purple, layers and layers of different shades of purple. She turned and smiled at Kate. She was like some character in a fairy tale, and Kate could not stop looking at her. This woman took up all the space her body inhabited; there was no shyness or apology. She looked life square in the face and dared it to challenge her, consequently life oozed from her as she sat quietly taking in her surroundings. She was captivating.

Kate noticed a large diamond ring on her left hand made of hundreds of small stones. Paste or real, she wondered. Unpracticed at small talk, and having nothing else to say, Kate asked her.

'Is that important to you?' the woman replied.

'What?'

'If something is real or not?' She accepted her espresso from the waiter.

'I suppose it must be, though I've never really thought about it.'

Colette-Maria smiled. 'Then do,' she said. 'I think you'll find it fascinating'

'Is it important to you?' Kate asked.

The woman shrugged. 'I can only tell what I believe.'

'Tell me.'

'I think it all illusion anyway, so we might as well make up what we want as truth,' she laughed and sipped her coffee.

'Where are you from?' Colette- Maria asked, returning her cup to the saucer.

'England, you?'

'Oh, lots of places,' she said with a wave of her hand.

'So you don't really know where you're from,' Kate suggested.

'Oh no, I know. In order to know where you're going, it's vital to know where you've come from. It's just...it's a long story, and I have learnt that, whilst I find it fascinating, few other people do,' she laughed again and drank off her coffee.

A flock of birds in the square lifted and Kate turned to watch them soaring round and round, catching eddies of wind, tilting this way and that, small movements in order to keep their balance. They finally came back down to rest. She turned the words round in her head likewise, allowing them to rest somewhere inside her, to nest and roost until their meaning rose up.

When she turned back, Colette-Maria was standing up and getting ready to leave.

'Thank you for sharing,' she said, and left.

Kate watched her walk across the square in a stream of purple, reflecting on what she had said. Several things had resonated with Kate in their short exchange. The woman's approach to being different, her sheer indifference to what was truth and what was illusion, and her resounding belief that you needed to know where you come from.

'Great things come to those who are different,' she had said and *'we might as well make up what we want as truth'* and finally, perhaps the most germane: *'In order to know where you're going, it's vital to know where you've come from.'*

Kate paid the bill and walked back to Las Ramblas, but as she walked into the busy road she suddenly felt disorientated. She wasn't sure if it was the heat or the strong coffee, but it all seemed strange and unreal, as if she were moving outside of her body. Unable to cope and wanting to get away from the overstimulation of the crowds, the noise and the hot sun, she plunged back into the little dark streets. They were still busy but quieter, and cooler in the shade.

She walked for some time, feeling disorientated. She needed to get off the streets, but she didn't want anymore coffee and she didn't want to go into a bar either. She toyed with the idea of collecting her case from the hotel and heading off to the airport, but it was too early for that. So she walked, hoping to stumble on a solution. She had just decided to find a cab to the hotel, when she came across a small square and found herself outside a church. She thought of Josh, and wondered where he was and what he was doing.

The clanging bells overhead assaulted her ears and she found herself drawing closer to the church, until finally she was inside. It was cool and dark, and Kate took a seat near the rear. The bells now muted, Kate could feel herself begin to relax.

There were about forty people scattered among the pews. Kate closed her eyes. Immediately her mind automatically began to probe. Here the thoughts were quieter, gentle hisses she couldn't quite make out. Realising she was being intrusive she made a conscious effort not to probe. These people were praying, and she wanted to respect their privacy, even though they were probably Spanish and therefore, she would not be able to understand. Instead, she allowed the hissing whisper of their prayers to wash over her, bathe her, and a softening occurred in her body, an opening.

She took a deep breath and she sighed quietly as she let it go. Her body relaxed, her tight heart opened and before she could stop herself, tears began to roll down her face. Organ music began and the congregation rose as one body. Kate hastily stood, sweeping the tears from her cheeks.

They began singing in Spanish, and Kate listened, unable to join in, as the priest and choir progressed up the aisle to the alter, carrying lighted candles and a large crucifix on a pole. After the hymn the priest chanted out some words and made the sign of the cross over his body. The congregation did the same and Kate followed a heartbeat later. Everyone sat.

Kate followed the service as best she could, standing, sitting or kneeling in delayed time, like some poorly rehearsed dancer. She couldn't join in the hymns, and didn't understand any of the words, so she simply allowed it to wash through her, enjoying the rhythm that appeared to underpin it all.

At the end of the service she joined the small queue to leave and shook the priests hand as those who had left before her had done.

'Thank you, gracias,' she said, finding herself bowing as if she was meeting royalty.

The priest, an aged man with wiry hair and buck teeth smiled, said something in spanish Kate did not understand, and bowed back, a glint of humor in his eye.

As she left the church and squinted into the bright sunshine she was lighter, a burden had been left behind on the pew. The confusion had gone. The answer to a question she wasn't even aware she was asking, had come to her in the service.

Josh would have said it was God given, she preferred to believe that the assured rhythm of the service had allowed the answer to bubble up from within her. Maybe, she thought, they were the same thing. It didn't matter. What mattered, was that Kate finally knew what she had to do.

Sam had a half day holiday due, so after the lunchtime rush she took a walk in the park. The weather was changeable at the moment, neither summer nor autumn, but in that halfway place that couldn't seem to make up its mind. Sam knew how it felt.

She found an empty bench by the river that ran straight through the park and sat down. She was aware she was procrastinating, deflecting the moment when she would have to face her husband with her decision, because she knew she had made it.

Sam looked at the river. A loud group of ducks had gathered by the river bank below with the mistaken belief she had come to feed them. She watched them swim around each other, seeming to glide across the water. One turned upside down, tipping its tail feathers up to the sky. It was comical, as if something had come up under the water and pulled it down.

It reminded Sam of the swimming baths on a Saturday morning when she was young. She could still remember who she went with: Jason Pillars, Shelly Drum and Jeremy Fields. They would pull each other under and horse around until their skin was wrinkly. With their clothes sticking to them, skin smelling of chlorine, they drank oxtail soup from the vending machine. Dreadful stuff, but it tasted like freedom to her. No parents, no chores, no one telling her what to do. Afterwards, regardless of the weather, and despite wet hair, they would come to this park and hang around for hours, not doing anything in particular.

She had kissed Mark Longstaff in the rose garden on the other side of the bridge. He was her first love. After a few weeks she 'packed him in', immediately regretting it, and two days later asked him back out. He said no and she was crestfallen. For a week. She smiled now at how she cried herself to sleep for a full three nights. Until David Barns came on the scene. How fickle the young.

But had she really grown up? What if the same thing happened with Paul? What if she went home, and told him, and their relationship ended, because it would, she knew it would, and then, a few weeks or months down the line, she realised she had made a mistake? She knew one thing for sure; it would take her a lot longer than three nights to get over this heartbreak.

But she didn't feel old enough to have a baby, she didn't feel ready. She wasn't sure what you were supposed to feel, but she was convinced this wasn't it.

Going home and telling Paul she was taking this job also told him she didn't want to have his children, at least for now. And if she was going to be honest with him, he would need to know that there was a part of her that was afraid she never would. She knew this made her look odd to a lot of people, but that wasn't a good reason to have a child. She knew it would be the end of her marriage, but that wasn't a good reason to have a child either.

Her mind felt like the inside of a golf ball, reams of tangled elastic. Her head was so mangled inside it had set. Hard. Intractable. She was full inside; there wasn't any room for a baby. Not in her life and not in her body.

Taking a deep breath she forced herself off the bench. Just because she knew what she should do, didn't make it easy.

The expression on the surgeon's face told Felix everything he needed to know, and the words 'I'm sorry' confirmed it. Phoebe fell into his arms sobbing. Felix thought the world had gone into slow motion and barely heard the surgeon's words.

'Thrombectomy unsuccessful...complications...shock...heart failure... deeply sorry...we did all we could...'

None of it mattered. His mother was gone. His last surviving parent. Now it was just him and Phoebe. He didn't feel the way he thought he would feel at the death of the old bag. He thought he would be relieved, joyful even, instead he wasn't sure he could contain the unexpected rage he felt. He wanted to hurt something, someone, lash out, do some damage. He squeezed Phoebe to him, his teeth clamped, as she sobbed into his shoulder.

Chapter Twenty-Six

'Katie, darling, how lovely to see you. Come in, come in.'

Kate entered the large entrance hall of her parent's detached bay windowed house. The trip back had exhausted her and she was pleased to see her mother and her childhood home. It made her feel safe.

'What's with the suitcase,' her mother asked.

She dropped the case in the hall. 'I've just flown back from Barcelona.'

'You! Flown! Really?' Jan said, as she closed the front door. 'I'm just making myself a sandwich,' she trotted down the hallway towards the kitchen. 'You want one?'

Kate followed, a hard knot wedged in her throat. 'No thanks.'

Jan resumed buttering the brown bread laid out on the kitchen counter. 'It's been a lovely day here today,' she said. 'This is a wonderful surprise. You should have called to tell us you were coming.'

Kate watched as her mother laid out the slices of cheese onto the bread.

'Your father's playing squash. We're eating out tonight. He'll be disappointed he missed you. Unless…are you going to stay? We could change our plans, or I could change the reservation? We're not eating till nine.'

Kate shook her head.

'Sit down, take off your coat, you look like you're about to speed out that door any minute.'

Kate half smiled. 'Sorry,' she said and shed her coat, plonking herself into one of the kitchen chairs at the oak table that dominated the centre of the room.

'You sure you won't have something to eat?' Jan asked, wiping her hands on a tea-towel.

Kate shook her head again.

'So, tell me, how was Barcelona?'

Kate felt her mother's eyes peering at her, scanning every fibre, checking on her daughter in the way only a mother's glance can do. 'It was good.'

'Did Sam go with you?'

'No, I went alone.'

'Alone! Why?'

Kate smiled at her mother's horror. 'Mum it's fine. I just wanted to spend some time away, alone.'

Jan began slicing iceberg lettuce. 'You spend too much time alone already. You always have.' She looked up, 'are you sure you're alright?'

'Mum I'm fine, honestly.' She watched her mother's shoulders drop in surrender.

Jan cut the sandwich in two, put it on the plate and turned to Kate. 'Darling have something to eat, you look so thin.'

'Really mum, don't fuss I'm fine,' the slice on Kate's voice silenced any further pleas.

'Tea then?' asked Jan, changing tack.

'Coffee would be better.'

They both fell silent as Kate watched her mother's hands move swiftly; filling the kettle, getting the mugs and milk jug, swilling the coffee pot. The sounds of the water, the clattering of the crockery and the tick of the kitchen clock filled the kitchen, fighting the quiet.

Eventually Jan joined her daughter at the table with a full pot of coffee, the milk jug and her sandwich in front of her.

'So, what's going on?'

'What d'you mean?'

'Katie, you don't turn up here like this without calling. You never do that. And to come direct from the airport like this…come on, what's going on?'

Kate's stomach tightened, contracting towards her spine. She took a deep breath and suddenly her plan seemed ludicrous. What would this solve? And yet, there was no alternative, now that the idea had come to her there was no going back.

'Katie please, I'm getting worried.'

'Mum, it's nothing I just…I have some questions.'

Her mother took a deep breath and sat back in her chair, the sandwich untouched.

'What?' asked Kate.

Jan shook her head. 'I've been expecting this. We thought, your father and I, we thought it was over. That now you were in your late-twenties it had passed. But I can't say I'm exactly surprised, especially after our conversation a couple of weeks back when we were horse riding.'

Neither spoke for a while. Kate examined the dry skin round her thumb nail. She really should take better care of her hands.

'So, what do you want to know?'

'I don't want to hurt you, or dad. It's just...I need to know.'

'Why now? I mean, I could understand it if you'd asked as a child or a teenager, and I was even prepared that, when you had children of your own, the subject would come up, but now, like this, out of the blue...why?'

'It's complicated. I'm not sure I can explain.' Kate swallowed, 'I'm sorry mum.'

Jan shook her head. 'Darling, there's no need for you to apologise. It's just a shock. Whenever your father and I tried to talk to you in the past, you would refuse to listen. You had no interest, quite the opposite in fact. I always thought that maybe you'd change your mind, one day, but...' Jan fell silent and picked at the crust of her sandwich.

Kate held her breath.

'I need your father here,' her mother said. There were tears in her eyes.

'Mum, please don't cry. I love you, I'll always love you.'

Jan shook her head and smiled. 'I'm not crying for me. I know you love us, there's no question about that. You have been nothing but a source of joy to us from the day we met you. It's not that.'

'Then what is it?'

'What happened to you...before you came to us, it's not...well, it's not pleasant.' Jan pulled her mouth into a smile, tears slipping down her face. 'And I guess we secretly hoped we would never have to tell you.'

Sam sat opposite Paul at the dining room table after dinner. She opened her mouth but nothing came out. They talked, but not about the one thing they needed to.

'You finished with that,' he asked her, pointing at the nearly full plate of macaroni cheese in front of her. She slid the plate across to him.

'What are your plans tonight?' she asked as lightly as she could.

'There's a documentary I want to watch.'

'Right.'

'And you?'

'I thought I'd try giving Kate another ring.'

'She out of communication again?'

It irked Sam, the way he said it.

'No,' she lied. 'I just haven't spoken to her for a while.'

'You don't need to have a tone with me – it wouldn't be the first time.'

She didn't trust herself to answer him so she said nothing. Instead, she left the table and dialled Kate's number from the phone in the hall. It went to voice mail and Sam left a message.

Frustrated she sat by the phone thinking. Anne Fletcher would want an answer in the next couple of days, it was a great opportunity: Managing Director, company car, running the whole show. It excited her. She had come home with every intension of sorting it out once and for all tonight. She had promised herself in the park, but every time she tried the words got stuck.

One thing Sam did know, she hated the idea of someone else doing that job. If she didn't take it, she couldn't stay, and if she didn't stay then...well, she was back to square one. What she really wanted was to talk to Kate.

Where was she now? Was she at home listening to her messages and ignoring them the way only she could? Sam picked up the phone and called Felix.

'Is she there?' she asked, forgoing the usual polite formality of a hello.

'Who?'

'Kate.'

'Oh, no, I don't think so. I haven't heard her moving around.' His voice sounded flat.

'Where is she?'

'Why are you asking me?'

'Don't get so tetchy.'

'Sorry, I've had some bad news today.'

'Oh?'

'Yes, my mum died.'

'Oh my god, Felix, I'm so sorry!'

'Thanks.'

'How are you?'

'Not sure...numb I guess. It hasn't really sunk in. She was fine a couple of days ago.'

'That really is awful, I am sorry.'

'Anyway, Kate isn't here. I think she's gone away, usually I hear her if she's just being unresponsive. Do you want me to give her a message when she turns up?'

'I need to talk to her about something. It can wait.' Sam heard Paul making his way from the kitchen. 'Anyway, let me know when she gets back won't you? Or better still, get her to call me, and sorry to hear your news.'

Sam replaced the receiver as Paul came to a halt in front of her.

'She's away,' she said.

'You want to come and watch this documentary with me?'

Sam had no interest in the programme, but recognised the truce he was offering and so agreed. Paul held out his hand and helped her from the telephone stool.

Sam followed him into the living room, realising that once again, she would not say what needed to be said.

Chapter Twenty-Seven

'Morning darling, coffee?'

Kate entered the kitchen and nodded as she sat down.

'You want some toast?'

'No, thanks mum, I'm not hungry. Where's dad?'

'He had to go in the office this morning. He didn't want to wake you. We both felt you needed some sleep after…everything.'

Kate took the mug of coffee from her mother. Jan pulled out the kitchen chair opposite and joined her.

'How are you feeling?'

'Okay. A little shell shocked, but alright.'

'It's a lot to take in all in one go.'

Kate sipped her coffee.

'Listen, your dad and I were talking and we think it would be a good idea if you stayed here for a few days. Let us look after you.'

'No, I'm okay mum, really.'

They listened to the clock.

'How are you…I mean *really*?'

'Mum, please, I'm fine.'

'Do you want to talk about it? You didn't say much last night.'

'What's there to say?'

'Will you go and visit your father? Your birth father I mean?'

'I don't know,' Kate put the mug down on the table and studied the blue flowered pattern. 'I don't think so.'

'Oh, Kate, I wish there was something I could do.'

Kate leaned over and placed her hand over one of her mother's. 'Mum, I'm fine, really. It's all a bit of a shock, but I'm okay. I need to go home and be on my own, let it all…sink in.'

'Shall I drive you?'

'I'd like that.'

'Good,' Jan stood up. 'What time do you want to leave?'

'When I've finished my coffee?'

'I'll just nip up and put my face on. I think we should stop on the way and pick you up some groceries too.'

'I don't need anything.'

'Milk, bread, that kind of thing,' Jan turned to leave, and then stopped. 'I know, we'll pick up a couple of tins of soup too. In case you get hungry later on and don't want the bother of cooking.'

Kate relented. 'Good idea,' she said. Her mother beamed an over bright smile and left.

Kate sat at the table tracing the wood knot patterns beneath her fingers. The clock ticked quietly in the background; the heating hummed gently, a car passed. Kate sat and took in these small sounds, holding onto them. They seemed the only real thing to her, the sounds and the feel of the wooden table beneath her fingers.

Whatever she was expecting yesterday, it wasn't what she was told. Although the death of her mother was a surprise at first, it wasn't the biggest shock. She had always been vaguely aware of a childhood before the adoption, and while she hadn't been able to remember anything concrete until recently, that single memory had suggested a mother who loved her. So the death of her mother hadn't been entirely a surprise, but the *way* she had died. Now Kate knew the story, the flashbacks made sense. It all made sense and pushed deep into her core.

Reality, truth, dreams, lies, voices, whispers. She didn't know what to do with it all. Emotions swirled round and through her, intense and black. She found herself on the edge, afraid of going in, convinced that she'd drown in it all. She felt sick with the swirling.

Jan's voice broke into Kate, pulling her back hard.

'You haven't drunk your coffee darling.'

'I don't want it.'

'You okay?'

'Mum, I'm fine, stop asking me.'

'I'm sorry, Shall we go?'

Kate stood up. 'Yes please.'

On the drive home the newspaper banner smacked Kate hard, "Police Find Body of Missing Girl".

'Lucy,' she whispered.

'What?' her mother said.

Kate, determined not to break until she was alone, said, 'Nothing.'

If she showed any weakness her mother would whisk her back to the family home, and Kate needed to be by herself now more than ever.

Felix put the last of his mother's things into the case that sat open on his bed. It felt strange and intrusive handling her things like this. He half expected her to appear in the doorway to give him grief about it.

Case packed he closed it and zipped it up. He wasn't sure what he was going to do with it now. Put it on top of the wardrobe? No, he would be able to see it from his bed, and he didn't want that reminder every morning and every night. Under the bed would be better.

Once the case was stowed he returned to the living room, unsure what to do with himself. He could make some tea, except he didn't want any. He wasn't hungry. He had cleaned the flat earlier, so there was nothing for him to do there. All his ironing was done. Kate hadn't returned home and besides, he wasn't sure if he could face her now.

He slumped into the sofa. He hadn't expected to feel so empty. Surely when you lose your last parent there should be more emotion than this? At first he thought it was just the shock of it, or that he was just being strong for Phoebe, but now, now there was no excuse. He had the space to grieve, but he found there was little to grieve for. He hadn't much cared to spend time with her when she was alive, had once beaten her so hard she nearly died, so why would he be sorry now she was dead. Of course, he wouldn't admit that to Phoebe…or anyone else.

What he did feel was unsettled, he needed to fill the day that stretched before him. Finally, he decided to go and get a paper. That would kill a couple of hours.

Jan set her daughter down outside her flat and despite her protestations Kate insisted she leave her there. She was fine, she could take care of herself from here, and she needed to be by herself. Needed the space. Reluctantly Jan Gregory drove away.

As soon as Kate opened the door to her flat it happened. A kind of disintegration of herself. Each step from the entrance hall through her home diminished her further. She left herself behind, crumbled, like wet sand on shoes, she fell off in clumps. Pieces broke away, fell and exploded onto the carpet. By the time she reached the bedroom it was all she could do to arrange the remainder on the bed.

Hours later she woke in a fug of prickly cotton wool. Grey and damp, red heat coursed through her. Every movement created an intense reality of her physical body, and a lessening of her surroundings.

Echoes, through water. Distorted sounds. Hooks of reality that slipped when she put any weight on them. Electrical tentacles of pain shot through her legs and arms. Neck and shoulders stiff, braced for the next red shock. Swimming deep. Breath held. Eyes bulging from the boiled head on her shoulders. Pressure pushing at her ear drums. Brain too big for the skull. An urgency, somewhere.

Slipping in and out. Unsure what was in and what was out. Were the curtains blue? Had she been swimming that afternoon? Did Felix bring her daises? Did she have creamy coffee with Josh this morning? Had she bought a red dress from Sam's place that afternoon? Was Lucy Newton dead?

The heat. The furnace in her brain, making thought bubble up and over, lapping down her body, bathing her in volcanic images. Red. No escape. It moved to her kneecap, there the memories flooded out. Her lower back twinged and out they poured. An ear lobe. A finger nail. Some muscle twitch in her face. No escape. She was trapped by her body. Held firm in the torment. *'In order to know where you're going, it's vital to know where you've come from.'*

She reached up. Searching for help. It was high above. In the blue. She pushed against the rubber bubble that surrounded her. No escape. Hard grey. Unbreakable.

She folded into herself, a cream cloud in coffee, and despair clawed its way through her veins. No escape. Voices. Distorted faces. She tentatively reached with her probe, feeling, attempting to connect. A click and she broke in, the combination revealed, a thief at a safe.

But this was not the whispers. Not the familiar friend. It was a memory. Josh, a voice she strained to hear. A message. And then she heard.

'God is like arithmetic - Omnipresent. Two plus two is four, wherever you are. There is no place when it is not.'

Like bread dough she folded herself in on herself again. Unclear. A scrabbling for meaning. It meant something. Her thoughts raged like buffalo on the plains, galloping without direction or destination. 'There is no place where it is not.'

'Truth and reality, what's the difference. Think about it.'

Minutes passed, or hours or days. It was difficult to tell. The blue rose over and engulfed her. A sob caught. A catcher's mitt throat, designed to seize the words. A punch from within. It popped and escaped. Clashed on the ear drums and vibrated through the body. She surfed the blue. The blue.

It tightened the throat. She knew, she saw, she watched. Small. The blue silk, the pink throat, the tightness. She watched. 'There is no place where God is not.' 'Truth and reality, what's the difference. Think about it.' 'Don't you just love to be different?'

She rode the blue and watched it pull the life from her mother. 'There is no place where God is not.' 'Truth and reality, what's the difference. Think about it.' 'Don't you just love to be different?' 'In order to know where you're going, it's vital to know where you've come from.'

The words rocked inside her. Gentle. They seeped in and rose up. She pushed again the rubber bubble to reach help. She collapsed into herself and then the green broke. 'Truth and reality, what's the difference. Think about it.' 'In order to know where you're going, it's vital to know where you've come from.'

'There is no place where God is not.' God was there. Inside her. She reached in. Heat waves rose from her groin and stomach. Green warmth spread out through the body. Her body. The blue terror receded. The green grew, opening her heart, healing her. Pulling the pieces back together. The voices returned. Familiar hissing. Gentle lullabies, the heart slowed. The blood eased and slowed its path. The green heat moved. Lapped through her body. Soothed, rocked, sang. Until finally, she slept.

He had been able to put it from his mind, had almost forgotten what he had done, until he saw the headlines. Then, there in the middle of the corner shop, in front of the rack of papers, it all came back to him, like a bad dream you recall in the middle of the day. His stomach turned over and he looked up, expecting everyone to be looking back at him with accusing eyes. There were only two people in the shop, both focused on their shopping. Stay calm, he reminded himself.

There was nothing linking him to the girl. The police had questioned him no more than anyone else who lived in the street. And he had an alibi. He had been visiting his mother that weekend; everyone would back up his story if asked, except Phoebe might mention he had been away from the house for a few hours on the Saturday afternoon, unless he asked her not to. Would she do that for him? Lie for him? Of course she would, she wouldn't suspect the truth, and if he explained that he could be arrested for something he hadn't done, she would protect him.

He considered anything else he had overlooked. There were DNA and fibres and stuff, he had seen that on CSI, but surely dumping her in the river would have washed that away? She had been in the boot of his VW for a couple of days, but he'd hovered that out, and besides, they wouldn't be checking his boot unless they suspected him, and why would they?

Breathing easier Felix picked up a Northern Echo and an Independent and took them to the counter.

'Terrible business isn't it?' said Dot Kimble, taking the five pound note from Felix.

'Yes,' he said.

'She often came in here,' Dot continued, as she rang up the sale. 'Such a sweet little thing,' she shook her head. 'I hope they catch the monster who did this.'

Felix took his change and left quickly, wanting to return to the flat. As he walked back, papers tucked under his arm, it reassured him that, all things considered, he was probably safe.

'She looks dreadful. How did you know?'

'I didn't, her keys were in her door when I got back from the shop, I nearly tripped over her suitcase.'

Sam and Felix sat at Kate's kitchen table drinking tea. Kate was sleeping.

'What did the Doc say?'

'Chest infection. She's on antibiotics now. She'll be back on her feet in a day or two.'

'Have you rang her mum?'

'Not yet.'

Sam drank her tea. Rain pattered on the kitchen window. It was getting dark earlier and earlier. Winter was on its way.

'It's a good job I dropped by, but you should have called me.'

Felix shrugged. 'I didn't think, I've had a lot on my mind.'

They drank more tea.

'Sorry to hear about your mum.'

Felix didn't say anything. It clogged his brain, making conversation. He wanted her to leave him alone with Kate. He wanted to take care of her.

Sam glanced at her watched as the silence descended and Felix noticed. 'Do you have to get back?'

'Not really. I was thinking I might stay over, take care of Kate, give you a break.'

'That's not necessary,' Felix said quickly. 'It's only been today, hardly taxing.'

'I know it's not necessary, but I want to. Kate's my friend.'

'She's my friend too,' he said.

Sam glared at him.

'It's all been...appropriate,' he said quickly. 'I wouldn't hurt her.'

A puzzled look crossed Sam's face. 'I know that,' she said. 'That isn't why I want to stay.'

'But I'm just downstairs…it's better if I do it-'

'Felix I'm staying,' Sam stood up and strode out of the kitchen, and he knew it was senseless to argue. He clenched his jaw against the rising tide of anger and hatred that bubbled up inside him. He'd had enough of Sam.

198

Chapter Twenty-Eight

It was 8am when Sam took Kate a cup of tea and a slice of toast. 'Here,' she put the toast on the bedside cabinet and turned to Kate, handing her the mug. 'You look a bit brighter.'

'I'm okay,' said Kate pushing herself up to a sitting position on the bed. 'Bit groggy, but not bad.'

'Sleep well?'

'Good thanks,' she took the tea

Sam perched on the edge of the bed.

'You been here all night?' Kate asked, rubbing at her hair with her free hand.

Sam nodded. 'Wanted to make sure you were okay.'

Kate was touched and surprised by her friend's unusual care. 'And Felix?'

'Scuttled back to his flat, but not without a fight.'

'My hair's a state,' Kate said, rubbing her head again, ignoring Sam's comment.

Sam laughed. 'You must be feeling better if you're worried about your appearance.'

Kate smiled. 'I suppose.'

'You still look tired though. You sure you're okay?'

Kate hesitated, unsure whether she was ready to share what had come to light recently. But it was too soon, too raw. She needed to hold it to herself a while longer. Make it part of her. 'These things take time,' she said.

Sam re-crossed her legs, making Kate bounce in the bed. 'I suppose.'

Kate could feel Sam's interest in her health receding and began to relax. 'So, what's going on with you?'

Sam, who had started to slouch, sat up straight. 'Anne Fletcher rang yesterday, chasing a decision. She said she'd have to go out to recruit if I turned it down.'

'Wow, Sam, well...well, I suppose that was inevitable, if you don't take it.' Kate saw the tension in her friend's forehead and reached out, probing until she found the barrier. Then she pulled back, not wanting to intrude further than was necessary. Her friend would share what she wanted to share, it was inappropriate for Kate to know more than that.

'But there's a problem right?'

Sam nodded. 'I still haven't told Paul my decision yet. I just can't bring myself to say anything, I just know it will all go pear-shaped. Us I mean.'

'How can you be so sure?'

'I just know that if I take this job it'll be the end of us, permanently. But on the other hand, if I don't take it I'll regret it, and probably end up resenting Paul, which could also be the end of us.'

'So what are you going to do?'

'I don't know,' Sam wailed. 'I know I've flitted about in the past. I know I can be…flaky, but I've really enjoyed working at the boutique.'

'Sam, a few weeks ago you were bored stiff and looking for a change!'

'I know, but I've been offered it now haven't I? I mean, everyday'll be different. I'll have lots of new challenges. I don't see myself getting bored with this for well, ages really.'

'Sounds like you really want this.'

'I do.'

'So hadn't you better tell Paul?'

'I know, I'm just…'

'Putting it off?'

'No! I'm thinking.'

'What are you thinking *about?*'

'Oh I don't know, if I'm really honest, I think our marriage might be over. We want different things, fundamental things,' she glanced at her watch. 'Look I've got to go otherwise I'm going to be late. I need to go home and change. Felix said he'll pop in later to make sure you're okay.'

'There's really no need. I'm fine now.'

Sam stood up and shrugged. 'I told him that, but he insisted,' she raised her eyebrows. 'I told you, he's a bit keen.'

Kate picked up a pillow and threatened Sam with it.

'Okay, okay I'm going. Oh, and your mum phoned last night, about nine-thirty. Asked if you could call her. She sounded a bit worried about you. I told her you were fine, just a twenty four hour bug, but call her anyway. Oh, and you need to eat that toast,' she pointed. 'Before you take your antibiotics.'

'Thanks, and Sam?' Sam turned back to her friend. 'Thanks for staying last night.'

Sam shrugged. 'It's what friends are for,' she said.

It was true, but Kate had never seen it from Sam. She liked it.

Kate got up after drinking the tea that Sam had brought her. She left the toast. It had gone cold and rubbery and besides, she had no appetite. She swallowed the antibiotics with a full glass of water, hoping it would negate the effects of taking them on an empty stomach. Then she showered for a long time, letting the hot water run in rivulets down her body. The pounding of the water on her head was pleasant. The thrumming chased everything else away. As she was towelling herself, she tried to understand what had been happening over the last few days, the last few weeks for that matter.

Certainly she'd had a fever, and the news she heard at her parents had been the catalyst for that…the final straw so to speak. But something else had happened as she fought the fever, she couldn't shake the feeling that it wasn't the only thing she fought yesterday.

As Kate padded into her bedroom to select her clothes she tried to grasp what it might be, but failed and dismissed it. Instead, dressed in jogging bottoms, a sloppy fisherman's sweater and thick wool socks, she sat at the kitchen table with a cup of coffee, picking her way through the newspaper.

They were looking for Lucy's killer and it squeezed Kate into a box of tension, as she read the profile of the man they were looking for. A loner, someone who kept themselves to themselves, and either lived alone or with their mother. Ray Mountford fitted the profile she thought, and then quickly dismissed the idea. She'd been down that route several times before to no avail. Besides, there was lots of man who lived alone, Felix for example.

She turned the page and there was a picture of Lucy; a school portrait taken when she was missing her front teeth. She looked adorable and the picture blurred. Beside it was a head shot of Rachael looking wretched and distraught, the woman had aged considerably over the last few weeks.

Kate jumped up and scrunched the paper, pushing it hard down into the bin. She allowed the bin lid to fall then washed the newsprint off her hands, and rinsed her face in an attempt to wipe away her sorrow. There was only one thing for it…work.

By the time Felix arrived at noon she was in the kitchen on the phone talking to Bruce about deadlines for work. She waved at Felix as he stood in the doorway and finished her call quickly. 'Made some fresh coffee if you want some,' she told him.

Felix put her keys on the table. 'Sorry to let myself in, but I didn't want to disturb you, wasn't expecting you to be up and about so soon. You looked like death yesterday.'

Kate didn't look up from the note she was making on the yellow post it. 'Thanks,' she said, as she stuck it to one of the packages that sat on the table in front of her.

'Good to see you up,' he said, still standing. 'You worried me yesterday.'

Kate glanced at him and gave him a tight smile, feeling self-conscious, unable to meet his gaze. 'I'm feeling much better. Thanks for looking after me,' she mumbled, pushing the package across the table for something to do.

He shrugged. 'No problem.'

He stood, she sat. Both looked elsewhere.

'Your mum phoned.'

'I've spoken to her.'

'Good, good,' Felix scratched his nose. 'She sounded worried.'

'Mums do, don't they?'

'Yes.'

Kate sat up straighter and looked at Felix, though not directly. 'How's your mum?'

There was a pause before Felix answered. 'She…died.'

'What! When?'

'Couple of days ago.'

'Oh my god! I had no idea.'

'You were away, and then,' he shrugged. 'You've been ill.'

'I don't know what to say.'

'There's nothing to say.'

'How did it happen, I thought she was fine?'

'Complications from the fall, a blood clot, they had to operate and…' he looked down at his feet.

'That's terrible.'

'Yes.'

'It's all terrible news at the moment,' she said quietly.

'Oh?'

'Lucy.'

'Lucy?'

'They found her body.'

A whisper rose and struck Kate.

'Oh, yes, that.'

Horrified, and for something to do, she stood up, poured her coffee down the sink and rinsed the cup.

'Look, Kate, about what I said...I was just...well, I'd rather have you as a friend than...this.'

Kate focused on wiping the drops off the stainless steel sink. Her chest hammered. It was uncomfortable, having him here, but not for the reason he thought. A shaft of guilt pushed deeper, was it true or was she imagining it? Could Felix really be capable of what was niggling at the back of her mind? Surely not...

She turned and leaned against the sink shaking her hands dry. 'I know. It is awkward isn't it?' She forced herself to smile, suddenly afraid of him.

He smiled back and shrugged. 'Just a bit.'

Kate opened the top drawer next to the sink and took out a clean tea towel, her mind racing. Was she in danger? Was she even sane? Given her recent illness, and all that had happened to her, could she rely on anything? After all, she had been mistaken before.

'And you?' he hesitated. 'Are you seeing that Josh bloke then?'

Drying her hands she focused on what she was doing as she spoke. 'Oh, no. We're just friends.'

'Friends like you and me?' His voice was hard, and Kate felt her body tense.

'No, it's...different.'

'Oh?'

Kate chose her words carefully. 'It's...professional,' she said, at last.

He seemed satisfied by this response. 'Well, I'd better get back to work; I just popped back in my lunch break to make sure you're okay.'

'Thanks, I appreciate that,' she said, and Felix left.

As she heard the door click below Kate relaxed, until her eyes rested on the keys that he'd left on the kitchen table. Would he?

Chapter Twenty- Nine

When Kate opened the external door the following day her jaw dropped in surprise. Josh was stood on the doorstep. Ten minutes later they were sat in Kate's living room with mugs of coffee, the late afternoon streaming in through the window. She had even had the awareness to place a plate of biscuits on the coffee table between them.

'What brings you here?'

'I saw Paul this morning. He told me you'd been unwell.'

It took Kate a moment to realise he meant Sam's Paul. 'Of course, I forgot he came to you. It was Sam who recommended you.'

Kate sighed. It all seemed so long ago now, her visit to him with a stiff neck. 'It was only a twenty-four hour bug, nothing life threatening.'

'You look...troubled.'

'Something and nothing,' she said.

'It's either something or nothing, but it can't be both.'

'Depends how you look at it.'

Josh smiled. 'True.' He sipped his coffee, not taking his eyes from her.

Kate was aware of him looking. 'What?'

'Just looking at you,' Josh said. 'Trying to work out what's different about you.'

Everything! She wanted to shout. Everything's different. Instead she took a deep breath and told him the story. She told him about her trip to Barcelona, how she finally realised what she had to do, how consequently she now understood the mysterious visions, and ended by telling him about her childhood and the death of her mother.

'My father was a drinker. A heavy drinker and abusive, he frequently beat my mother. I remember it all now. I would hide either behind the sofa with my face pressed hard against the patterned back, or behind the dresser, my nose pushed up to the wood grain, as I listened to my mother's pleading and the hard crack of the slaps he administered.

'It never lasted long. He was not a fit man, and once he had expelled the little energy he had, he would leave, breathing heavily from the exertion. I would crawl from my hiding place to where my mum lay, weeping and pat her forehead, hoping to stop the crying, hoping to kiss it better, the way she did for me when I fell. Silly really, but I was only three, four at most.

'Sometimes the police came. I was always pleased to see them. They seemed like these giants in dark blue uniforms with shiny buttons who quietened things down, and sometimes took my father away. I understand now why I always feel so reassured when I see a police officer. But he always came back.

'The last time my father lost his temper my mother had pushed me behind the sofa to hide. I tripped and fell hard, twisting my shoulder and neck.'

'The childhood injury I mentioned that first time you came to see me?'

Kate nodded. 'I was too afraid to move, and lay with my face in the carpet, the pain in my shoulder causing my eyes to water, but I knew better than to call out or make a fuss when my father was in the mood he was in. I can still remember the dusty smell of the carpet filling my nostrils, nearly choking me at the time.'

Kate placed her cup on the coffee table and sat back. 'My father charged into the living room bellowing. "No Adam please," my mother begged. There was a moment's silence, a split second and then red splattered across the wall. I thought it was red paint gleaming in a line. My mother screamed and something was thrown across the room. I didn't know what it was, but it crashed on the wall above me, and sprinkled me with broken shards of itself.

'It must have caught the light because it started to sway up and down the wall. My mother started screaming. It was different to her usual crying and made me shake. My father bellowed and slapped her. This usually quietened her, but this night , for some reason, she screamed louder. And then she stopped.

'Instead of the usual noises, mum made a gurgling sound. It was like the sound I'd once made when I hadn't chewed a jammy dodger properly, and a piece got stuck on the way down.

'It went on for a long time, and then it stopped, and my father staggered across the room panting. He didn't slam the living room door behind him and stomp up the stairs like he usually did, instead he left the house. Quietly creeping away.'

Kate stopped and took a deep breath before continuing. 'I crawled across the floor to my mum, the broken shards biting into my legs. My mum wasn't crying. Her eyes stood out, unblinking, like my broken tiny tears that would not close her eyes when she was laid down. Mum had a long cut down her arm and she was covered in blood, but she had stopped bleeding. There wasn't usually blood. I curled up beside her, and eventually fell asleep. That's how the police found us the next morning, me curled up beside my mother's cold corpse.'

They sat in the dying winter light, Josh and Kate, the story between them. Both acclimatising to the air, like trekkers up the Himalayas.

Finally she broke the silence, and told Josh about her fever and how she thought she had connected with the God within.

'Sounds crazy doesn't it?'

'No. Not to me. It's sounds like you've been on quite an adventure.'

'I'm still a little shaken, but I'm back at work.'

'So soon?'

'It helps.'

'I guess. So what's next?'

'I dunno. When I first came to see you I'd spent most of my life plagued by other people's thoughts, voices battling for attention inside my tiny head. Then I had those awful visions. That's been a nightmare. I was convinced they were about Lucy, and all the time they were about me.'

'Do you still have the voices?'

'If I want them. They're now under my control.'

Josh looked down and for the first time since she met him he looked uncomfortable.

'What is it?'

'They found the girl.'

'I know, I read about it in the papers.'

He nodded, relieved that she knew.

The visions had all been hers. Something had dislodged it; it may have been the chiropractic adjustment, perhaps it was Lucy's abduction. It didn't matter. In a way, Kate felt Lucy's abduction had started to heal her past, enabled her to regain control over her life and accept who she was. It wasn't she who was saving Lucy Newton. It was Lucy Newton saving her. She started to explain it to Josh, but grief bubbled up, clogging her words.

He sat next to her, took her in his arms and rocked her, anchored her while she wept.

'Why didn't you tell me? Why didn't either of you tell me?'

Felix held his breath, waiting for Phoebe to speak. They were sat in the window seats of Café Nero in town. Phoebe had called that morning and asked him to meet her there. He thought they were going to discuss the funeral arrangements. He hadn't expected this.

'Well?'

'It's...complicated.'

'Like how?'

'It wasn't really any of our business.'

'How did you know?'

'I saw it Felix.'

'I didn't. Why didn't I see it?'

'You saw what you wanted to see. It happens all the time, one person sees one thing, another person sees something different. Besides, you were ill.'

'But don't you think it might have made a difference...if I'd known'

Phoebe played with the handle of her cup, tracing it with her finger nail. She looked up. 'How? How would it have made a difference?'

'My relationship with mum for a start. I always wondered how you could be so much more...' he stopped, groping blindly for the word.

'Felix, it wouldn't have mattered,' she said.

'Not to you it wouldn't, but to me...if I'd known the truth I would have been...different...with both of them.'

'But that's the point, don't you see? It really wouldn't have made a difference, not really. And besides, you were going through enough. We all were.'

Felix decided to ignore the second reference to his illness. 'Did he really leave her with nothing?'

Phoebe nodded. 'Worse than that. His gambling left her in debt and his life policy was void because of the suicide. He'd re-mortgaged the house, but she didn't know that until he died. She didn't know any of it. After he was gone, she picked up the payments to keep the house till it nearly crippled her. She used up all her savings, that's why she held down two jobs. It was a miracle she managed to keep the house for as long as she did. When you went into hospital after...well, after mum, she had to sell. She was too...damaged.'

He had done that to her.

'So there was no equity at all?'

'None.'

'So how did she manage to buy the other house then?'

'David and I-' she stopped.

'Why didn't you tell me,' he wailed again. 'I could have helped.'

'No you couldn't. You were just a kid, and you had, all that stuff going on. Besides, Mum was really clear; she didn't want you to know. I'm sorry.'

'But why?'

'You know why.'

'You should have told me anyway.'

Phoebe shrugged. 'She refused to let us help her if we told you. I'm sorry Felix, I really was over a barrel.'

'I didn't know him,' he said quietly. 'He was my father and I didn't know him at all,' he looked at her. 'I...don't know any of you.'

'Yes, you do. Stop it. He was your dad, end of subject. I'm guessing mum didn't want to interfere with that, or his memory, especially with everything else going on for you. Maybe she thought we'd never get you back if you knew the truth.'

'But what about my relationship with *her*?'

'I suppose she thought it was the sacrifice she had to make.'

'And you?'

'And me what?'

'You and David, it's the same all over again isn't it?'

'How do you make that out?'

'Ignoring his bad behaviour; not expecting the best for you.'

'I don't know about that, I never talked to mum about how she felt. Maybe it's the same, maybe it's different. It's academic now. I love David and it works for us. That's what love is; sometimes love doesn't fit into these conventional little boxes. You just make the best of what you've got.'

'How can you say that?'

Phoebe sighed. 'It's really very simple. My relationship is my relationship. Mum and dad's was there's.'

'But it's bound to have had an effect on us.'

'Felix, you didn't even know anything was going on until I just told you.'

'Yeah, but on some level, some deep level. Maybe that's why I got schizophrenia?'

'Oh god Felix! There was no "deep level", it was in dad's DNA. He suffered it, that's why he committed suicide in the end. Well, that and the mess he'd made of the finances. Who knows? But there was no "deep level". I was lucky, I didn't. You weren't so lucky.'

'Okay, maybe no deep levels for me, but you and your relationship with David? You're ignoring David's bad behaviour in the way that mum ignored dad's."

'You could argue that I'm repeating the pattern; I'd argue that by learning from my parent's relationship I've developed the ability to avoid a lot of pain in my life. It really depends on how you look at it. But I'm happy Felix, believe it or not I have no deep levels.'

'But you were always so…spiritual.'

'When?'

'When you wanted to go to the kibbutz.'

'God, Felix, I was just a kid then. I also wanted to save the whale and become a go-go dancer, but I didn't go and study marine biology nor, as you know, did I do any go-going. It was just a phase.'

The café door opened and they watched a group of young people come in and settle round a table.

Felix turned back to Phoebe. 'What about the baby?'

'There is no baby.'

'Choosing to ignore that too?'

'In a way I suppose, but to me it never was a baby. It was potential, nothing more.'

'And now there's no potential?'

'I've had the abortion if that's what you mean?' Her tone cut into his flesh.

Felix looked out of the window and watched someone park their car, trying to breathe away the pain, comprehend everything that was being said.

Phoebe sighed. 'Look Felix, can't you just accept that we look at things a little differently, you and I? I am not this perfect ideal you seem to think I am.'

Felix looked at her. 'You don't understand. I…I have…I…' he couldn't make sense of it anymore. He wanted to tell her what he'd done, to come clean. Yes, clean was a good word for it. He wanted to confess so he could put it all to rest. Start again. None of it made sense anymore. The familiar confusion clouded his brain, making it difficult to find the words he needed. Drugs...that's what he needed. Or vengeance.

Phoebe leaned forward. 'What is it Felix?'

He looked at the concern in his sisters arresting blue eyes. Could he tell her? Could she help him? He felt as if everything was slowing falling away from him. He opened his mouth for the words to form.

'I have…'

She put a hand over his. 'What is it? What do you have?'

'I have…' his voice came out as a whisper. He couldn't find the words to explain what he had done. He tried to put the words in order in his mind, but they were scrambled up again. He could feel the confusion pressing down on him.

'What Felix? What is it?'

It would be such a relief to tell someone, to off-load this secret, to confess. He wanted to ease this pressure that built up in his head.

'I am…confused,' he said finally.

'And?' Phoebe asked, urging him to say more.

He looked at her concerned face and shook his head. The moment had passed and he had regained control. 'I'm fine. Just a little…overwhelmed by it all, that's all.'

'God, you worried me then Felix. You are such a drama queen.' Phoebe sat back, visibly relieved. 'Mind you, to be fair, this must have all come as quite a shock.'

Felix nodded. It had, it was and it made him feel foolish and powerless. There was no feeling he hated more.

'I have a favour to ask,' he said.

'What's that?'

'You know the weekend we spent at mum's?'

Phoebe nodded.

'I took off for a few hours, remember?'

She nodded again.

'If you're ever asked can you say I was with you all weekend?'

'Why?'

'Can you just do this one thing for me?'

'Of course, but why?'

'Can you?'

'Felix, you haven't hurt anyone have you?'

'Just do it? No questions? It's the least you can do after shutting me out like this.'

Phoebe hesitated.

210

He pressed her, 'please.'

Finally she agreed, and Felix relaxed back into his chair. *Now* he was definitely safe.

Paul was in the kitchen when Sam arrived home. 'I'd almost given you up. Where've you been?'

Sam stretched up and kissed his cheek, his evening stubble prickled her lips. 'Got held up,' she said. 'Smells good.'

'Chilli,' he grinned at her, and Sam's body tightened. He was back, and this was going to be hard.

Was she doing another Mark Longstaff she wondered, only this time it wasn't a teeny bopper love affair that would crush her for a week, this was her marriage. This was her husband.

'Be about fifteen minutes, just waiting for the rice.'

'Great. I'll just go up and get changed.'

She dragged her body up the stairs. Her heavy, dense, desperate body filled with a swollen heart.

Sam hung up her maroon Calvin skirt suit, threw the blouse into the laundry basket ,and stood in front of the full length mirror in her underwear. Her figure was all right, not the fashionable waif figure currently in vogue, or the athletic lean look Kate had. Sam's was a softer, more curvaceous body. Paul had always commented favourably on her breasts, bum and thighs. She ran her hand over the slight rounded belly, wondering what it would be like if it were stretched full and round. It was an uncomfortable thought, like carrying an alien inside her, feeding off her, literally. The thought horrified her. No, she couldn't do it. She simply couldn't.

Paul's voice sailed up the stairs and enveloped her in sadness. 'Sam, dinner's in five.'

She turned away from the mirror and slipped into her white Susien Chong cotton trousers and loose shirt combo. This had been her must have this summer and, because of the price tag, she planned on wearing it next year too. She took a few moments to admire the cut of the material and the way it draped from her, before joining Paul downstairs at the dining table.

'Good day?' he asked, helping himself to a large portion of brown rice.

Sam hated brown rice and had told Paul many times. He would nod and smile, but still serve it. She didn't say anything tonight, what was the point? Tiredness sank into her bones, pulling her into the chair, robbing her of her appetite.

'Not hungry?' he asked.

Sam couldn't respond. She needed to distance herself from him before she struck the final blow. She watched him tuck into his meal, forking it down like some industrial mastication machine, great jaws clamping down.

When it came, it came like a great rush, a flood of words that nearly choked her.

'Anne Fletcher rang me today about that promotion.'

Paul stopped the fork in mid-flow. He lowered it to his plate before he spoke. 'And you said?'

But she could see he knew. It was written across his face. In the tense jaw line; in the eyes that had moved from the deep blue of enjoyment to a cool distant grey.

Sam tilted her jaw. 'I said I'd take it.'

'Right,' he said, and nodded, as if he agreed with her.

They sat on opposite sides of the table with the meal cooling between them. They heard their neighbour's door bell and the dog barking in response. The wind was picking up outside. The dog quietened and they sat staring down at their dinner plates.

Finally Paul spoke. 'This is serious,' he said.

'Yes.' Sam focused on the pattern round the rim of her dinner plate. Forest green leaf and gold, a wedding present. They had chosen the design themselves. Young, excited about the wedding, in love. It was this or a navy geometric pattern. Sam had preferred the latter because it was more modern, but Paul thought it would date quickly. She had conceded, not really caring that much.

Was her disinterest in crockery a warning sign, there from the start if they had just stopped a moment to look? Like looking back after a bad accident and remembering that you did see a sign, only you were going too fast to let it register?

'Does this mean...what does this mean?' he asked, his voice cracking.

Sam had expected coldness, or fury, or both, but not this, not this stillness, this charged emotion.

'It means I'm getting promoted,' she tried to sound light.

It was a mistake. Paul banged his fist on the table making Sam and the plates jump.

'Don't play games with me, Sam.'

She looked at him. 'I'm not, it really doesn't have to mean anything else.'

'But it does, we both know it does. Everything we talked about, our plans-'

'No Paul, no. Everything *you* talked about, *your* plans. You didn't fall in love with me because I washed up, kept house and wanted babies, did you?'

'Of course not.'

'So why did you fall in love with me? What was it about me?'

'What has this got-'

'Everything, please, answer the question.'

'You. Who you are.'

'But this *is* me Paul, this is who I am, and this is what I want.'

She watched him rest his head in his hands, his elbows on the table, and she wished everything could be different.

'What has this all been about?' he asked, in a quiet voice.

Sam thought for a moment before answering. 'Love?'

Paul raised his head and looked at her. 'But that's where love takes you... to a family. It's a natural progression.'

'Not necessarily. Some couples never have a family.'

'But that's what I want. It's what I need, I need it all, wife, children, a dog, a family, everything.'

Sam was surprised by the tears that blurred her vision, she wasn't one for crying. 'Then I'm not the one Paul and,' she paused to swallow. 'And I think we've both known it for a while now.'

He nodded and looked at her; the pain in his eyes pierced her body and left her gasping. She imagined butterflies had the same experience in the hands of a lepidopterist.

'Then that's it,' he said quietly.

'I guess it is.'

He took a deep breath and let it out slowly. 'I'll move out.'

'No,' Sam said quickly, 'I will. I need to. Just give me the weekend to sort something out. This is my doing, if I'd been more honest, if I'd...' she stopped, unsure of what else to say. 'Besides, this house has always been more yours than mine.'

'I'll get it valued. I'll buy your share.'

'Fine. That would be…useful.'

Paul reached over and took her hand. She laid her free hand over his. As dusk fell, and the day ended, they sat together, until the dark took over.

Chapter Thirty

'Ever thought about using that talent?' Josh asked Kate the following day. He had called in to check up on her, and had prepared the scrambled eggs they were now eating at the kitchen table.

'Talent? I've never thought of it like that before.'

'Maybe you should.'

'And do what exactly? Get a job in a circus? Besides, after the fiasco with Lucy, I'm not sure I could go through this sort of thing again.'

A few moments passed before Josh asked the question they were both thinking. 'Have you decided what you're going to do?'

After crying in Josh's arms the previous day, Kate had confided her suspicions to him about Felix.

'As I said, I'm not sure I could go through all that again.'

'Can you afford not to?'

Kate stared out of the window in abject misery, the remainder of her eggs growing cold on the plate in front of her.

'Kate, what if you're right this time?'

She rounded on Josh. 'And what if I'm wrong, *again*. I couldn't stand it.'

'This isn't about your pride.'

'No, you're right, it's about accusing an innocent man. Can you imagine the harm I could have done to Ray?'

Josh nodded. 'You're right, I'm sorry. I didn't think.'

'Well, I have. I've done nothing but think. I am so confused with thinking Josh, I don't know what to believe, and what not to believe. I don't know the truth of anything anymore.'

Josh shrugged. 'Who does?'

'It's funny, I met a woman briefly in Barcelona who said a similar thing.'

'Oh?'

Kate nodded. 'She said she believed it was all an illusion, so we might as well make up the truth the way we want it.'

'She has a point.'

'Yes, but not if a man's reputation is at stake.'

'True. So what *are* you going to do?'

'I don't know yet. I really don't know.'
'There is one thing you could do.'
'What's that?'
'Get more information.'
'How?'
'Listen. Use the voices.'
Kate shuddered. 'I'll think about it.'

Chapter Thirty-One

'You okay?' Kate asked, putting coffee in front of Sam the following morning. Sam had rung Kate the night before to ask if she could stay, and had arrived that evening. They had shared a bottle of wine and talked long into the night.

'Yes, and there's nothing more to say. We have finally faced the fact that we want different things in life. Marriage over.'

'But you still love each other, isn't there a compromise?'

'Not about this. Paul wants children, I don't.'

The toaster popped and Kate left the table.

'Toast?'

'No, thanks.'

'Won't you change your mind?' Kate asked, as she buttered the toast.

'Who knows? Maybe, but what if I don't? It wouldn't be fair on either of us. The pressure on me, the waiting for him…'

Kate returned to the table with her plate and sat down. 'But what if, in a couple of years you change your mind?' Kate bit into her toast.

'I might and I might not. Paul and I have been living like this for the past five years. It's too stressful for us, and neither of us is prepared to put up with the stress any longer. It's better this way.'

'And you're sure?'

Sam nodded. Kate saw the dark circles under her friend's eyes, her unhappiness evident. She was tempted to probe, but thought better of it. Besides, it was all there in front of her to see, why look any deeper?

'You're putting on a brave face,' she challenged.

Sam glared at her. 'Course I fricking am, what d'you expect? What's the use of curling up in a ball in the corner?'

Kate raised her arms. 'I surrender,' she said.

Sam slumped at the table. 'Sorry.'

'Understandable. You're forgiven.'

Sam glanced at her watch. 'I should go, don't want to be late.'

'Congratulations, on the new job.   Is that appropriate under the circumstances?'

'Yes,' Sam smiled as she stood up. 'And thanks for the bed.'

'No problem,' said Kate. 'I'll see you later.'

After a brief call to Bruce to clarify priorities, Kate worked steadily through the transcripts on her desk, taking regular coffee breaks. She was aware she still wasn't in full health, and refused to compromise herself as she had in the past. At the end of the day, when she packed up, she was on target, and without the usual punishment to her physical body. Unfortunately, the contentment she usually gleamed from her work was disturbed by Sam's disrupted personal life.

Kate sat on the sofa with a glass of wine, mulling over Sam's predicament, wondering how she might help. If the whispers were portends of the future, Kate thought, they would be so much more useful. Simply being able to hear someone's thoughts, even their unconscious ones, was no use at all.

Josh's suggestion yesterday morning over their late breakfast to, 'listen in', also niggled at her. She still hadn't done it. What was she so afraid of? Being right...or being wrong? The idea that Felix could really do what she felt he had done was...well, unbelievable. And yet, it was so clear. So clear it had terrified her at the time. But, hadn't she been as equally convinced of Ray's guilt, more so?

Later, as Kate began washing up the breakfast pots before starting the evening meal, she heard the outer door. She knew it wasn't Sam; she was going to call home for a few clothes and personal effects, and wouldn't be back for at least another hour. If it wasn't Sam downstairs, it must be Felix.

Thinking about him gave Kate a basket of worms for a stomach. If she didn't resolve this one way or another, there was a chance that she might go quietly mad. Besides, until she had resolved the issue of Lucy, she didn't feel she could move on in her own life, and there were things that needed settling there.

Kate left the washing up and, as she dried her hands, decided she could put this off no longer. It had to be faced, *he* had to be faced. Moments later she was knocking on his door.

When Felix opened it they stood looking at each other for a long half minute.

'Hi,' Kate said, eventually. 'Can I some in? We need to talk.'

'Um, not here,' he said. 'Your place. Give me five minutes,' and with that, without waiting for a reply, he closed the door.

As she made her way back upstairs she struggled to make sense of what had just happened. He had never kept her on the doorstep like that, much less closed the door in her face. She entered her lounge at a loss, an inexplicable fear gripping her insides.

When the knock on her door finally came, she considered not answering it, but that was foolish, he knew she was here. The thought sent a shiver through her. He knew she was here.

Sam was on the phone to Mrs. Hyde-Stephenson's daughter discussing an appointment for her to come and look at the new autumn range, when Anne Fletcher entered her office.

Sam finished the call, made a note in the large store diary, and then focused her full attention on the woman sitting on the opposite side of the desk.

'You look tired Sam, are you all right?'

Sam nodded. 'I'm fine thanks.' She felt Anne's eyes running over her. 'Another booking to view the new lines,' she indicated the diary. 'It's happening regularly now, private viewings. Time consuming but worthwhile, they tend to spend, on average, at least forty per cent more than if they just came in to browse. Of course, it may mean we'll have to recruit more staff if that side of the business continues to grow.'

Anne nodded but said nothing.

'What can I do for you?' Sam said, finally.

'Is there something you're not telling me Sam?'

'About what?'

'About the MD job.'

'Like what?'

'Who knows, but you look terrible, not what I'd expect from someone who's just been so spectacularly promoted.'

Sam wasn't sure if it was the shock of Anne's concern, the heavy heart or the poor night's sleep, but she couldn't help slumping into the office chair.

'Thought so,' said Anne. 'What is it?'

'It's...personal,' Sam said.

'Not when you come into work looking like that it isn't.'

Sam took a deep breath and faltering, attempted to explain the complexity that was, or rather was not, her marriage.

Anne raised an eyebrow. 'You must really want this job,' she said.

'I suppose I do,' Sam said.

'And yet, correct me if I'm wrong, you were all itching to leave a few weeks ago.'

Sam's head snapped up to look at Anne.

Anne smiled. 'Sam, I've been running my own business for nearly forty years. You learn to read people.'

'I just needed a new challenge,' Sam mumbled, embarrassed at being found out.

'Don't you think I know that? Would I have offered you the job if I thought you'd just up and leave?'

'Suppose not.'

'Still, it needs some thinking about.'

'What?'

'Your decision,' Anne stopped for a moment to think. 'You were going to leave a few weeks back, and now you're ready to chuck in your marriage to stay?'

'But it's not the same job.'

'No, but have you thought how you might feel in three year's time?'

'No-one knows how they'll feel in the future.'

'We can make a good guess if we know ourselves well enough, and I guess, from what I know of you, that you'll be as bored of this new job as you are of the one you have now.'

'If you think that why offer me the job?'

'Because you're good, because I want someone now, and three years is a long time. You can get someone else trained up to take over when you've had enough. Let's just say it suits me,' she stopped and leaned forward. 'But does it suit you?'

Sam sat very still, unable to respond. Anne was right; she probably would get fed up in a few years time, and then what?

'I only ever had two children, but I never got bored of being a mother. It seemed that just when I thought I had a handle on it, they'd up and grow and give me some new set of problems and dilemmas. Now some women aren't cut out to be a mother, but I'm not so sure about you Sam.'

'I don't think I am.'

'Well, you need to grow up a bit, be a bit less self-absorbed, but children have a way of making you do that. And you'd never be bored, that's for sure.'

'I don't know.'

'I know, that's my point. Like I said, it needs more consideration,' Anne stood up. 'But what do I know? Come on, we're near closing, let me take you for a drink.'

Sam nodded and collected her bag, Anne's words ringing in her ears.

Felix and Kate sat in her lounge. The air was thick with electricity, the way it was before a thunderstorm. Kate pulled air in, but her body didn't seem to be able to get the oxygen it needed.

'Still awkward eh?' said Felix, with a laugh.

Kate decided to play along with his misunderstanding of the situation. 'That's why I knocked,' she said.

'It's difficult to put everything back the way it was,' he said.

Kate nodded, and unsure of what to say, waited for him to continue.

'But you'll see, in time we'll forget about it, as we both move on.'

'There's something else,' she said.

'Oh?'

It pained her to see the gleam of hope in his eyes. 'It's about Lucy,' she added quickly.

His body tensed. 'What about her?'

'I…I…thought…' she stopped, unable to continue, unable to tell him of her suspicions. What use would it be anyway? No, she had to probe; there was no other way to do this.

She relaxed and moved her attention out towards him. His agitation was palpable and what she heard horrified her. She froze as she listened.

'Oh god…what does she know? Can she tell? Maybe she saw my car? I never thought about that, but no, she'd have said something before now. She'd have told the police. I just need to stay calm, breathe, don't let anything slip out. No one knows, no one knows…'

Abruptly she slammed out of his mind and back into hers. Tears welled.

'Kate, what is it?' he asked.

She shook her head causing the tears to fall. She thought frantically about what to say next, realising she could be in danger. 'I thought she'd be found alive,' she said eventually. His answer chilled her bones and confirmed her suspicions.

'There was no hope of that.'

When Sam got back that night Kate was packing a transcript for Toby the courier to collect the following morning. Sam stood in the doorway to the living room, watching Kate meticulously write out the address label. It reminded her of Paul's attention to detail.

Whenever Sam sent anything she just took a large marker pen and scrawled the address in big black letters across the envelope, but Paul would line up the address and print it out in capital letters, ensuring it was centralised with some magical internal measuring device he possessed. She supposed that's what made him a good architect, that internal measuring device. She felt a pang of loneliness and Anne Fletcher's words came back to her. Was she making a mistake? Was she cut out to be a mother after all? It might be just what she needed. And she missed Paul terribly.

'I'm thinking of going back to Paul,' she said.

Kate's head jerked up. 'What?'

'I'm thinking of going back to Paul.'

Kate left what she was doing and came to stand by her friend. Sam saw a familiar expression on her friend's face, and knew that in a few short moments Kate would fully understand, without the need for any further explanation. It was one of the things Sam loved about Kate. Few people understood her, and she often felt she could spend her life explaining her actions, if she cared enough, but never with Kate.

After a few moments the haze cleared from Kate's face, she nodded and headed down the hall to the kitchen. 'I'm putting the kettle on, want one?'

Sam followed, dropping her bag and coat over the bannister. When she entered the kitchen, Kate was washing up mugs in a sink full of this morning's dishes.

'Haven't done the washing up today. Didn't get round to it,' Kate said, in a flat voice.

Sam was too caught up in wanting to talk about her indecision to recognise the anomaly in Kate's behaviour.

'So I was talking to Mrs. F, Anne, today, and she pointed out that I'd get bored in a few years and then what? And I really miss him Kate.'

'I know,' she turned and smiled, drying a mug with a tea towel.

'He hasn't pressured me, you know?'

Kate nodded. 'I know.'

'How do you do that?'

'What?' Kate had her back to Sam, getting the coffee out of the cupboard.

'You're so sure of stuff. You just seem to know everything.'

Kate turned and looked at Sam. 'Are you kidding? Have you any idea of the mess I've been in the past few weeks? The confusion? Has it ever occurred to you to wonder why I drive myself so hard, why I cut myself off from life, why I have to hibernate from time to time?'

'Sometimes.' It was then that Sam noticed the dark circles under her friend's eyes.

Kate turned back and spooned coffee into the mugs. 'Felix came round.'

'And?'

'And what?'

'And…why are you telling me this?'

Kate finished making the coffee, put a mug in front of Sam and sat at the table with her.

'Do you really want to know?'

Anne Fletcher's words about her self-absorption came back to her now, and for the first time in their friendship, Sam was worried and wanted to hear what Kate had to say.

'I'm listening.'

So Kate began. She told Sam everything. About her childhood; her mother and father; about the voices and whispers; the chiropractor adjustment; the visions; Lucy; Ray; her feelings for Josh. It all came pouring out.

Sam sat in stunned silence, listening, soaking up the story, the words binding them into a deeper friendship than either had ever experienced. As Kate found her voice, Sam discovered the joy of being a true friend.

Finally, Kate told Sam about Felix.

'Are you sure?'

'I wasn't until today.'

'And this isn't another…Ray thing.'

Kate shook her head. 'I thought the same thing, which is why I went to see him today.'

'What are you going to do about it?'

'Well, apologise to Ray for a start!'

'But what about Felix?'

Kate shrugged. 'I don't know what to do. What can I do?'

'Tell the police.'

'I don't have any evidence, and after the fiasco with Ray, I don't think they'd consider me a credible witness.'

'Tell them what you just told me.'

'I think they'll lock me up.'

'And you think he has a key to your place?'

'I'm not sure, but I suspect so.'

'Then it isn't safe here.'

'I thought that earlier today, but I've had time to absorb it all. *If* he has one, I can just drop the latch.'

'Even if there's a chance he can get in, you can't stay here.'

'I don't think he'd hurt me. From what I could gather, he usually hurts small things, animals, that sort of thing.'

'But Kate, he killed Lucy, and was she the first?'

'I don't know. When I found out the truth today I was so shocked I just slammed back into my body.'

'Then we have to find out more, gather some evidence, find something that we can take to the police.'

The two women sat still as stone, as the horror of their predicament sank in.

Chapter Thirty-Two

Phoebe thought the service had been too impersonal, but Felix considered it acceptably poignant all things considered. They stood in small miserable circles, conversation low and respectful, in a grimy pub in the centre of town. The carpet was worn and sticky, the ceiling browned from cigarette smoke before the ban, the air thick with the smell of the culmination of stale beer.

Felix wondered what had possessed Phoebe to hold the reception in such a dive, but resisted commenting, realising he had offered her little support in organising it.

The turnout was poor. Their mother's social life had narrowed considerably since their father's death, and consequently, so had her social circle. There were a couple of neighbours that they hadn't met before, and a couple of their mother's old friends, who neither recognised at first, but vaguely remembered once prompted. All in all it was a dire affair, and Felix couldn't wait for it to be over.

Phoebe came and stood with Felix. 'How you feeling?'

'You know,' he shrugged.

'No, I don't, that's why I'm asking.'

'Weird. It's all happened so fast, I can't really take it in to be honest. It's not just mum's death either.'

Phoebe had the grace to look abashed. 'Sorry,' she muttered.

Felix sighed. 'No, it's not your fault. I can see you had no choice. I just wish I'd known that's all.'

Phoebe nodded. 'Can I ask you a question?'

'What?'

'You know you asked me to do you that favour?'

Felix nodded, wondering where she was going with it.

'Does it have anything to do with that missing girl?'

Shit, he thought, and hoped his face didn't betray him. 'Why do you ask?'

'I'm not sure, I suppose I just think it's an odd thing to ask me to do.'

Felix looked around the dingy room to see if anyone was listening, then turned back to Phoebe. 'Yes it is,' he said, in a lowered voice.

'But why lie? Felix you haven't…?'

'No! The girl lives in our street, when they questioned me I didn't think anything of it, just told them I was at my mum's,' he paused before he continued. 'I forgot about the run out until later, but by then it was too late. I was worried if I changed my story it would look bad, especially with my history.'

Phoebe nodded.

'Do you see where I'm coming from?'

'Yes, but...' she stopped, and Felix held his breath waiting for her to say something.

'What?' he said eventually.

Phoebe shook her head. 'Nothing.'

'It isn't the same Phoebe, honest. I know I hurt mum, and badly, but this isn't the same thing at all. This is about kidnapping and murdering a small child. Do you think I'm capable of that?'

'No, no of course not.'

'Besides, I have support now, Dr. Carmichael, a treatment programme. So will you help me? Please?'

'Of course I will.'

The neighbours approached to say their goodbyes, and soon after the old friends did likewise. They sat at one of the tables, alone in the room.

'God, that was grim,' Phoebe said.

'Indeed.'

'Janet suggested this place. Apparently she and mum used to come here all the time when they were young. It's on a bus route.'

Felix nodded. 'Right.'

'Dreadful isn't it?'

'Now you ask, I'd say it's not one of your finest decisions. Speaking of which, where's David?'

'Don't start. He's looking after the boys. I didn't want to bring them.'

'Couldn't the au pair do it?'

She raised an eyebrow. 'We haven't found a replacement yet.'

'All too young and beautiful eh?'

'Don't Felix, not today.'

'Sorry.'

They sat some time before Phoebe spoke. 'This missing girl...'

Felix sighed, 'what about her?'

'Did you know her?'

Felix shook his head. 'Not really.'

'Dreadful business.'

'Yes.'

'I'm not sure what I would do if the boys…' tears filled Phoebe's eyes.

Felix put his hand over hers. 'Don't torture yourself like that,' he said.

'No, you're right, it's probably just the emotions of the day, you know? Still, dreadful dreadful business.'

'Yes.'

'I hope they catch whoever's responsible.'

'We all want that,' Felix said, squeezing her hand.

'What would convince the police that Felix did it?' asked Sam.

'I don't know,' Kate hugged the cushion tighter to her.

The two women were sat in Kate's living room. Sam was walking back and forth.

She stopped. 'Could we give them an anonymous tip off? You know, just call them?' suggested Sam.

'What would we say?'

'That Felix did it of course.'

'No, that won't work, they'll just think it's a crank call. They probably get loads of that sort of thing.'

'But they'd have to check it out. They'll be some procedure won't there?' Sam insisted, sitting on the sofa next to Kate.

'I don't know,' Kate sounded miserable. 'And even if they do, all they'll probably do is question him, and they've done that before.'

They sat in contemplation.

Sam started. 'I know. Can't you get into his head? You know, find out something only the killer would know? That way when we made the call, they'd know we knew what we were talking about.'

Kate shuddered at the thought. 'What sort of thing would convince them?'

'It would have to be something that wasn't in the papers. We know where she was found, and how she died, so it would have to be something else.'

'This is madness,' she said to Sam.

Sam nodded in agreement. 'I know, but we have to do something.'

'I just wish I hadn't got it so wrong in the first place.'

Sam placed her hand on Kate's arm, 'it wasn't your fault you know?'

'I know I just, god what a mess, and the thought of going back in there, into his head...' Kate rubbed her eyes hard.

'I have an idea,' Sam said.

'Another one?' asked Kate looking at her friend. 'You're just bursting with them today.'

Sam smiled. 'Why don't we take Felix to the pub? I'll chat to him and distract him, while you probe him with your magic powers.'

'I'm not sure I want to be anywhere near him to be honest, let alone in his head again. There has to be another way.'

They slumped into silence again, frantically trying to think of a solution that didn't result in Kate having to go into Felix's mind. When the landline rang it made both women jump. Kate ran to answer it, her nerves jangling.

'Hi, was just wondering how you're doing?' It was Josh.

Kate couldn't stop herself from smiling, despite everything. 'I'm fine, Sam's here. We're trying to find a solution to our problem,' she put her hand over the phone and mouthed 'it's Josh.'

It took Sam a moment to realise who she was referring to, and then felt her face flush at the memory of their lunch. She would have to apologise to the man, especially if he and Kate were going to be an item in the future, which looked very likely from the ridiculous grin on her face.

'The Felix conundrum?' Josh asked.

'Yes.'

'I've been thinking about it, and I think I might have a solution, but you have to promise me you'll be careful.'

'Oh?' she spun round to Sam. 'Josh thinks he has a solution,' she turned back to the phone. 'Okay what is it?'

When Felix returned home he felt restless. His mother's death, Phoebe's revelation about his father, and the funeral all seemed to be some sort of dream. He couldn't hold onto anything. Nothing felt real anymore.

He thought of going to see Kate, and then remembered their tryst and decided against it. It infuriated him that there was this rift between them. She was so god damn stupid!

Agitated he prowled round the flat, looking for something to ease his restlessness. After putting some laundry on and cleaning the fridge, he finally sat down with his box. Inside were trinkets he had collected over the years, and although he didn't take it out often, pouring through them always calmed him.

Now, as he picked up one item after another, remembering how he had come by it, he found his breathing deepen and his body relax. Most were trips he'd taken or reminders of happy times. He picked up his father's watch. He hadn't had an opportunity to process all the things he had learnt recently. It all still fizzed and popped in his brain. He returned the watch and took out Lucy's silver bracelet.

It had been an accident. He'd just wanted to take care of her, but she screamed, made a lot of fuss. He only meant to keep her quiet, not kill her.

I'm not a bad man, he decided, I just do bad things from time to time.

Sam had gone to work and Kate was left alone. After her conversation with Josh she had discussed it with Sam, and both women agreed it was the best solution.

Now it was up to Kate and she felt nervous. It was all resting on her. What if the whispers, the voices, let her down now of all times? What if she couldn't hear anything? What if she could hear, but it wasn't helpful? The doubt, confusion and worry clouded her mind, until eventually she couldn't sit still any longer.

She sprang up off the sofa and decided she needed to get some fresh air, go for a walk to calm down before she attempted this. And then she wondered if she was merely procrastinating.

Cross for second guessing her every move, Kate grabbed her coat, pulled on her trainers and set in the direction of the corner shop, remembering as she did, the day she watched Lucy walk down the street eating a lolly pop.

So much had happened since then, and Kate was now on the cusp of a new life. Josh and Sam had been taken into her confidence, and both had accepted her. It felt good to share this with them, she was no longer alone.

She continued passed the corner shop, not sure where she was going, just needing to walk until her body relaxed.

The revelation about her parents had helped too. Despite her denial, she now realised that there was always a feeling that a small piece of her was missing. That feeling wasn't there anymore, although she recognised there was some unfinished business with her father. Still, that would have to wait until after she had resolved the problem she had in front of her.

Finally, as she turned home an hour later, she thought about Josh and her feelings towards him. She liked him, a lot. And she thought he might feel the same way. Could this be the start of something important in her life? Again, it would have to wait.

It would all have to wait, she thought, as she let herself back into the flat, until she had put an end to all this business, until she had ensured that the killer of Lucy was brought to justice.

After removing her shoes and coat, she settled on the sofa to begin. More confident and relaxed than she had felt earlier that day.

That evening Kate had to let Sam into the flat.

'My key wouldn't work,' Sam told her, as they climbed the stairs.

'I know, I changed the locks.'

'You did what?'

When Sam heard the full story she nodded her head in agreement. 'Good decision,' she said.

Kate nodded. 'Sam?'

'Yeah?'

'I'm scared.'

'Me too.'

Chapter Thirty-Three

'Are you sure it's absolutely necessary?'

Kate nodded. 'I need to be certain before alerting the police. I can't be wrong again.'

'But you said you were sure.'

'I am...I am, but I just need to double check. After Ray I just-'

Sam lay a hand on Kate's arm. 'I understand. I'm just concerned it might be dangerous.'

'No, I'll wait until Felix has left for work. He might come back at lunchtime, but not before then. It'll be perfectly safe,' she hoped she sounded more confident than she felt.

'And how are you going to get in?'

'I've got his spare key from watering his plants last year.'

'Okay, if you're sure. Call me when you're done, just so I know you're okay.'

'Will do.'

After Sam left for work Kate listened for the front door, and then from her front room window she watched Felix get into his VW and drive off.

She left it for a full ten minutes, just in case he returned for anything, and then, with a thumping heart, she made her way downstairs, his spare key in her hand.

It wasn't until Felix arrived at his desk at work that he realised he'd left his phone at home. He could see it now, on the kitchen top by the kettle, he'd been checking his emails while waiting for it to boil and forgotten to put the phone back in his pocket.

He flopped into his chair and leaned his head in his hands in exasperation. Life felt as it were closing in on him, and he was surprised that the extent of the repercussions of his current state of mind wasn't more severe that just leaving his phone behind. Still, it was frustrating.

'You okay?' asked John, coming into the office with a mug of coffee. 'I'd have made one but you weren't in when I went down.'

Felix looked up at his colleague and shook his head. 'Don't want one just yet.'

'You look like you have the world on your shoulders. You alright mate?'

'Yeah, left my phone at home.'

'That's a bugger.'

'Tell me about it.'

'Why don't you nip back and get it? I'll cover for you.'

Since his mother's death he had noticed how much more amiable his work colleagues had been. 'Nah, it'll wait till lunchtime.'

'Well, I'm in all morning if you change you're mind. All it'll cost you is a pint on Friday.'

Felix laughed. 'Thanks, I'll bear that in mind.'

Kate slipped the key into the lock and it turned easily. For some inexplicable reason she hadn't expected it to work. She pushed the door open and stepped into the empty flat.

A faint smell of coffee and toast still lingered in the air, and made Kate even more aware that Felix could come back at any second. She now realised that perhaps she should have developed some excuse for the break-in, just in case he came back unexpectedly. She dismissed the thought, it would be fine, Felix never came home during the day, apart from the odd lunchtime and that was, she glanced at her watch, not for another three hours at least. She'd be long gone by then. Besides, the distinct roar of his VW would give her plenty of warning.

Kate knew what she was looking for, at least, she thought she did, but she wasn't sure where it would be. She tiptoed into the living room and then stopped, why was she tiptoeing? She'd be better off moving round naturally to enable her to get out of there faster.

She considered the most obvious place to look and decided that she'd probably keep it in the bottom of the wardrobe. Decision made she hurried into the bedroom. The bed hadn't been made, which was unusual for Felix, being so fastidious, bordering on OCD in her opinion, and there was an acrid stale body smell in the room, which also surprised her. Dismissing her observations she moved to the wardrobe and searched along the neat rows of shoes. Nothing.

She wondered what size it was, what it looked like, the things she had picked up through her delving of his mind had been unpleasant and revealing, but unfortunately people rarely described something in their mind they were familiar with. Her teeth clenched in frustration. So close and yet...she knew it was in this flat somewhere.

There was only one thing for it, she would have to systematically search the place from top to bottom until she found it. She decided to start with the kitchen cupboards.

Sam sat at her desk waiting for her phone to ring. What was keeping Kate? Had she been caught in the act? Was she now, as Sam sat here drumming her fingers, in danger? Should she do something, call or...something...but what? Still, it hadn't been more than thirty minutes, maybe Kate hadn't been able to put her hands on it straight away. But if her friend was in danger, Sam would never forgive herself for doing nothing. She cursed herself, she should never have let Kate do this, at least, not on her own.

As she wrangled with indecision one of the girls came into the office to tell her the next appointment had arrived, and Sam felt torn. Finally she resolved that if there wasn't a message from Kate by the time she'd finished with her next client, she'd call her. Decision made she hurried out to greet her nine thirty.

An hour later Felix felt as if he'd lost his arm. 'I didn't realise how often I checked my phone,' he told John.

'You changing your mind?'

'Might be.'

'I would, you'll be there and back in fifteen minutes at this time of day, twenty tops.'

'Do you mind?'

'Nah, told you, you can buy us a pint on Friday.'

'You're on,' said Felix standing up. 'Thanks mate. I won't be long.'

After turning out every cupboard and drawer Kate was convinced it wasn't in the kitchen. She had no idea Felix had so much kitchen equipment but then, he did like his gadgets. She had moved into the bathroom, but it didn't take long to conclude there were no hiding places there. She checked the cistern, remembering a scene in a film she had watched once. Nothing.

She moved into the bedroom and stood at the door, unsure where to start. She had checked the wardrobe, but there was also a chest of drawers and of course under the bed, although that seemed a little obvious. Top of the wardrobe was another obvious but possible place.

Then she heard the outside door and froze, her ears pricked for every noise, hoping it was just the postman, but no, that someone had a key, they were letting themselves in. It couldn't be Felix, surely she would have heard his car?

Her heart leapt into her mouth as she frantically looked around for somewhere to hide, hoping that perhaps it was Sam, but needing to hide just to be on the safe side. In desperation she lay down and scurried under the bed, bumping into a large suitcase. Was that where he was keeping it, she wondered, as she shoved the case over to make room. If it stuck out too much on the other side he might notice, but otherwise she wasn't hidden, and there was no where else.

She lay on her back, barely breathing, listening to every sound. Whoever it was, Sam or Felix, they were now outside in the hall, she could hear the jangle of keys.

'Please go upstairs, please go upstairs,' she whispered, and then, with a sick feeling in her stomach, she heard a key being inserted into Felix's front door.

She held her breath as she heard footsteps cross the living room to the kitchen. He didn't know she was here, all she had to do was lie quietly and wait, clearly he had left something behind. It was then that the small black box caught her eye, tucked between the slats of the bed and the mattress. Of course, an ideal place to hide something. It seemed obvious now.

She turned her attention to Felix. He'd be gone in a few minutes, the logical side of her brain reasoned, the other side was sending the blood around her body so fast it was sending her into a blind panic. She felt sick, her head was swimming, and her heart beat so fast she was sure it was being broadcast though the floor.

Then she remembered the mobile in her pocket. She hadn't switched it off. She decided sod's law it would go off now, so moving slowly and carefully, she reached in her pocket to put it on silent.

Sam returned to the office to check the answer machine on her desk. Nothing. She picked up her mobile and checked that too, nothing again. No call, no text, nothing. She chewed her lip, Kate was taking too long for this to be good news.

She scrolled down her contacts, selected Kate's mobile number and pushed call.

Kate pulled her phone from her pocket and as her finger was poised over the silent button it rang, making Kate jump so high she banged her head on the bed frame. She quickly pressed any button to stop it, cursing herself for her stupidity. It had only rung once, and Kate held her breath, hoping against all the odds, that Felix had not heard, listening to see if he was approaching the bedroom.

Moments later she heard his quickened footsteps heading her way. Of course he'd heard it, he'd have to be deaf not to. There was nothing she could do and no where she could go. Her mouth dried up; unable to think with a head full of cotton wool panic. If she was found here, under the bed, there was nothing she would be able to say that could save her.

Sam stared down at her phone confused. It had rang once and then gone straight onto answer machine, as if Kate didn't want to take the call, which was odd. Her finger hovered over the call button again, but something stopped her. Something wasn't right, so Sam called Josh's office.

She was informed he was with a patient, but would be available in the next fifteen minutes. She left a message for him to call her urgently, along with her mobile number, and then sat back in her chair contemplating her next move.

She glanced at her watch. It was gone eleven now, which meant that Kate had been in Felix's flat for over an hour and a half. She may not have found anything, but that didn't stop her answering her phone, and if she'd pressed the wrong button and cut Sam off by accident, she would have called back by now.

Perhaps she was being overly cautious, but Sam decided that while she was waiting for Josh's call, she would return to the flat, just to reassure herself.

She would phone Josh again on the way, leave a second message with more details this time, so someone somewhere knew what the two women were up to. Just in case. Just in case what, she wondered, with fear gnawing at her stomach.

She could see Felix's brown shoes beside the bed. He didn't know she was under there, yet. Kate held her breath, her heart pounding in her ears, her stomach tight with tension. What could she do?

Moving as slowly as she could she switched the phone to silent and then quickly typed the following text to Sam:

'Hiding under bed, Felix here, don't call, get help x'

She pressed send and then let her head rest on the floor to wait for help to arrive, praying it would get there in time.

Sam got off the phone to Josh's receptionist as she pulled into Kate's street. It was busy but she eventually found a parking space and, as she picked up her phone she saw the text from Kate.

'Shit!'

She called the police immediately, trying to explain the gravity of the situation and utterly failing. Eventually she resorted to a lie, 'there's a man attacking a woman next door. She's screaming, please send someone quickly.'

Sam looked down the quiet road as she spoke, needs must, she thought.

Once off the phone she climbed out of the car, walked quickly to the flat and let herself into the building. Standing in the hallway she was unsure what to do next. She couldn't hear anything, but couldn't decide if that was good or bad. Perhaps Felix hadn't found Kate...or perhaps he had.

Felix walked around the bed to the other side and paused by the window. She could tell he was looking out because his shoes were pointing away from her towards the window. She noticed one of the heels needed replacing. Would he see the suitcase sticking out?

She wondered what was going through his mind and then, realising what she just thought, nearly laughed out loud. If she could just relax she'd be able to find out.

Kate took a deep breath through her mouth and released it quietly, trying to release some of the tension in her body. Meanwhile, she sent out the tendrils to see if, by any chance, she was able to reach into Felix's mind.

Moments later Felix moved and made Kate's nerves skip. Any chance she had of accessing his thoughts gone, she was too tense, it was hopeless.

All she could do, was pray.

Sam stood fixed to the floor in the hallway, indecision rooting her. What was stopping her banging on the door? What was stopping her charging in to save her friend? But she knew the answer, and the shame of it made her want to scurry back to the boutique like the rat that she was.

Instead, she stood paralysed, her limbs powerless to move, unable to push herself forward to bang on the door and save her friend, incapable of retreating. The truth of who she was screamed in her face, she was too afraid for her own safety, and all she could do was stand in the hall and hope her friend was safe beyond the door.

Rather than remain in shame any longer, Sam finally turned and went to wait for the police in the car, horrified by her inaction, unable to do anything to absolve her unforgivable cowardice, and too shocked to cry.

Perhaps he hadn't heard the phone, Kate thought as she watched Felix walk back round the bed to the door. Was he leaving? Her body stilled in hope. Then he stopped, his feet pointing towards her.

She lay and waited, her breath held, her blood banging so hard through her body she thought she might explode. Suddenly his face appeared inches from hers, so distorted it no longer looked like Felix.

Had Kate any breath in her body she would have screamed, but instead her body let out a quiet hiss and leapt involuntarily, banging her head again on the frame above her.

Felix reached out and grabbed at her, she tried to scuttle out of his reach, but the suitcase impeded her exit. He leaned in further, desperately trying to get a hold of her.

From somewhere inside, she found the voice to scream.

Sam heard the scream as she was walking back to the car, and she knew she had to do something. Shaking, she turned round and stood for a moment, unsure. Then, before she knew what she was doing, she ran to a neighbour's house and started banging on the door.

An ill kept man opened the door and a stale essence wafted from him that made Sam take a step back.

Undeterred she started to speak. 'I'm sorry,' she said, 'but I need help. My friend, Kate, needs help. Please.'

The man blinked at her, and she wasn't sure for a moment if he'd understood. He looked half-witted, and Sam turned to the street wondering what she could do next to help her friend.

'Kate?' the man said.

Sam spun round. 'Yes, yes my friend Kate. She's hiding and Felix is there and I think he might hurt her.'

'Felix?' he said, and Sam was worried again that he was, after all, a simpleton.

Then he hurried towards Kate's place and Sam followed him.

'Do you have a key?' he asked.

Sam handed him her key and he opened the door into the hallway. 'Where is she?'

'In there,' Sam said, indicating the door to Felix's flat.

Ray thumped on the door and Sam noticed for the first time his physical size and colossal hands. There was no reply.

Ray turned to her. 'You sure someone's in there?' he asked.

'Yes,' she said. 'I got a text.' She said this as if it explained everything.

He didn't ask her to elaborate, instead he banged on the door again, pounding harder this time.

Kate and Felix froze when they heard the noise. Felix had his arm outstretched under the bed, still trying to get a purchase on Kate. Kate was millimetres from his reach, but knew it was only a matter of time before he got his hands on her, and then what?

The noise was a relief. 'I'm in here,' she said loudly, but she knew it wasn't loud enough.

Felix glared at her. 'It's over Felix,' she said.

He didn't say anything, just swiped at her again.

The banging occurred again. 'Let them in,' she said. 'Hand yourself in.' As she was speaking she pushed the suitcase away from her to give her more room.

Felix's face was fearfully distorted, and Kate knew that when, no if, he got hold of her, he would do her some damage. The thought froze the blood in her body.

'Open up!' said a voice from the hall way and Kate knew immediately, ironically, who her rescuer was.

'Felix it's over,' she said again, her words full of blocked tears.

Felix scrambled to the other side of the bed and Kate, spotting her chance, scuttled out from under the bed, and dived for the bedroom door, shouting.

She heard Felix's footsteps behind her, and hoped she could reach the front door before he reached her.

Sam and Ray heard the shouting, which made Ray pummel the front door so hard Sam thought it would break beneath his bare hands.

'Haven't you got a key?' he asked, he sounded out of breath.

'Why would I?' she answered.

She knew it was ridiculous that she should have an attitude with the man who was trying to assist her, but she couldn't help herself.

'Can't you break down the door?' she asked, thinking it shouldn't be difficult, given his size.

'I'll give it a try, doesn't look too sturdy.'

With that Ray stepped back and slammed his gigantic frame into the door. The shouting continued from the other side.

At least she's alive, Sam thought. Then it went quiet.

Kate felt Felix beside her moments before he pushed her. She hit the floor hard and all the air left her body. He was on her instantly, turning her over on her back and pinning her arms to the floor as he sat astride her.

'What are you doing here?' he hissed.

Kate, winded by the fall, was unable to respond. Felix, frustrated, shook her hard, banging her head off the floor.

'I said, what are you doing here?'

There was another slam against the door. Finally, knowing her only hope was to keep him talking, Kate found her voice. 'Looking for something,' she rasped the words out.

'What?' he was out of breath now with the effort.

'Your...' she wasn't sure what to call it. 'Your...trophies box?' she said.

'My what?'

'Trophies box.'

'Trophies box?'

'Yes,' another slam against the door.

Felix looked puzzled.

'The things you took from the girls you...' she couldn't finish the sentence.

Realisation dawned on Felix's face. 'How did you know?'

Ray crashed against the door again. How much longer could the door hold out? How much longer could she hold out?

'I...I...' she wasn't sure where to start, how to explain. 'It's difficult to explain,' she said, eventually.

Felix sat back, releasing his grip on her. Kate knew it was an opportunity to lash out, fight back, but she was too afraid. She couldn't move.

Felix stood up as the door started to splinter. Kate was transfixed.

Ray crashed against the door again and again. After four attempts it began to make a cracking sound, but Sam couldn't hear any sounds coming from the flat now.

'Keep going,' Sam instructed.

After another two body slams the door flew open.

'Stay here,' Ray said, and Sam was happy to oblige.

Kate sat up, shaking. 'Felix?' she said, unsure what she was going to say.

'I didn't mean to,' he said. The distortion in his face, the anger, the monster he had been moments ago vanished, replaced by a forsaken boy. He sank down, his arms wrapped round his body, and began to weep, words spluttering out between sobs like a bubbling coffee pot. She was unable to understand anything.

'It was...accident...didn't realise...they deserve...trouble...struggle...

Kate sat in a tumult of emotions, as her body involuntarily shook. The gripping fear subsided into an exhausted relief, but anger rose tsunami like. She wanted to lash out at this pitiful blubbering man before her. She took a gulp of air, trying to calm down. If she struck him now, when he was in such a wretched state, she was no better than him. So she watched him confess, on his knees before her, not trusting herself to do anything.

'My mother...father...it was all wrong...I needed to get away. Lucy was, was, Lucy was just there...on the corner...I thought she was lost...I needed some...I was angry. It was boiling in me. We were just talking and then she started getting...silly. She started shouting.' Felix started to cry again.

Kate remembered Lucy in the street when she had tried to talk to her, talk her out of talking to Ray, how frustrating it felt to be misunderstood, but Kate was trying to save her whereas Felix...

'What were you talking to her about?'

He shook his head. 'I can't remember, all sorts of things. Animals I think. Frogs, kittens, puppies. I just needed some...comfort. I wanted a hug. She got scared. I got scared.'

The door splintered some more in the background. If she could just keep him talking for a little longer, they might be able to get in and help her.

241

'What did you do Felix?'

'She shouted and I panicked. Put my hand over her mouth. I pressed on hard. She made me so *angry*. She wanted to get me into trouble. She kicked me. What is it with you women? Why do you always want to get me into trouble, huh? Always. You want to hurt me.' Spittle flew from between his clenched teeth and landed down his chin.

She held up her hand to try and calm him down, her mouth dry, her breath shallow. 'Felix it's okay, I'm your friend, remember?'

'My friend? My *friend*?' He sounded angry.

'That's right. We, we nearly have a...a...thing going. Didn't we?' She wasn't sure if it was the right thing to say. It could either remind him of her rejection of him, or suggest there might be hope.

'But...you said,' he looked confused, but calmer. He was thinking it through. It seemed to be working.

'I didn't say anything. You didn't ask. Remember?'

'But now, with Lucy, with...'

Kate knew he was referring to the other girl he had killed, years ago, when he was younger. The door splintered further, they were so close. What could she do now?

'Felix, you can get help. I can help you get it. Let me, won't you?'

He dropped to his hands and crawled over to her. The fear returned, was he going to attack her again? When he got to her he held out his arms, begging for consolation.

At first she was unsure what to do, seeing him there, on his knees beside her, his arms outstretched, appealing for help. After a few moments she did the only thing she could do under the circumstances. She took him in her arms as he wept.

When the door burst open, this was how Ray found them.

Chapter Thirty-Four

A week later Josh and Kate were sat in her living room.

'I'm done talking about it for now,' Kate said.

'It's good to talk,' Josh insisted.

'I have been talking about it. To you, to Sam, to mum, the police...I'm all talked out.'

'I mean properly.'

'I don't need you to counsel me,' she said.

'I agree. That would be disastrous. I'm too close. But I think you need to talk to someone, at some point, maybe not right now, but in the future.'

'I don't know.' She noticed he said he was 'too close' and she suppressed a smile, not wanting Josh to think she wasn't taking his suggestion seriously. In truth, she did think it was a good idea, she just didn't want to do it at the moment. She really was all talked out.

'Will you at least think about it? For me?'

'Of course.'

'Thank you,' he smiled, and sat back into the sofa. 'Now we have that cleared up, there's something else I wanted to discuss with you.'

'Oh?' she fluttered inside.

'I realise I'm in danger of repeating myself here, but have you thought any more about using this...you don't like it to be called a gift, so...whatever you call it.'

Kate was disappointed but answered, 'curse?'

'You still think like that after what you did?'

Kate shook her head. 'No, I don't.'

'Good. It doesn't have to be police work; there are other things you could do.'

'Like opening a Gypsy Rose Lee booth in Redcar?'

Josh laughed. 'I was thinking more along the lines of counselling.'

'How would that work?'

'Often people need help to overcome problems; addictions, habits, negative self worth, confidence problems, that sort of thing. You could help them.'

'How, by reading their minds?'

'Yes. Don't you see?' Josh sat forward, suddenly animated. 'You'd be able to get past all the rubbish, tap right underneath it all. You could find out what belief is underlying the problem. Then all you'd have to do is use your counselling skills to help them draw it out for themselves. They'd never know you were actually reading their thoughts.'

'I don't have any counselling skills.'

'Then get some.'

She thought for a moment. 'That's what that book is about, the one I found at the indoor market,' she paused before adding. 'Do you really believe all that stuff about beliefs creating our reality?'

'It makes total sense to me.'

'I'm not sure.'

Josh sat back. 'Think about it. You could make a difference to people's lives.'

'You know, it's quite a big step for me? I've spent all my life avoiding this thing, at least, as soon as I was old enough to realise it was weird. Now you're suggesting I launch myself into a career with it!'

'What I'm suggesting Kate, is that instead of running away from who you are, you embrace it.'

'I could do a lot of damage messing with people's heads like that.'

'That's why I'm suggesting you get proper training.'

'Maybe.'

They sat listening to the sounds of the outside world permeate the room. A pushchair clunked by, a dog barked on the other side of the road. They could hear some children at the other end of the road shouting to each other and scuffling after a ball.

'Before I 'embrace it' as you suggest,' Kate said eventually. 'There's something I need to do, something I need to complete. When I'm ready, will you help me?'

'Of course.'

Paul was in the kitchen cooking cannelloni, he turned and jumped, throwing the wooden salt cellar over his shoulder involuntarily.

'For crying out loud woman, you nearly gave me a heart attack.'

'Sorry,' said Sam.

244

Paul retrieved the salt cellar from the floor and threw a couple of crystals over his left shoulder to ward off bad luck. He was a man full on contradictions, Sam thought. Didn't believe in mumbo jumbo and yet he had these silly superstitions.

'What are you doing here?' he asked, not unkindly.

'I needed to pick up a few things. Sorry, realise now I should have called.'

He nodded, but said nothing, turning the cellar in his hands. 'You okay?'

'Not bad.'

He looked at her. 'You look well.'

'Thanks. I've been thinking,' she said.

'Dodgy,' he said, pointing the salt cellar at her and smiling. He turned and ground salt into the sauce then stirred it carefully.

She knew then he was as nervous as her, Paul was never careful in the kitchen, it was another one of those contradictions of his. It gave her the courage to continue.

'I was thinking that I'd probably get bored of this new job after two or three years.'

'Probably,' he said, but she saw his body become rigid with anticipation.

'And then what would I have?' she laughed, a high emission of notes that bounced round the room. The sauce in the pan bubbled and popped gently. 'So I wondered if you could be a little more patient? Give me a couple more years to...grow up?'

Paul turned. 'We've been through this, we said it all. What could have happened in a week that could change any of that?'

Sam smiled. 'You'd be surprised. How about sleeping on Kate's couch?' she saw Paul's pained expression. 'Okay, okay I'm sorry. All joking aside, you would not believe it if I told you.'

He shook his head as if exasperated.

'Okay, it was something Mrs. F said. She came into the office last week and quizzed me on why I looked so glum, given I'd just been promoted, and I told her...I told her about us.'

'You did what?' Paul snapped.

'I know, I know, but she caught me off guard. I was miserable. Anyway, I'm glad I did because she starting talking about her experience of being a mum and she made it sound...well, not how I'd thought it would. She also said she thought I'd make a great mum.'

'Well, I know that!'

'You do?'

'Of course.'

'You never said.'

'I never thought I needed to.'

'What, you just thought I'd know I'd be a good mum?'

'Er...yeah.'

'But I didn't.'

He looked dumbfounded so she continued.

'Mrs F also said I needed to be a little less self-absorbed.'

'I know that too.'

'You're not that funny you know?'

'Sorry.'

'Anyway, I've been thinking and I wondered if...' She stopped, hoping he would fill in the silence for her. She looked at him, he looked at her, neither spoke for a long time.

'You want me to wait a couple of more years?' Paul said.

Sam nodded. 'Three at most.'

'And what if you still don't want them then?'

'We cross that bridge when we come to it?'

She looked at him, holding her breath, waiting for him to say something. She could see the struggle on his face, knew he still loved her, but this was a dilemma.

'So, what do you think? Can we try again?' she pressed.

'Sam, I...'

He shook his head, and as she heard his words, she shattered inside.

'I know it's tough, but no. I...can't.'

Josh had left and Kate had taken the opportunity, before Sam returned, of finishing some transcribing. She saved the files and thought about playing the Sims game, but switched off her computer. She didn't need to anymore, not now she had a life.

There was a new looseness in her limbs that she enjoyed. Was this how people normally felt? Her jaw, usually so tight, moved easily, and her back didn't stiffen up the way it used to when she walked away from the computer.

Kate moved into the kitchen and began preparing a ham sandwich. As she worked her mind began to mull over her future options.

She had very little idea how she was going to use the voices, but she had dismissed Josh's idea of counselling. She was not a people person, and she couldn't see how she could go from the quiet existence she had, to a life open to all sorts of strangers walking in and demanding something from her. Perhaps something would reveal itself in time.

When she thought of little Lucy Newton her heart ached. Once again Kate had been powerless to help someone. Lucy's death, and Kate's inability to stop it, scratched at her guts. She toyed with the idea of working for the police. She knew she would be able to convince them of her ability in time, but was that what she wanted to do with her life? Spend her time probing into the minds of disturbed people?

Her gaze fell on the little hard backed book she'd bought on the market stall, it sat on the counter, on top of her unopened post. She finished making her sandwich, wiped her hands and picked it up.

She posed the question 'what can I do with the voices?' and opened it. It read:

'Realised, your mind can torment and deceive you, but in the service of the heart it is a great and noble ally. The trick is to face those demons that torment and terrify, and come to realise you give them power; and you can take it away again. You decide.'

She had let so much be taken from her because she had been afraid to act. It wouldn't happen again. She was ready to do what needed to be done to lay the ghosts of her life to rest.

Kate returned with her sandwich and fired up her computer again. When it was ready she typed, 'Adam Firth', into the search engine and pressed enter. It took barely fifteen seconds for the search to finish. Since Jan had told her the name of her father it had rolled around her head like an oversized marble. Firth. Firth. Kate Firth. It wasn't her, it was some stranger, some other being she might have been if things had been different. She imagined her school books with the name, her reports, her qualifications, her passport, her household bills, No, she decided, she was not Kate Firth.

There were over seven million matches and she wasn't sure whether to be relieved or disappointed. As she scrolled through she was able to eliminate several of them straight away, and in the obituaries they were too old to be her father. But it still left millions to go through. Then on page five she saw something that might narrow down her search. It was a long shot, but the alternative was either months of searching, or going through the more formal routes, and she wasn't sure she was ready for that. If she were honest, she was just curious.

There were twelve Adam Firths who had a profile on Linked in. She clicked on the web site, her breath shortening as she scanned the twelve profiles quickly. She suddenly realised that, other than his name, she knew nothing about him, he might even be living abroad now. And then she saw it.

There it was, third on the list. Under the summary heading where his profile should be, he had written: 'I am looking for my daughter Kate, born 11th February 1978, adopted at the age of four after my wife died.' There was no further details, no picture, no occupation past or present, no location, no eduction, nothing.

Reading it, a rage welled up inside her. He wrote as if they were a family who had been struck by tragedy. They were, she supposed, but not the way it sounded in his description.

She clicked on his profile and was presented with a blue rectangular button with the words 'connect'. Did she want to 'connect' with her father? All she had to do was press the button and a request would be sent to him. He might even be on-line now. They could be 'connecting' within minutes.

'...after my wife died,' he had written. She didn't die, Kate wanted to shout at the screen, you murdered her. Maybe that would be her first message to him. Just the one word...'MURDERER'. She sat for several minutes, the cursor hand pointing it's finger at the connect button.

Then she closed down the computer. She wasn't ready afterall.

Chapter Thirty-Five

'So how are you?' Sam asked down the phone the following day. Kate was surprised by the question.

Sam had returned the previous night, distraught at her aborted attempt to return home. She had also confessed her cowardice, convinced that she had put Kate's life at risk. It had taken a lot of reassuring and consoling to convince Sam otherwise. So when Kate saw Sam's name flashing on her mobile, she had thought the call was going to be all about Sam.

'I'm okay, not sleeping as well as I'd like, but that's to be expected. And you?'

Sam ignored Kate's question. 'I'll say, it's not every day you discover you live above a murderer!'

The words reminded Kate about her aborted search for her father. She knew she had to face him, but the thought literally sent shivers down her spine.

Sam interrupted her thoughts. 'Have you decided what you're going to do yet?'

'About what?'

Sam laughed. 'Your career, your love life, your father…?'

It was Kate's turn to laugh. 'I could fire the question straight back at you!'

'Paul and I are over, he made that very clear last night.'

'And how do you feel now you've slept on it?'

Sam laughed. 'I didn't!'

'Oh, Sam, I'm sorry.'

'It's okay, he's right, I know he's right. Trouble is, just because you know you shouldn't be together, doesn't necessarily make it easier.'

'No, I suppose not.' Kate hadn't had much experience in this area. 'So what are you going to do?'

'I think I've found a flat.'

'That was quick!'

'No point hanging around.'

'I suppose. Look, Sam, really you don't-'

'I know, I know, but I can't sleep on your sofa for much longer.'

'Really, I don't mind.'

'I do! It's breaking my back!'

Kate laughed. 'Ah, yes, good point.'

'I'm going to see it tonight. I thought I'd rent at first, until I've got my head sorted out.'

'Good idea.'

'Now, stop avoiding the question Kate.'

'Oh I don't know Sam, I don't think I can make any decision about my future until I close the door on my past.'

'Close the door?'

'No that's the wrong expression...I think 'closure' is the word I'm looking for.'

'So you want to go and meet your father?'

'Yes and no, I'm not sure what good it will do, or even why I want to.'

'Perhaps you're just curious.'

'Is that a good enough reason to turn someone's life upside down?'

'I'm not sure you need to worry about him in all this, think about you and what you need.'

'Maybe.'

'Or are you just scared?'

'A little, to be honest.'

'That's understandable.'

'Thanks for listening,' Kate said, suddenly.

Sam laughed. 'It's this new thing I'm doing these days. But seriously, I think you need to do it. If I can help...?'

'Thanks, but Josh has said he would.'

'And how are things with you and the lovely Josh?'

'Good, we're taking things slowly, but good.'

'I'm glad he's forgiven me.'

'He's not a one to hold grudges.'

'No, thank god! I am mortified you know?'

Kate laughed. 'Don't worry, it's all in the past.'

'Yes, and it's where your's should be too, the past belongs in the past.'

When Kate rang off from her call to Sam she was in turmoil, but she knew Sam was right.

She picked up the phone and called Josh. When he answered she said, 'I'm ready.'

'Good,' he said.

Chapter Thirty-Six

On a cold November day, Kate slid out from the car into a long windy street, and looked over at the small terraced building that was home to Adam Firth . It was only an hour's drive from her and her parent's home, and it seemed strange that he should be living within travelling distance. In her mind these mystical birth parents had been on some other dimension, and she wondered, not for the first time, if that was why she was visiting today. It would make him concrete, would make him real, it might even make him human.

Kate had learned that he was released after serving eight years. Eight years! She hadn't even been a teenager by then. He had murdered her mother, stolen her childhood and hadn't even served a childhood's worth of time in jail. Why was she doing this, what was the point?

'I'll be right here.' It was Josh, in the driver's seat of the car. He must have sensed her hesitation. 'Remember, what's happened in the past, is just preparation for today.'

She bent down and smiled at him. 'Thanks.'

'It's tough, but you're tougher.'

She nodded and smiled. If he came out with another clique she might scream, besides, she didn't feel tough as she turned round to face the house.

She took a deep breath and smoothed her hands over her jeans for reassurance. She had spent hours the previous night tossing and turning, wondering what she would wear, what she would say. Who did she want him to think she was? A smart business women, the girl next door, a church goer, a fashion icon? In the end she had settled on jeans, a sweater and flat suede boots. It was easier, less of a statement. Besides, in spite of everything, or perhaps because of it, it was who she was. A simple, down to earth woman. A jeans and a sweater girl.

She walked up to the front door. This was it. This was her foray into a past she had little recollection of. She was suddenly small, standing at the edge of a very deep very cold lake, to plunge into this house, into her past, was akin to jumping in. No, worse, at least with freezing water you knew that if you swam hard enough the initial shock would pass. Here, she didn't know what to expect.

If she remembered nothing, if this man was meaningless to her, would that be better or worse? And if she remembered it all, what would be the quality of those memories, given the scene that had wiped all that had gone before? Her stomach lurched and her hands shook as she reached out to lift the door knocker.

She heard movement inside and her body tightened, her breath shortened, her heart quickened. What would he look like? Would she recognise anything about him? She found herself wanting him to like her. Why?

The door rattled as someone on the other side began to open it and Kate had a million butterflies frantically trying to escape the small space that was her stomach. She thought she would throw up.

The door opened and there he stood.

He was much smaller than she imagined, he stood only about an inch taller than her. His black hair, that stood up in tufts much like her own, was greying considerably on the sides. Deep lines were chiselled into his craggy, rock-like face. He had a small pointed nose and large dark eyes. She searched and found the similarities between their facial features. The hair of course, but also the eyes and nose, they were definitely the same. He was a familiar stranger.

'Adam Firth?' she asked, though she knew. She held out her hand. 'I'm Kate.' It was very formal under the circumstances she realised, but she was unsure how else to do this. There were no etiquette books on this sort of social situation.

The man took her hand and shook it. It was warm and strong, and surprisingly big for a man of his size. A flash of the damage they had done shot into her mind, but she pushed it to one side.

Adam stood back and opened the door wide.

'Please come in,' he said.

His voice was deep and quiet, not the voice of the man Kate remembered. She stepped into the hall, glancing back briefly to see Josh stood against the car, with his arms folded, watching.

'Does your friend want to come in too?' Adam asked her.

Kate shook her head. 'I don't think so.'

As Adam closed the door behind her, a small wave of panic rose. This was a murderer; he could do anything to her. It froze her to the spot for a moment, thoughts of her fight with Felix came roaring up, all she could do was watch the man walk through a door to the left and disappear.

He reappeared. 'Please join me,' he said.

The words were like a magic spell, and Kate unfroze and followed him into the lounge.

It was small, dimly lit and dated, but clean. The sparse furnishing included a brown cord two-seater sofa, and matching armchair, a portable TV in the corner and a cheap teak coffee table, set with a tray.

'I thought we'd have some tea,' he said. 'Unless you prefer coffee?'

Kate hated tea but found herself saying, 'tea will be fine.'

He bustled with pleasure. 'Sit down,' he said, pointing to the sofa.

He poured the tea and handed her a cup. 'Sugar? Milk?'

It was all absurdly civilised and Kate wondered if it was a dream.

'Just milk thanks.' She held her cup still and watched the milk pour from the pink jug to her cup, clouding the black tea.

As the man busied himself serving, Kate thought she recognised a familiar smell, a perfume, that permeated the room. It pulled at somewhere deep and mingled in her memory with another more personal smell. It gave her a feeling of warmth.

Then she remembered sitting beside her mother, with her mother's arm around her, listening to the story of the three little pigs. She could clearly see the small ladybird book, with the brightly coloured pictures of the pigs in britches, and the big bad wolf wearing a battered top hat.

Oh it was there, so clear, so clean a memory; a moment of softness in her young life. Some of it was good. Some of it had been normal.

'What's that smell?'

'What smell?' he asked, as he sat in the armchair.

'There's a perfume smell.'

'You recognise it?' he beamed.

'Vaguely. What is it?'

'It's "Charlie" a perfume your mother used to use. I thought it might help. They told me that you'd lost your memory after…everything, so I thought it might jog something.

She wasn't sure what she thought about that. Wasn't it a bit weird that he would want her to remember? Wasn't he just ever so slightly off key? Perhaps he wasn't sane.

'Well this is nice. I've thought a lot about you. A lot about how you were doing, what you looked like, what kind of person you were, and here you are, in the flesh.' He stopped and looked down at his tea.

Kate sat holding her cup and saucer, the feeling of unreality spreading.

'It was hard and I want to say I'm sorry. I was ill; I didn't know what I was doing. It was…difficult.'

The gas fire hissed. Kate thought of Josh sat out in the car and hoped he wasn't too cold. She thought of things she needed to pick up from the supermarket, and whether Josh would mind stopping off on the way home. Would it be cheeky to ask?

'Aren't you going to say something?' he asked.

'Like what?'

He shrugged. 'Tell me what you do for a living, that's a start.'

She realised she didn't want a start, she didn't want anything. This was a mistake, sitting down to tea. All she had wanted, was to look at him. Now she was trapped. How could she leave?

She took a deep breath and forced the words out. 'I'm a transcriber.'

'Oh, that's nice.'

She knew he didn't know what it was and was pleased.

'Are you married?'

'No.'

'Well, there's time yet, you're still young.'

'Yes.'

'Do you remember the "American pie"? Your mother put it on the record player and you two would dance, sometimes I would join in. Do you remember?'

Kate took another breath. 'Yes.'

He nodded and smiled. He was shy, but Kate didn't care to put him at ease. She was beginning to feel the anger that lay quietly under the surface. This man had destroyed it, destroyed it all. Murdered her mother and stolen her childhood, her real one, the one she should have had with the mother she loved. Then she had a twinge of guilt. She loved Jan too, and Jan couldn't have given her a better childhood, couldn't have loved her more.

Adam jumped up and it made Kate start out of her revere.

'I have something,' he left the room and returned a few moments later carrying a child's painting. He handed it to her. 'I kept this all this time,' he said proudly, as if he'd accomplished something amazing.

The paper was soft suede beneath her fingers. It had been folded, the four creases quartering the painting of a boat on the high seas, with crashing waves beneath it. She remembered this. She had painted it in nursery school. The school had selected her picture to be on the front page of their magazine. Her father had showed the magazine to everyone, pointing out the white foam she had painted round the ship. Kate hadn't wanted to show her father the original picture, because she hadn't painted the foam; it was just how it came out in the printing, so her mother had agreed to put it away for her. In the special memories box.

'Everyone should have one Katie-loo, because sometimes we forget things.'

Kate could hear her soft voice, smell her perfume, feel her arms round her. The sing song voice came through clearly now, the lost voice of her mother, and it broke something inside Kate. She began to cry.

'Hey, hey, I didn't mean to...I just thought with you not remembering... I...I...' he stopped.

She looked up at him and saw that he had tears in his eyes. How dare he cry! How dare he? He had no right to cry! This was all his fault!

'You murdered her,' she said it quietly, softly, and yet, the raging anger came out with every word. She glared at him as she said it. Watched him bend and cringe under the statement.

He nodded. 'I know, and I am sorry,' his tears had dried now, and Kate was shocked that he was over his grief so quickly.

'I think I need to go,' she said, and she put the cup onto the coffee table untouched.

'I'm sorry,' he said. 'About making a fool of myself,' he indicated that he meant the tears.

'It's the least you should feel sorry for.'

He hung his head, there was nothing for her to rally against, nothing for her to push at or fight with. She wasn't sure what she was expecting, but this hadn't been it. She wanted to rage at him and beat him, but the monster she remembered as her father had gone, and the man who stood before her now was a shadow, not the man who had killed her mother. He had gone a long time ago. This man, was more broken than she had ever been, thanks to Jan and Phil.

She understood, for the first time since finding out the truth, she had been loved as she grew, and the fact was, the alternative childhood she had been grieving for of late, would have been one in a home filled with violence and fear.

She couldn't love the man in front of her, she didn't even want him in her life, but she could forgive him. She had to. For her own sake.

'It's over,' she said. 'It happened a long time ago. We're all different now.'

'Thank you,' he whispered.

Kate moved towards the living room door, but he stood in the way. 'Will you come back and see me?'

She shook her head.

He nodded.

As they walked out into the hall Adam remembered something, 'wait, I have one more thing for you.'

He disappeared into a room down the end of the hall and returned carrying a small book, as he passed it to her she realised it was a photo album.

'There hasn't been much kept from the past. Your picture, some photos... anyways, I put this together for you.' He pushed it at her.

'Thanks.' A million questions bubbled into her mind, but she didn't want to ask anything of this man, this Adam, this father of hers. They stood in the hall, a taunt silence stringing them together, holding them in place.

'I don't want anything from you, you know?' he said. 'I just wanted...I don't know, I suppose I just wanted to check you were okay.'

'I'm okay,' she told him.

He stepped forward and opened the door. 'You look a lot like her,' he said.

Kate smiled. 'Thank you.'

She stepped into the street, gripping the photo album and the folded picture. The cold air assaulted her. Kate pulled her coat tight around her and walked back to the car. She didn't look back until she was in the passenger seat. When she did, Adam was stood in the doorway watching her. Her heart squeezed for a moment with pity and concern, and a sadness of what they might have had together, if things had been different. If *everything* had been different, she reminded herself.

'You okay?' Josh asked.

'I'm fine,' she turned to him and smiled.

He squeezed her hand. 'You look alright.'

'Thank you.'

Josh started the car and Kate looked back at her father. As the car moved by she raised a hand in a final farewell.

Chapter Thirty-Seven

Kate was packing a small bag for her Christmas visit to her parents. Josh was due to pick her up in an hour. When she finished packing, she placed the bag at the top of the stairs, then went to the living room to stand by the window to look out for him.

Rachael was stood across the road, framed in the doorway of her front door, smoking a cigarette. Was it the same brand Lucy had tried to buy that day in the corner shop? Kate wondered. A gulf of emotion swept over her, to see Rachael stood there like that, as if she were looking for her child, calling her in for her tea.

The two women looked at each other, Kate down at Rachael, Rachael up at Kate. They stood like that for a long time, until Rachael nodded and Kate replied similarly. Moments later, the woman threw her cigarette into the garden and, rubbing her arms against the cold, turned back into the house, closing the door behind her. Kate stared at the closed door.

Life was changing for her, opening up and fanning out in all sorts of new directions. Doors were opening and, for once, Kate didn't feel afraid to walk through one or two of them. Possibilities were limitless, she had realised.

She hadn't used her gift since watching Felix being taken away, and she wasn't sure she ever would again. Josh and she had discussed it at length, and she had tried to explain that, although he saw it as a gift, for her it had never been like that and possibly never would be. It was packed away in the back of her mind, like fine linen wrapped in layers of tissue paper in a bottom drawer.

Josh joked that he was relieved she wouldn't be poking around in his head, and she joked that he shouldn't relax too much. It hadn't been mentioned since, and Kate liked that. Now her future, their future, lay before them.

Her thoughts turned to Lucy Newton and all the things the little girl wouldn't do. She wouldn't learn to drive or swim, get a job, leave a job, get married, have children, travel on a train, attend a yoga class or practice Tai Chi in the park. She wouldn't argue with someone she loved in the morning, and make love to them that evening. She wouldn't attend her child's school play, read them a bedtime story, or kiss scrapped knees better. She wouldn't learn how to bake a great apple pie, or cook a Christmas dinner for her family. She wouldn't see her child win an award, fail an exam, pass their driving test or break her heart when they left home. She wouldn't watch her children fall in love and have their hearts broken, she wouldn't knit her first grandchild a pair of booties and watch them grow out of them, or watch her husband age and be glad to be alive to see it.

Kate wasn't sure what life had in store for her, but whatever she experienced, whatever she did, whatever life experiences came her way, good and bad, Kate would live it for Lucy, she would do it for both of them. She would be that lost voice.

THE END